F O R S Y T H I A

2 0 1 9

AN IMPRINT OF CODHILL PRESS

THE
CATCHER
IN THE
LOFT

BY CH'ŎN UN-YŎNG

TRANSLATED BY BRUCE AND JU-CHAN FULTON

AN IMPRINT OF

CODHILL
PRESS

FORSYTHIA

Codhill books are published by David Appelbaum for Codhill Press

THE CATCHER IN THE LOFT

Originally published as: 생강 by Ch'ŏn Un-yŏng
Copyright ©2011 Ch'ŏn Un-yŏng

Publication is with the kind and generous support of the Sunshik Min
Endowment for the Advancement of Korean Literature at the Korea Institute,
Harvard University; and of the Literature Translation Institute
of Korea (LTI Korea).

Book Design by Jana Potashnik
BAIRDesign, Inc. • bairdesign.com

ISBN978-1-949933-05-5

Printed in the United States of America

For all who work on behalf of restorative justice and reconciliation on the Korean Peninsula and elsewhere in the world.

CHAPTER 1

It's a thing of beauty. Inevitably. You'll see—mastery of technique is beautiful, and triumph makes beauty its own. And absolute triumph requires unconditional submission.

What's the rush? You think he'll submit if you're barking like a mad dog? No—what you need is economy of movement, attention to detail. Each gesture, every eye signal has a purpose; nothing's left to chance. There's one end to the process and one end only, and that's terror. Not till you extract raw terror can you bring him to his knees.

Violence for its own sake doesn't work. All you get from brute violence is hatred and resistance. The distillation of terror involves a sequence, it requires fundamentals. Perfect your technique, and you can bring him to his knees with the tip of your pen.

I'm going to teach you how beautiful it can be.

First you strip him. But don't touch him—make the kid do it himself. And when he's buck naked you leave him be and let the humiliation sink in. Make him understand he has nothing. You leave him alone till his rosy cheeks turn pale, till his slumping shoulders start to shake, till his balls shrivel.

Then you turn the light on him. Flood his face with it, and when he shuts his eyes you pass it over his body. Make him feel the light on his skin, and watch the skin react—the blue of the veins stands out and the pores open up. But not too long—you don't want the light making him warm.

Whatever warmth there is, get rid of it. Cold water's just the thing. Give him a good blast of it, let him feel the sting of ice-cold water, let it gouge terror into his flesh. Make him burn like fire, fire that makes darkness darker than dark. Whether it's water, fire, light, or darkness, he has nothing to cling to, nothing he can make sense of. And *that's* when terror begins. A body that's awakened to terror is ready for the artist.

Before you begin you leave him alone for half a day. Priming time. Time for the kid to play out the drama of his life, to recall every crime, every sin he ever committed, maybe some he hasn't gotten around to yet. Time to remember when he used to be happy, time even for hope. After half a day, his last meal's digested—nothing to vomit, nothing to block the airways, he's not going to die on you.

Now you're set. It's time to get serious and lay him out on the Board of Death. What, you never heard of the Board of Death? Well, it's a little bit of heaven you can take with you to the next world, the heaven whose North Star beacon shines calmly, lighting your way. Beautiful, isn't it? I made it myself, a plank from a birch tree. Lay the kid out on it—secure the ankles, then prop the head up so he's nice and comfy. Now cover his sorry carcass with a blanket. You don't want any visible damage—leave the bruises on the inside, deep down to the bone. Bind him fast with the four straps and show him what an honor it is to be joined with the lovely Board of Death.

Isn't he lovable. Look at the little guy, all swaddled up, still as a newborn. Ready to take mommy's tit. So we'll give it to him nice and sweet.

Cover the face with a wet towel. You don't want him breathing freely. Now start the water, just a dribble, but keep it going—it has to go in through the nose and down the throat. Don't stop till you fill his throat. He'll try to keep his mouth shut, till he realizes he can't breathe. Then the mouth opens up, and in goes the water. The more he resists, the longer he suffers. Can you hear him gasping for breath? Do you see his chest bulging out? Now turn up the flow. More of it's coming out than going in, but no matter. Keep it running till it leaks out of his eyes, till his yap stops twitching.

Did it stop? All right, then turn the North Star toward heaven. Flip the kid over so the board's on top and he throws up the water. Once he vomits he'll come back to his senses, and then you flip the board back over and turn on the water again. Simple, isn't it? It's a splendid contrivance. You don't need to waste energy sticking his head in the bathtub, you don't have to manhandle your little rag doll. All you do is flip him over and he turns into a faucet.

You want him waterlogged. Till every pore, every hole in his body is oozing water. He'll piss himself for sure and it'll come out his other end too. Spit, sweat, piss—make it all come out. And the more that comes out, the more you put back into him. Add a pinch of red pepper for seasoning. Then tilt the board up and keep replenishing those precious bodily fluids.

Don't stop now, no rest for the wicked, keep that water flowing. That's not a man there, it's a rock. Or a tree, grass, a bucking donkey, a dog, a goat. Let's call him a rock, a rock you'll squeeze tears from. Don't lose control. Mask your tender feelings and keep cool. Don't get worked up—put on an icy face and cool your hot blood, pretend you're not even breathing. Don't work up a sweat, and no moaning or groaning.

We're at war. We're fighting for our lives. Our enemy is armed with the power of evil, and they'll attack us unless we crush them first. They lie and they cheat and they steal, they're pawns of the devil, a wicked mob with fantasies of violence and struggle and subversion, minions of darkness who wish to taint and contaminate our world order. And we are warriors who combat the power of evil with good.

Now lay the board back down, unstrap the kid, and remove the blanket. Handle him gently. We have now a body that's receptive to every conceivable sensation, a sweet little body that responds to the faintest breath, that trembles at a feathery touch. To such a body static electricity will feel like lightning. He'll feel like the stars are coming out of him, the sun is rising inside him, like he's been hit by a tidal wave, like he's blossoming with flowers and birdsong. The kid's body will experience everything between heaven and earth, it'll experience Creation.

Awake now? How's our little rag doll. He's been crying? He wet himself? No worries. We'll dry him out soon enough. Now why the sad face—he's not being treated right? Well, he has only himself to blame for his crimes—he'd *better* feel sorry for himself. He wants to confess? No, not yet. First he needs a taste of the essence of my mastery. He's suffering? Well, heaven's not far away. I'll show him heaven, I'll let him hear the angels sing. And after it's over he'll bow down before me.

Now get some salt into him, we need to replenish the electrolytes and keep him hydrated, we don't want him exhausted. Hook up his little toes, the right one to negative, the left one to positive. Positive and negative—the principle of heaven and earth. Now turn on the juice and listen to what comes out of his mouth. Listen to him bray like a mad donkey. Watch his tongue roll up, watch that little tit in the back of his throat swell up.

Now gag that mad donkey and watch his red lips go purple, see the whites of his eyes turn red. Let's jack up the current and watch the electricity dry everything up. When the moisture's gone, sprinkle him with salty water—it's the ideal conductor. Look for when the water dries up and the salt crystals appear. Watch with your own eyes for that exquisite moment when the goose bumps go down and the fine hair of the body comes up.

Watch the electricity make the hair stand up and gather in one direction. Fine hair charged with electricity. Savor it. Isn't it breathtaking? *This* is genuine beauty, absolute proof of perfect skill.

"Sir!"

What the hell? Who dares interfere in this electrifying moment, when total submission is at hand, when absolute triumph lies before my eyes?

"Sir!"

"What!"

"I think you need to stop. There might be a problem."

"What problem?"

"A casualty."

"Where?"

"Room 201."

"Team three?"

"Yes sir."

"The rookies. . . . And?"

"We've been ordered to stop all interrogation."

"What!"

Stop just when our little friend's mouth is wide open, head drooping to the side, dried-up lips twitching and ready to spill out his crimes? My god, he's ready, all we need now is his signature. My hands are trembling. I clench my fists.

***

When the king's head got chopped off the dogs had the time of their life, baring their teeth and running wild. No more tails between legs, no more tail wagging and cozying up to the master. Those dogs joined the ones penned up, and they're roaming around in packs.

It's my shit luck. Mad dogs need to be slaughtered, their seed needs exterminating before they can run riot. Why didn't I muzzle those goddamned animals?

It's all because of that son of a bitch. That crap hound foaming at the mouth, dying to be top dog. That sniveling sissy who begged me for his life, who licked the floor, who shit himself, that bastard finally did it. He got my mug posted in their rag, along with that rambling article about my artistry—that son of a bitch.

I take that back. It's those damned rookies. If the rookies don't fuck up, no one comes in alive and goes out dead. If not for a kid dying from the rookies' stupidity, the dogs in hiding don't run amok and the king still has his head. If the king has his head, that asshole I stuck in jail doesn't get pardoned, and if that asshole isn't released, then my face isn't made public for all the world to see. Damned rookies aren't up to the job—they're always fucking up.

I take that back. It's the eyes. The rookies should have read the eyes, they should have pushed the eyelids back up, they should have known how to read the fading of the pupils. They shouldn't have been running on automatic, they should have known the difference between eyes fading at the moment of sleep and eyes fading at the moment of death. They should have known when to stop. Goddamned rookies.

You have to read the eyes. It's an instinct you develop into the skill of knowing a boundary, a stopping point, the crucial moment when the will to resist weakens, when the decision is made to submit, the moment when the clinging hands drop and the feeling of oppression gives way to freedom. It's the moment when anxiety and ease transpose, when seething hostility changes to respect. When you recognize those boundaries you've finally approached truth.

You don't cross those boundaries. There's a moment when the tiny blood vessels in the whites of the eyes burst from tension, like a taut string snaps. And like a fluorescent light flares up before it fails and goes dark, there's a moment at the very end when the eyes light up, when the cornea loses moisture and grows hazy. The moisture and the haze go back and forth, one retreating and the other returning, and then the cornea expands and contracts one last time—that's the moment that separates life and death. You have to stop before that point, and that's what requires genuine skill.

It's all in the eyes, believe me. Look in the eyes and you see truth. To read the eyes is to read everything about a man. It starts and ends with the eyes. The rest of the body you can't trust. The tongue lies and the body exaggerates, but the eyes are honest, they don't lie, you won't be deceived by them, ever. When you read the eyes you approach truth.

I take my Smith and Wesson .38 from its holster. It's a classic of simplicity and precision. Feeding the cartridges into the chamber, giving the cylinder a spin, firing the bullets, ejecting the casings—it's beautiful. The crosshatch grip looks small but it sits snug in my palm.

My .38 is loaded with blanks. I pop the cylinder and empty it, then snap it shut again. I pull back the hammer. The click of the cylinder turning one notch, that's a sweet sound. I pull the trigger. The spring releases and *snap!* goes the hammer spur. Hammer, cylinder, trigger. Let's do it again. Point the muzzle straight at the wall, aim, pull the trigger. Sight in on the light bulb, aim, pull the trigger. Arm against the ear, point toward the ceiling, pull the trigger. And then one shot to my temple—*snap!*

The hammer striking the empty chamber vibrates against my temple. I make myself dead still, imagine a warm, sticky flow down my cheek. I lower the gun, pop the cylinder, reload the blanks, then raise the gun and target a splotch on the wall. That splotch is the skull of a mad dog. I pull back the hammer. I'm ready for you sons of bitches, just tell me when and where. I close one eye and imagine I'm pulling the trigger—*bang!*

Time to go. My gun goes back in the holster, my sneakers under the desk. I put on my dress shoes, throw on my jacket, and leave. The click of my shoe heels on the floor echoes quietly down the long hall. Those I meet are quick to look away. Eyes that used to hold respect and envy are filled with censure and resentment. Those eyes are telling me something, they're saying it's all because of me, that I was the one who killed him. They're the eyes of an accomplice who wants to weasel out. Don't all of you do the same work I do? It was the rookies who killed that kid, not me.

I walk tall. I go down the stairs and let myself out, cross the yard to the gate, look back at the building, a gray building shrouded in silence. Strange—I don't remember it ever being this quiet.

The gate opens. Out I go, the gate closing behind me, metal screeching against metal in the dark. I look around. There's a wall in front of me and a wall in back. The alley is still and there's a chill to the air. I ease back against the wall and light a cigarette. Looking down the alley, I blow blue smoke into the night.

A black sedan turns into the alley. I crush out my cigarette against the wall. The car comes to a stop. I reach for the door handle and down comes a window exactly one hand span.

"Did you clean up after yourself?" Pak growls.

I jerk my hand back. "How did they found out?" I ask, bringing my face close to the opening.

"You know how persistent those bastards are."

"So what do I do now?"

"You need to take off. At least till things quiet down."

"Take off where?"

"Doesn't matter."

The tone is curt, the message clear—no more questions. Pak is concealed inside the car, his voice the only indication of his existence.

"Where am I supposed to go—my mug is plastered everywhere."

"For now just hide—we'll take care of the rest. Sit tight till we contact you. If you're caught now it gets too big to handle and the whole organization could come down. Make absolutely sure you don't get caught."

A manila envelope slides out through the opening. I straighten up and stare at it. It's sealed. I feel myself tightening up.

"Go on, take it. Everything you need is there." Pak is starting to sound irritated.

I take it.

"So I just wait?"

"So you go get lost, now!"

The window goes up, punctuating the sentence.

"Till when?" I ask, placing my hands against the window.

Silence. I tap-tap at the window. I grab at the door—it's locked. And suddenly the car's in motion with my hand still gripping the door handle. A lurch, and *plop*—down I go. The car disappears into the gloom, leaving a cloud of smoke. A weird thrumming hangs over the alley. I gape at the darkness.

There on the pavement, the manila envelope. *Make absolutely sure you don't get caught.* I jump to my feet, pick up the envelope, clutch it in my fist, and run, eyes dead ahead, like a hunter who's come across his prey.

But I'm not a hunter—I'm the prey, an animal released from its pen, a target. I'm a man on the run.

I press myself against the wall of the dark alley and scan the plaza in front of the train station. A cat darts in front of me. I tell myself to walk tall, then cross the plaza. *Take your time, but don't look around, don't act anxious. So what if they purge you—you still have your dignity.* I climb with measured steps to the waiting room.

The last train has left and the waiting room is a den of tramps, rag-covered lumps of humanity who have taken over the seats and are scattered about the floor, every one of them fast asleep except for a babbling old man who's keeping himself company with a bottle of *soju*. I weave among the ragged lumps to the timetable on the wall.

I need a place to go lose myself.

The first train leaves at five-ten—four hours from now. I walk past more of the ragged people to the bathroom. I lock the door and check the stalls—all clear. I choose a stall in the middle, lock it, sit on the pot, and steady my breathing.

The manila envelope is thick and heavy. There's a deadly purpose to whatever's inside. I try the tape but it's too much bother, so I work my little finger into the crease above and rip it open. A heavy little box falls out—bullets. What are bullets for if I'm supposed to be hiding?

A true warrior knows when to use the knife—Pak's voice echoes in my mind. He means you have to know the exact moment to slit someone's throat, or cut open your belly. You must always be calm when you use the knife. That's the way of the warrior, the spirit we must possess. That's how Pak ends his pep talks. And what does the warrior die for? Loyalty and righteousness, that's what. He offers up his life for those two things only. That's the spirit we must possess.

Do they doubt my loyalty, my sense of justice? Are they testing me? I know when to use the knife. What do warriors prove by cutting open their belly? Is *that* loyalty and righteousness? No. To prove you can put a gun to your head is not loyalty or righteousness. It's a coward's way out. I am a loyal and just man. That is a fact. They can test me all they want, but they can't shake my loyalty and my righteousness.

The box of ammo goes into the outer pocket of my coat. Next, some cash, million-*wŏn* stacks, three of them. And the newspaper that tells me when the next contact will be—let's see, okay, three days later. I stuff the cash and the newspaper in my inner pocket. Time to go. I take a deep breath, get up, and open the door.

I stand before the sink and look at myself in the mirror. I see the face of a starving animal, eyes shot through with fear. Is that really me? It's a face that tries to look commanding but instead it's anxious, afraid, confused, a face that doesn't know what to make of its own image, an animal frozen by the sight of a hunter. That can't be me. My nose is running and there's a tingle to it.

I splash water on my face, and in that water I feel cold, hard reality. I'm not going to hide in this stinking bathroom for the next four hours, or stay with those hobos in the waiting room. I kick the door open and march out.

A ragged lump is in my way. I stop and look down. A hand touches the tip of my shoe, the filthy, prune-like hand of an old woman. There's only that hand; the rest of her is covered in rags. I pull my foot away then bring it to rest on her hand, pressing gently at first, then harder. Her hoarse scream breaks the silence. The rags flip open and out comes the hag, her hair a rat's nest.

"What fucking bastard. . . ."

The hag's eyes are bloodshot. My eyes make contact with those eyes—*rise and shine*—and the hag jerks her head away and retreats inside her rags, her hand still trapped beneath my shoe. I look about. The stir from her squawking dies down and the station lapses back into silence. The *soju* sot gives me a stuporous look with hazy eyes. The rest are hiding inside their rags, trying to hold their breath, which is coming out in fits and starts. They know all too well their only defense is their spinelessness.

I grind my shoe down one last time, then allow the hand to recoil inside the rags.

The waiting room grows still again.

I fling open the door and the cold wind rushes in. I pause on the steps and look out over the plaza. Four more hours and then I go get lost. I pull up the collar of my jacket and down the steps I go. At the plaza I hear the old woman cawing at me from above.

"Hey! You scum, you son of a bitch!"

I look up and there she is with her rat-nest hair, shaking her little fist, a bottle in her other hand. She's backed by three men who look just as pathetic. The hag throws the bottle at me. It hits the steps with an empty ring before tottering to a stop, shy of the plaza. The hag dusts off her hands—*so there*—and scuttles back inside. The men remain at the door, gazing ruefully at the empty bottle. I turn and walk away.

I cross the plaza and go down the alley where the windows are lit up in red. The alley is deserted—the vice squad must have paid a visit. At the end of the alley is a squalid place with a small, dimly lit window. Hunched up outside is a girl warming herself at a coal-briquette stove. She gives me a sheepish grin. I go inside and down the cramped hall to a tiny square room. The girl is right behind me.

The first thing you see is the mirror on the wall opposite, and in that mirror I see the girl come in behind me, holding my shoes. The red light accents the weary look of her face. She's so small she looks like a tween. She's just standing there in the middle of the room, and then whoosh—off comes her dress. It's time to get down to business. She's a bony little thing with dark blotches on her skin. There are white, dried-up sores around her belly, and scabs where she scratches her neck and the insides of her arms. Shivering, she gathers her hands in her crotch for warmth.

"Put your clothes back on if you're cold!"

The girl shakes her head. I take off my jacket and hand it to her. She hangs it from the wall. Such a docile little thing. Next I unbuckle my holstered gun. This item she hangs more quickly, as if she's touched something forbidden. I take off my belt and toss it to the floor, then remove my clothes. Tie, dress shirt, undershirt— each article she folds and places atop the previous one. Crowning the pile are my briefs with the check pattern.

Her gaze is glued to my feet. She picks up the belt and closes her eyes. She's seen the violence in the belt and she's ready for it.

I grab her wrist. She squirms and whimpers, and I let go. She takes a step back, rubbing the red mark I've left there. I take a step forward. She retreats no farther, looks me square in the eye. Her eyes are wet. I put my mouth to her ear.

"Take the buckle and wrap the belt around your hand. If you don't do it right you'll get hurt."

"Don't you want to do me instead?" she recites, eyes downcast.

I smile.

Realizing it's no use, she does what I tell her. I kneel at her feet. She takes a deep breath and steps back. I lean forward, palms to the floor. Up goes her arm with the belt. Like a little girl praying I gather my hands and close my eyes. I hear the belt cleave the air and feel the free end wrap itself about the small of my back. I bellow like an animal.

"If you don't draw blood I'll draw it from you!"

She lashes down as hard as she can. I see a flash of red. A moan escapes from deep inside me. Her arm flails wildly. Tears flow from my eyes. The whipping gets faster and faster. She's really into it now. I crawl along the floor, wailing. She grabs my hair and climbs onto my back. I'm a gutless bastard and I'm in ecstasy. The girl and I are giving the performance of our lives.

Blood oozes from the insides of my thighs. That's better. Panting, the girl slumps to the floor. I sink prone, limbs splayed, and a languid happiness washes over me. The girl is trembling spasmodically, still clutching my belt, an actress caught up in the emotions of her role even though the show is over. Her breathing eases and she crawls onto me, puts her hands in my armpits, and presses her face against my back, so close it's like we're one body. She dozes off, and I ease my breathing so it matches hers. I see her bony form in the mirror. And then she's gently rocking, like a boat on water.

"You know who I am?" I softly ask the mirror.

Her eyes open and then close again. She pulls on my arms and rubs her face into my back.

"The one who can make a rock cry."

"That's right."

"Who says he's a rock and then he's a rock. Who says he's tears and then he's tears."

"That's right."

"Who can see in the dark."

"That's right."

"What do people call you, mister?"

"The Half-Moon Bear. Number Two Man at the Funeral Home. An, Head of Security."

"I like Half-Moon Bear the best."

"Good. Now take what you want from my wallet—I won't be back for a while."

"Are you going somewhere?"

"Yeah, I'm going to get lost."

***

I'm in the middle of the compartment, on the aisle. There's a bathroom up front. I scan the other passengers. Up ahead a party of four in hiking getup, with the forward seat reversed so they're facing one another. Closer to me a baby and its mom, a pair of soldiers, and a scattering of people in window seats. No one to be concerned about.

I go past my assigned seat to the last row, set down my pack in the aisle seat, and sink back in the window seat. I'm out of sight back here and can move quickly if I have to. It's a good place to sit through a long trip and keep a low profile.

The train clunks into motion and in no time we're out of the city and chugging through fields. I see the outlines of low hills, scattered patches of snow, then more fields. It's not light yet. We're heading south.

I rest my forehead against the window. My eyes keep closing. The steady rhythm of wheel on rail is beckoning me to dreamland. I need to stay alert but I keep nodding off. The baby's crying. I open my eyes. I wish the crying would go away. The mother gives the fussing baby a whack on the back, and now listen to it bawl. I smell breast milk and the sour stink of booze and the musty odor of unwashed bodies. I ease myself out of my seat and slip into the space between this compartment and the next one back.

I can feel the cold air—that's better. I step down into the exit stairwell and light up. The smoke from my cigarette vanishes in the wind. I hear the announcement for the next stop, toss my butt into the night, and go back inside. The train comes to a stop. I sit back down and close my eyes but I'm still on full alert. I sense danger in the air, lurking among the sounds. I always analyze silences and disturbances. But now everything's calm. The train's moving again, picking up speed.

I open my eyes and see two kids standing there, looking down at me and slouching the way guys do when something's bothering them. The air is pulsing with the reek of booze—they must have been drinking all this time.

"These are our seats, mister—could you check your ticket?"

"There's plenty of other seats—can't you sit somewhere else?"

"What if we like these seats?"

"And want me to move. Like I said, there's plenty of other seats."

Kids—wet behind the ears. You guys are testing me? Wanting to see what I've got? Trying to sound threatening? A couple of bad-asses. Sticking the chin out, giving me the hard look. But you don't know what to do with me, do you. How come your legs are shaking? Are you going to swat me with that rolled-up newspaper? Think that's going to make me move my butt? Wrong. I'm not going anywhere. Fucking kids.

I give them a hard look. One kid gives it right back. The other one chickens out, tugging discreetly at his pal.

"Come on, let's go," says the second kid in a low voice. And then to me, "All right, help yourself, it's all yours."

"What do you mean?" says the first kid. "We didn't do anything wrong. These are our seats—what's the problem? Isn't that right, mister? Fuck, you're old enough to know better but you think you can give us that look and it's all over? You want to try something? Then get up off your fat ass."

What makes you so uppity? Two of you and one of me, is that it? The seat numbers printed on your tickets? Is it the hot blood of youth? You're convinced you're right and I'm wrong? Which is it? Outnumbering me means nothing. You want to make an issue out of seat numbers? Hot blood is reckless, you're living in a bubble. But you kids don't know that yet. You're a couple of cubs—no match for me.

"Hush up and get lost."

"Fuck you, big shot trying to throw your weight around. Are we supposed to apologize or something?"

"Hey, let it go." His pal looks annoyed and starts to haul him away.

"Fuck this—really!"

He's aggravated all right but it's all a bluff. They stumble up the aisle and plop down a few rows ahead of me. A couple of muttered obscenities and that's that. I close my eyes. Much ado over nothing. A couple of punks trying to be tough guys.

The baby's not crying anymore and it's dead quiet except for the steady rhythm of the wheels. The train comes to a stop and there's an announcement—we're letting an express go by. One of the kids has his head buried in his newspaper. Sounds like he's still worked up—he's making too much noise turning the pages. With the train stopped it's even more still, the only noise coming from the kid and his newspaper.

The train starts up again. Just when I'm thinking it's all right to close my eyes for a moment, the kid's head snaps around and he looks in my direction. Like he wants to check on something. *Warning*. His head whips back around and the next moment he's shoving the newspaper at the other kid. They're motioning back and forth. *Warning*.

The first kid gets up, slow and careful, and goes up the aisle, his back toward me, stiff and awkward, like he's shit his pants. He slides open the door at the far end and goes out, the door sliding shut behind him. The bathroom light stays green—he's not in the bathroom. *Warning*. I gather my pack and it makes a rustling sound—my nerves are on edge. Up front I see the other kid fold the newspaper and sneak it into his pocket.

I'm near the tail end of a moving train. Up front are the conductor's cubicle and the engine room. The bathroom light's still green. Pak's voice rings in my ears—*if you get caught, the organization's in danger*. And if the organization's in danger, there's no way out for me.

That son of a bitch, that bloodsucker, I tried to reason with him, I really did, and what does he do—he puts my face out there for everybody to see. I need to cool off. I get up and approach the kid with the newspaper. I rest one arm on the seatback in front of him, the other arm on his seatback. I make eye contact with the kid and whisper.

"If you're done with your newspaper, mind if I have a look?"

It's like I've put a spell on the kid—he produces the newspaper and hands it to me. I hold his gaze as I take the newspaper and put it in my jacket pocket. I grab the kid by the scruff of his neck and bring his head close. I give his neck a little squeeze then let go. His head stays where it is, near my waist. Like he's putting his head on his father's shoulder to tell him he's been a bad boy.

They're little kids, stupid, restless little kids, running wild with no idea where to—little boys for sure. I smooth the kid's hair, back off, return to where I was sitting. The kid hasn't budged. His shoulders are trembling and it looks like he's crying.

I put on my pack and go out the rear of the compartment into the exit space. The door clunks shut. I turn and look through the glass panel and see the kid sneaking a look back at me. That's right, you need to look, you need to make sure, you need to know there's still a pair of eyes fixed on you.

The door to the next car forward opens and there's the conductor, with the first kid right behind him. He sticks his head out to see if I'm still there. He looks so confident, him and his bloodhound. Go ahead, your bloodhound is a conductor, that's all. What's he going to do—the train's in motion. Then again I've got two cars behind me and I don't know when the next stop is. Those puppies are coming my way. Time to fly.

Quick—I open the door to the second-to-last car and head down the aisle, my pack bumping and catching against seatbacks. Quick—I go for the rear door, my eyes focused ahead. A snack cart—one of those volunteer groups—is blocking it. I squeeze by and there I am at the door. If I open it and cross the exit space to the door to the last compartment, that's it—no more doors. Every step is taking me closer to the worst-case scenario. I turn the handle, slide the door open, and a blast of air hits me.

It's a fierce wind and it won't die down. There's no shelter, no place to hide. The clack of the wheels beats against my eardrums. All I can see through the windows of the exit doors are the tracks stretching into the distance. Game time. And lucky me—the train's

16

slowing down. Steel shrieking against steel, the train goes around a curve.

I go back toward the next-to-last compartment and consider my options. Out the exit door to the right is a rock wall where the road bed's been carved out of the mountainside—not enough room. Out the exit door to the left is a low hill—enough room, but we're going around a curve and the centrifugal force will make for a greater impact. I have to choose before we get around that curve. I go left. Open the door, take out the newspaper and throw it. *Whap*—it opens up like it has wings and flies off into the darkness. I take a deep breath. The snow will ease the impact but god only knows what's hiding underneath it.

There, the hill flattening out to cropland. This is it—danger and opportunity. I throw the pack and then myself.

Tuck—make yourself into a ball! Can't land on your head, can't land on your feet. Tuck your chin and curl up, land on your left side. And then I hit, landing on the left side of my back, the impact like a punch to my chin. I brake with my right arm, soften the impact, and roll. Branches scrape my eyelids, frozen snow drives into my clothes, jagged rocks poke my back. I hit the crest of the hill, bounce off it, come to a stop. I let out a deep breath. The snow inside my clothes is already melting—cold. I try out my arms— there's some pain, but that's to be expected. My hips feel stiff. My nose is full of the smoky stink of oil from the tracks.

The clack of the train wheels fades in the distance. Over there— one of my shoes.

I stand myself up, limp over to the shoe, and put it back on, then half-walk, half-run along the cross ties. The rails are still whispering from the passing of the train.

Everything's far away, like in a dream.

CHAPTER 2

Finally—I'm having my ears pierced. Item number one on my off-to-university wish list. But I've chickened out a few times—do I really want this? The beauty shop lady is getting annoyed, I can tell. Just when I accept that there's no turning back, no more changing my mind, *bang!* goes the gun and I'm quivering all over.

Nothing to it. Just like Chini said. And the second ear is a breeze. I look in the mirror. Now that I'm over the big bang, I can see the little cube studs, their proud, ruby-red gleam. There, I'm a university student—I earned it.

Everything is beautiful, the sunlight dazzling in its brilliance, the wind fresh and energizing. A record-low temperature today, but what's recorded in me is a midsummer night festival— firecrackers going off, music in the air. The wind is biting but that's not the reason for the flush in my cheeks; no, it's because I'm giddy with anticipation and excitement. A little kid walks by and I give him a tap on his fur cap—I feel impish, I feel like prancing around.

I'm gadding about, checking out the shops. Yes, ma'am, a daypack for school. Those are the mufflers university girls like? Okay, I'll take one. In every shop I go I stick out my chest—I'm proud to be at a university. Before I know it I'm lugging a full shopping bag in each hand. But something's missing. Yes, last but not least.

There's a first time for everything—here I am in the dressing room in a lingerie shop to check my bust size for a bra. During school physicals I used to hunch up to make my chest smaller. Not anymore. Now I can stick out my chest, lift my arms, and let the discreet hands of a lingerie specialist do their thing. Time to kiss those Kitty bras goodbye—sorry, Mom, I know you bought them for me. Voila—a lacy, pink 34B bra—that's what a university girl wears. It's so pretty!

Mom has made the cake. It's not a surprise party, but still, a cake with frosting is special. And Mom loves to celebrate all the firsts and the special days, all the birthdays and the anniversaries, like my first period and coming in first in the essay contest. You should see the healthy glow on her cheeks when she lights the two candles.

"Oh, I almost forgot." Mom holds out an envelope. "Dad says to buy yourself something nice to wear. He's sorry he has to miss out on all the fun."

"Should I give him a call and say hello?"

"Later. When something urgent comes up, it's hard to reach him. You know how it is."

Of course I do. We're lucky if we get to see his face once a month. And I know he's overjoyed that I got into the university we wanted. It was Dad who chose which school and which department I should apply to. And I agreed with him all the way—we think along the same lines. Still, I feel kind of sorry he won't be here.

I show Mom my earlobes. She strokes them gently. "Did it hurt?"

"Not really, it was like someone screeching into my ear. Chini said her mom did hers when she was in kindergarten—with a needle."

"She's a tough girl, that one."

"She's brave, that's why. We're going to have a party in the loft tonight. Can you give her mom a call?"

"Okay, but no candles. And I don't want you making a racket like last time, understand?"

The two candles in the cake flutter. Mom should be humming by now—she hums when she's happy—but mostly she's just watching the candles. A party without Dad isn't a party. At a time like this Mom should tell me a love story. A story that goes with a frosting-topped cake.

"Mom, tell me that story. You know, before you were married."

"When I worked at the beauty shop?"

"Yeah, the time you met Dad."

She blushes—like she does when she's embarrassed, or when she's proud of something, or is daydreaming, or singing.

"I was really pretty back then."

Asking her to tell that story is like casting a spell over her—it transports her back to the past. And now I complete that spell by saying, "You still are."

"It was the only beauty parlor in town. I started out running errands, but after two months they gave me my first pair of scissors. I guess the word got around about how good I was with the curling irons—I had some steady customers from the big city by then. In all honesty I *was* the best."

"But Mom, you're still the best with the curling irons. There has to be more to it than that."

"Well of course there were always young guys from the neighborhood hanging around. Fools, all of them, not worth the time of day. So, no looks in their direction, no small talk. And then one day . . ."

The pause. This was the moment—enter Dad!

". . . your dad came in. He was built like a mountain, but he got red in the face like he was embarrassed, and when he got red in the face he had this habit of scratching his head."

It was rare for a young man to actually come into the beauty parlor, and Dad's appearance caused a stir—but a silent stir. He didn't say anything but everyone pretty much figured out he was there for Mom. He just stood there scratching his head, and finally he bellowed, *I want my head cut too!* One of the older women said, *What, you want someone to cut off your head?* And the beauty parlor erupted in laughter. The young man didn't know what to do. Laugh along with the women? Turn tail and leave? All he did was give Mom a piercing gaze. Mom fell for this huge man whose cheeks turned red as apples. She wanted to hear more of his resonant voice. It was a lazy spring afternoon, women in towel-wrapped heads nodding off to a radio drama, the snip-snip of the scissors working on them like a lullaby.

I rest my head against Mom's shoulder. Her voice is soothing, like the snip of the scissors on that spring afternoon. Hidden in her voice is that of Dad—through her voice Dad can join our party and through Dad our family is stronger. I can almost hear the *snip-snip* of the scissors. Our parties aren't complete without that sound. *Snip-snip*.

I flick the switch and the hundred-watt bulb in the ceiling comes on. The chill air has an acrid smell, musty and dusty, the smell of my loft. I'm in my very own castle, my hideaway.

I love everything in my loft. It's attached to the beauty parlor and hidden above it. I love hearing the *chuck-chuck* of Mom working her curling irons. And the cackling of the women. My secret books that I take such pleasure in reading while I listen to those off-and-on sounds—the young-adult romances and the boy-meets-girl comic book stories. The faint whiff of the caustic chemicals used for a perm. All the objects imbued with reminiscences from childhood, the boxes they're kept in, the boxes hidden within boxes.

One of those hidden boxes is my treasure chest. I open the lid and hear the tune. I've lost the ballerina that danced to the music, but the music is clear as ever. And there's the canine tooth on its bed of dark red velvet—the only one of my baby teeth I've kept. I remember when it was coming loose. It hurt when I touched it but I never thought of having it pulled. Looking at that tooth, I hear a Monami ball-point pen go *click*. I like that *click* when you press the button and the spring releases.

Dad held that pen up in front of me and pressed the button and *click* went the spring. He did it again—*click*. I can see myself mouth open, mesmerized by the click. And then there was another *click* and it did something to my tooth—it just fell down onto my tongue. Did it really happen? It was all over in an instant and it didn't hurt. It was magic. Dad said he could do anything with that pen. He didn't say what, but I knew for certain—that pen could remove a tooth and it wouldn't hurt.

I want my head cut too! I try to mimic the young man with the bushy hair and picture the flushed cheeks of the young woman who fell in love with him. I'm going to fall in love at first sight like Mom did. But I can't be giving away looks to some drooling fool. It has to be a gallant young man that I fall in love with, like the one with the bushy hair. But I'd like him to have nice hands, not the big, thick hands of Bushy Hair. When I meet a man with nice hands the first thing I'll do is lace my fingers through his and put our hands in my pocket. And I'll enjoy the touch and the workings of those hands, hidden from view, whether they're cool and clammy or warm and tingling.

There's a small hole in the corner of the loft floor. I drop the lamp cord through it, then go down to the washroom, unplug the hot-water heater, and plug in the lamp. It's a small lamp I bought at a gift shop, but it's elegant enough to set the mood. And now it's party time!

Chini has brought beer and snacks. We're snuggled up in a quilt, the lamp between us, sipping beer and giggling. We put our foreheads together and laugh until our eyes are oozing tears. Then push our makeshift box table out of the way and drum our feet on the floor calling out "Hurray!"

We're so happy we keep thinking up toasts to each other. Innocent happiness, innocent toasts, nothing dishonest. We don't have to hide our happiness if we're comforting someone who's sad, we don't have to wear a mask of consolation and pretend to share her sadness. That's why we're still pure. And it's through our purity that we're beautiful.

"Sŏna, what do you want to do at the university?"

"I don't know, I haven't really thought about it—what about you?"

"I'm thinking about media—the newspaper, the radio station, you know."

"Yeah, broadcasting—that's you. You really wowed everyone at the speech contest—you have such a nice voice and you speak so clearly."

"Are you trying to embarrass me? That was in *middle* school."

"What do you mean, embarrass? Look at all the prizes you won."

"Yeah, for being a puppet. For taking something someone else wrote and going out there and making noise—it's not my real voice you're hearing. Back to you—what do you want to do? Tell me."

"Hmm. . . . " I wonder if she'll look down on me. Well, candid is best. "I want to be in a CC."

"CC? As in 'campus couple'?"

"What, you don't approve?"

"Sure I do. You get to have dates, you go to orientation together. CC—yeah, that's good."

She sticks her chin out and closes her eyes. That's what she does when she disagrees with something or she has something to say. I hope Chini doesn't criticize me. Criticism is never fair. As long as I'm being honest, my honesty should be respected. If I told Chini she'll never be part of a CC because she looks like a stick figure in glasses, it's the truth, I wouldn't be criticizing her.

"But you know . . . now that we're in college, shouldn't we be different somehow?"

"Different how?"

"I feel like we should do something meaningful."

"Such as?"

"Something that gets your heart pounding. Something you can do because you're in college. Something you can only do when you're young. You know."

Is she criticizing me? Or is she telling herself what *she* needs to do? Well, what about love—doesn't that get your heart pounding? I want to tell her that. *That's* something you can do because you're young. You do what you can to get your heart pounding, and you live on. These words are on the tip of my tongue. But instead of letting them loose I bring in the words she said to me. And inscribe them in my own heart—*something to get your heart pounding, something you have to do when you're young, something meaningful.*

Sheepishly I bump shoulders with Chini. Bump bump. I've set the rhythm and she gets into it, touching her shoulder to mine— she's been waiting. It's never awkward making contact like this— because we care for each other and we can feel that. Chini smiles. I smile. Chini takes my hand in hers. I place my other hand on top.

"Anyway, we're going to be new—a new you and a new me," Chini says.

"Yes, and doing something that gets our heart pounding," I say.

I'm going to be in college. I'll do everything I ever wanted but couldn't. I'm going to open the crossbar to my body and soul and enjoy myself to the limit. I'm going to get my heart pounding. I'm going to love.

***

You fill in the line with tiny feathery strokes, like you're planting each of the hairs, Mom tells me as she works with the eyebrow pencil. The idea is to make a gentle arch, longer on the inside than the outside, with the length just right for the shape of your face. No fancy eye shadow—just highlight the shape of the eye with eyeliner.

I want her to leave my cheeks alone—they're naturally rosy. My lips need to be a perky red. Add gloss to the lipstick to liven the effect, and I'm all set. But then she wonders out loud if just the lip gloss would be better.

"Mom, I don't want to be late."

"Just a sec—let's try a different color of lipstick."

So again I stick out my lips. There's enough time. But I'm itching to see myself all dolled up. Mom's hands give off a lemon scent. I like the soft, moist touch of her hands brushing against my cheeks. She finishes with the new lipstick and examines my face.

"Are we done? Can I have the mirror?" I say, pursing my lips so I won't smudge them as I speak. Her expression tells me she's not completely satisfied—Mom the perfectionist. She hands me the mirror, and I look in vain for the smoky eyeliner and the purple lipstick I've seen on the ladies who sell cosmetics. I want to look a little more grown-up. But Mom always says the natural look is best.

She takes something out of the cabinet. A shoe box! I open it. The shoes are wrapped in tissue. Carefully I unveil them, the rustle of the paper promising elegance. I peel back several layers and the glossy shoes finally appear. I trace their contours with my finger. Wow—look at the heels! I ease my feet inside them. They're so snug and inviting the way they wrap my insteps. I lift my foot a few inches and the next moment my chest has pushed forward and my back is straight. My chin is up, I'm standing tall—it's magic.

"Take a few steps. Maybe the heels are too high? Do you think you can manage?"

Yes I can manage. These shoes are fantastic! I stick my chest out even more and take my first step. *Tap-tap.* A little tight but no problem otherwise. The tap of those heels will make people take notice. *Tap-tap.* My confidence swells and my waist narrows with each step I take. Beautiful, stately me. *Tap-tap.*

I look at myself in the full-length mirror—my short skirt, ending above the knee, and my turtleneck, both of them picked out by Mom. I try on a scarf and then the muffler I bought, and toss both items aside. Mom and I are surrounded by scattered clothes.

"Do I look all right? Is anything too showy? Do I really look like a college girl? Aren't the shoes too pointy? Don't they look like crocodiles? Mom, why aren't you answering?"

She's looking out the window, expressionless, arms limp at her sides. Her face is draped in shadow, and beneath her eyes I catch a glimpse of something even darker. But the next moment she's looking my way with a beaming smile.

That smile on her just-shaded face—what a contrast between light and dark.

Which is it that belongs to Mom, the shade that's left by light or the shadow that's left by a smile? Something's on her mind, but whatever it is, it doesn't feel like a big concern.

"I'm just being a worry wart—your first day and all." Mom smooths my clothing. "Have a blast," she says as I walk out the door.

I prance down the steps to the entry, luxuriating in my new

high-heels, and promptly bump into someone. I feel a twinge in my ankle. It's a man, and there's mail scattered at his feet. He gathers and pockets it and hurries outside. I check our mailbox. No new mail, only the same junk mail piling up. Not a good start crashing into someone first thing in the morning, but it's my big day so I'll give him the benefit of the doubt.

I swagger off, relishing the sound of my heels against the sidewalk. *Tap-tap.* The breeze feels nice. *Tap-tap.* I wonder who I'll be hanging out with the next four years. I hope I meet more kids like Chini. And I hope I can keep old friends like her when I make new friends.

I stop to catch my breath. My foot feels like it was stepped on and got twisted. I feel a tightening from my foot to my chest. Partly because the shoes aren't broken in yet, but maybe also when I bumped into the man? Or are my shoes a size too small? I'm afraid my big toe will rip through the leather.

I set off again. It's like all my nerves are running down to my foot. Now it's pain, not confidence, that's building with each step I take. Pain from cramping, pain rubbing and digging into my foot. It's scary how a nagging pain can possess you to the point that you lose your balance.

I arrive at the steps going up to the station. What now? Those steps look impossibly high. I'll have to change trains and from the station at the other end there's the climb up to the school. Now I realize my new high heels are overkill. A woman rushes past me and up the steps. *Taptaptaptap.* What a chirpy sound, the heels higher and more slender than mine—the real thing. With her hair streaming behind her, *she* doesn't look uncomfortable. Well, one of these days high heels will be part of me. I'm not going to let a little soreness bother me. I stick out my chin again—I'm back in control. Up the steps I go. *Tap-tap.* Back in control—I'm elegant. *Tap-tap.*

We're sitting in a circle on the amphitheater grass, the flag with the department logo rising from our midst. I like the bright red color but the lettering doesn't cut it—it's not cool, too extreme. Newspapers are spread out among us, and on them sit *soju, makkŏlli*, and snacks. I never expected booze for the reception for the new students. Am I the only one who's dressed up? I can't keep my legs together, can't keep them apart. The dry grass is poking my calves. A short skirt's a problem if you want to sit with your knees up. Someone spreads out a newspaper for me and I move onto it. Someone else gives me his jacket and I place it over my lap. That's better.

I tell myself to sit straight—that way my neckline will look nice, or so they say. I tense my bottom, straighten myself from the small of the back, put on a haughty look. Uh-oh, that makes my chest stick out too much. Then again the tip of my shoe looks so cute peeking out from the jacket.

The president of the Student Association is standing in the middle of the circle welcoming the new students. She's short but looks rough and ready. Her voice is clear, crisp, engaging—she's very articulate. She finishes to cheers and applause. Next up are the Student Association staffers. They all talk alike. I feel I'm listening to a gathering of speech-contest winners like Chini. Is this how university students talk? Silently I mimic them. My confidence is growing.

It's time for the new students to introduce themselves. I've been too obsessed about my appearance to prepare for this. We're told to be ourselves, let our personality show, say what makes us distinct—how am I supposed to do that? The first of the new students gets up, a girl with dragonfly glasses. She says she's from Pusan. Probably the only thing I'll remember is her Kyŏngsang accent. Next up is a girl with a perm who says she finally got admitted on this, her third try. And then she sits back down, forgetting to give her name. No clapping or cheers for her. I can tell from the wave that her perm is half-a-year old. It's hard to get excited about an unhip, third-time-lucky girl.

My turn is getting near and I feel a sense of urgency. Five people ahead of me.

Since we all wanted to get into this department, we probably have similar concerns. Now there are four of us left. Who's going to be impressed that I live in a satellite city? Now three people to go. I don't want to talk about Campus Couple stuff. Now we're down to two. A skinny boy gets up and launches into a song, a dirty, disgusting song. And then it's the last one before me.

"The reality is that innocent young men and women are being killed in this land of ours. . . ."

I look up. It's the boy next to me. I can't see his face except for his chin jutting out proudly as he stands there, hands clasped respectfully behind his back, intent on what he has to say.

"Last summer I witnessed a demonstration by university students—they were so passionate. I couldn't be part of that group, I could only hold my breath and watch. But now I'm ready to join those warm hearts and that hot blood. Please, teach us what we as young people must do. I promise to learn from you and to do my part, whatever it takes."

The young people of this land, hot blood, something that gets your heart pounding? Is there a cram school that teaches you this stuff? Is this how you're supposed to introduce yourself? Why do they all talk like that?

The boy sits back down. His knees brush against mine. I don't make eye contact; my gaze goes instead to his filthy blue jeans. The bottoms are frayed and tattered. The boy sits cross-legged like a gentleman, hands resting on his knees.

And then I realize *my* heart is pounding.

What a beautiful hand. Virile and yet lovely. Long, slender fingers, short, neatly-trimmed fingernails, soft fine hair between the knuckles and joints, the pink flesh of the fingertips. That hand makes contact with me. Not to feel me, not coming to rest on me, but just a touch. Like the wind in my hair. And now that hand is talking to me: two gentle taps on my knee—"Your turn."

Your turn. Yes, my turn. I look up. All eyes are on me. Of course—I'm the last one to introduce myself. I can't look like a weakling. I remove the jacket from my knees and stand.

"Well. . . . " It's so quiet. Only the sound of the fluttering flag playing about my ears. "Well, I. . ." And then it comes to me. ". . . want to do something meaningful." I proudly square my shoulders and let it roll off my tongue. And now that I've begun, that tongue takes on a life of its own. I don't think about what I'm saying and there's no time for the words to sink in. The eyes of those who are lending me their ears get my tongue loosened up even more. "We have to do things differently now that we're in college. Because we're young men and women. I want to do something that gets my heart pounding."

But it's not my voice. It's Chini's voice in the speech contest, her proclaiming voice. It's the beat of Chini's heart, not mine. I'm a puppet, a parrot, a petty thief. But am I ashamed of myself? Of course not. I'm not lying. Chini and I have a lot of thoughts in common, so who's to say whose thought was whose originally? Love is what will get *my* heart pounding. But because I'm like Chini in thinking of doing things that get my heart pounding, we're the same. And I'm not stealing from her because I'm not planning to go into media like she is. I just want to look good. Actually it's my seething heart that wants me to look good. I found the right answer, didn't I? That's what your eyes are telling me, aren't they? Yes, I said the right thing. I did well, yes I did.

Here I am, back to our alley already. I hardly remember changing trains. All I've thought about is that gathering. I keep thinking about the gentle tap of that handsome hand on my body. I stop and take a deep breath. A voice calling my name, someone coming up from behind me—how I wish. And then a sudden movement, like a black curtain sweeping across—someone's there, blocking my way.

Who is he? He's too close. So close I can hear him breathing— raspy, irregular breaths. My feet take me back a step. I look at him, see pain and melancholy on his face. I have a bad feeling about that face, I'm afraid I'll get infected by its pain simply from looking at it.

He advances a step.

"You live here?"

I take another step back.

"Why . . . do you ask?"

"An—is that your father's name?"

"Who . . . are you?"

"Your father—he's An, right?"

Frozen in place, I look at him. I can't retreat, can't get out of the way. Part of me thinks I've seen him before, part of me not. His mouth is clamped shut, the lips quivering. He smells like damp laundry. Like an old fishbowl or wash bucket, stale, moldy, like he's wet his pants.

His hand is on my shoulder. His breathing is rougher. He's gritting his teeth. "Where's your father?" he hisses.

There's menace in his tone and I imagine him grinding his teeth. His voice is muffled but has a vicious edge to it. I try to slip away and the hand presses down harder.

"What are you doing? Let go!"

"Where did your father go? Where's he hiding—where! Does he think he can hide and we won't find him? Where'd he disappear to? Tell me—speak up!"

Now he's shouting. And he's shaking me. I don't understand what he means. "You're hurting my shoulders, let go! You're *hurting* me. It hurts, you idiot!"

His grip on me loosens and I plop down onto the pavement. The man's arms fall limp to his sides, as if all the energy has been sucked out of him. He gazes in shock at his hands, as if they've just strangled someone. Then he walks away. I gape at his rounded back. The surroundings fade, sounds grow dim, and all I see is the slumping man, hands in his pockets as he staggers off. His back grows dim and blends into the gloom. I hear his voice in my mind: *Where's he hiding?*

Father has disappeared? He's in hiding? No, not Father. Hiding is what embezzlers do, or criminals who break out of jail, or serial killers. But Father's not a criminal, he's a policeman.

Father's in hiding? He must have gotten mixed up in some conspiracy. He's in danger—someone must have slandered him or threatened him. If he's done something wrong he would have turned himself in to face the music. That's the kind of man he is, righteous and brave, able to capture robbers barehanded. Somewhere in the loft he's got the plaques and medals to prove it.

I hoist myself to my feet and trudge home. I feel like a remote-controlled robot. I open the door to the multiplex, go up the steps, take out my key, open our door, and like I've done countless times, like a kid returning after a long day of study, I close the door behind me then turn and slide the bolt.

"I'm back."

Everything's dark, making the whir of the refrigerator sound unreal. It's creepy and chilly. I fumble along the wall and find the light switch. That's when I notice my feet are bare. What happened to my beautiful new shoes? And then I notice Mom. She's standing in the middle of the living room.

"Mom?" I call out in a soft voice. No movement.

"I'm back."

I slowly approach, get right up close to her. But there's no reaction, no expression on her face—it's like she's in shock. I take her arm. She flinches.

"Is that you, sweetie?" I can barely hear her.

"Mom . . . how come Dad's in hiding?"

"Where'd you hear that!"

"So it's true? Why would Dad go into—"

"Don't you believe it—they're lying."

"Lying about what?"

She flings my arm aside and turns away. Her back is like a wall and the message is clear—no more questions. That only makes me more determined. I turn Mom around so she's facing me.

"Just now some man asked me where Dad was hiding. He was shouting at me: 'Where's he hiding?' Where is he? Isn't he on emergency duty?"

"He didn't do anything wrong. It's all because of that Red son of a bitch!"

Red son of a bitch? The words give me a chill—my mother doesn't talk like that. *Red? Son of a bitch?* How could such expressions come out of that lovely mouth of hers?

She grips my hand. "Sŏna, you believe in your dad, don't you?" She's practically pleading. "That bastard. It's because of that bastard."

"Who, Mom? And what did Father do to him?"

"All your father did was slap him a few times. But his eardrum was ruptured—an unfortunate accident, your father said. Sŏna, he's a bad one, really bad. He was in jail. Why would he be in jail unless he was guilty of something, right? He has a grudge against your father, and now he's acting out. Sŏna, Dad didn't do anything wrong. You know what kind of man he is—don't you? And you believe in him, don't you? Because of that scumbag bastard, our innocent father. . . . "

She's talking a blue streak, like she has to keep talking or else she'll die. Or she's going to die and she's frantic to say something first.

"Yes. Yes, I believe in him." I say it over and over. Otherwise Mom's mumbling will never end and she'll be possessed forever. Mom cups my cheeks and squeezes. There's a vicious energy in those hands, like they want to strip the flesh from my cheekbones.

"Sŏna, listen carefully. When people are carrying out their job they sometimes make mistakes. It's happened to everybody. Well, there's been a fuss, and they told your dad to take some time off. All you need to do is keep believing in him. Just believe in your dad, and soon the truth will come out. In the meantime you can devote yourself to your studies without any worries. Do you hear what I'm saying? Don't you dare believe what other people say. They're lying. Do you understand? Tell me. You understand, don't you!"

"Yes, I understand. I believe in him. Yes."

Over and over I nod, until finally Mom removes her hands. Her eyes are moist.

"Is Dad all right?"

Mom nods. "Yes, of course he's all right."

I take a deep breath and then I'm shuddering the way people do when they've cried their eyes out and are trying to steady their breathing. I snuggle up to Mom. I stroke her back but it feels like I'm stroking my own back. I don't know what else to do.

I should have told Chini about the new-student reception. But the words felt like a lump in my throat and I kept swallowing them. I didn't mean to keep it a secret, but with Chini talking nonstop about her own reception and orientation, I could scarcely get a word in. She was even more worked up than when she told me she'd gotten into her university.

I'm in my room, staring at everything I might need for my own orientation—it's two nights and three days. I can't figure out what I'll really need and what will prove extra—I should have picked Chini's brain about that. My toiletries and warmup outfit are ready, but I should buy a small pouch for my makeup and socks. And since it's two nights, should I take my pajamas?

I throw on a jacket and leave, through the beauty parlor and outside. I freeze. That man. He's in front of the record shop across the street. His hands are buried in his pockets and his head is down, but I know it's him. Or rather I *feel* it's him, my body and not my brain telling me so—the pressure on my shoulders and the buzzing in my ears.

I ease myself back inside the beauty parlor. I draw the bolt and lower the blinds and then call home. After several rings Mom picks up. I tell her about the man. There's a long sigh at the other end.

"Stay where you are—don't go out."

"What about you, Mom?"

"Don't worry—I know what to do."

"Should I keep the door—"

I'm cut off. "Mom?" All I hear is the emptiness of the dial tone. Mom, I feel like an orphan here.

I peek out through the blinds just in time to see the man take a quick look about and then start across the street. I flinch and step back, then return to the blinds and peek again. He's almost here. I press myself against the wall. The door rattles. I close my eyes. He can't see me—it's too dark. And the blinds are closed. Has he left? Did I lock the door tight? Did he see me then? How long has he been out there? Did he follow me from home? But why is it me that has to hide? If it's like Mom said and it's the man who did something wrong and not Dad, then why am I acting like this?

I move away from the wall. If you want to take a look, go ahead. Do you want to come in? Be my guest, scumbag. But no way are you going to push me around. I stand at the door. It's quiet—no sound of anyone lurking outside. Again I look through the blinds—he's back in front of the record shop. I ease myself against the wall and keep him in sight.

His hands are in his pockets and he's stamping his feet to keep warm. He lights a cigarette, takes a look this way, and breathes out a long stream of smoke. He tosses the butt to the pavement and crushes it out. His gaze is fixed on the beauty parlor. Here we are keeping watch on each other, only the street dividing us. What's the point? We're just wasting time.

Everything was smooth sailing until that man appeared. I got into the university and I'll have heart-pounding experiences and romances galore. And here I am hiding out, trapped like a rat.

"Red son of a bitch!" I spit out the words. That's better. Now I feel braver, more righteous. I'm not going to hide like a rat. I unbolt the door, open it, and march across the street.

"What do you think you're doing, mister? What are you snooping around here for? Huh?"

The man takes a cigarette from his pocket. Without removing his eyes from me he produces a lighter and lights up. He blows smoke in my face. I'm not going to close my eyes, I'm not going to cough. I'm not going to be afraid, not going to plop down like I did last time. I'm not going to run away, I'm not going to hide. You want to shout at me, go ahead. I'll scream so loud you'll never show your face here again.

"All I want to know is where your father is."

"Even if I knew, you think I'd tell someone like you, mister? I know who you are. You're the one my dad slapped around, aren't you? I heard all about it from my mom. And you're the one who was stealing our mail, weren't you, mister?"

"Slapped around?"

"And you were in jail too, weren't you. While my dad was getting three medals from the government—three! You think you can come around here and we're just going to kneel down in front of you? If you do something wrong you need to come clean and admit it and then get on with your life, instead of harassing us."

"What? You don't know? You really don't know, or you're only pretending?"

"That's right, I don't know. So tell me what I don't know. What about my dad?"

"You really want to know? You want to know how he got those medals?"

"Yeah, tell me!"

Go ahead and tell me, you arrogant Red son of a bitch. I stick out my chest and glare at the man.

Without any warning he raises his hand. I close my eyes and cover my face, certain he's going to hit me. But instead he grabs my wrist and yanks it.

"Let go—what are you doing?"

"I'm going to show you who your father is. You're coming with me, let's go." He drags me away. I sense glances from passersby but no one comes over to us.

The man is practically running and he's breathing hard. Finally he stops at a newsstand. With his free hand he searches his pocket and comes out with some money, which he places next to a stack of leftover newspapers. He picks up a copy and shoves it in my face.

"Okay—look!" But the next moment, "That's strange, he's not there. I was sure they'd show him again. He was in yesterday's, that's for damn sure. And the day before it was a picture of that poor guy Hwang that he worked over. Say, mister, can I see the paper from the day before yesterday?"

"From two days ago? You'll need to find the distributor or else go to a library."

"So where's the distributor?"

He's anxious and fretful and he's not paying attention. He relaxes his grip on my wrist. Quick—I pull my hand free and off I run. No looking back. Red son of a bitch, you Red son of a bitch—

that's all I'm thinking. And then I realize I was too hasty. I didn't think it through. I was only pretending I was fearless. I'm afraid the man's going to grab me. I'm panting like a dog, my tongue feels bone dry. No looking back. I round a corner, another corner, down a narrow alley, out to a street, across the street to a sidewalk, car horns blaring—run, just run. The breath from my mouth is hot.

I feel like there's grit in my eyes, like I'm caught in a sandstorm. The sunlight is blinding me. I feel like I'm burning up, vein by artery, cell by cell. The rays of the sun are piercing me. I need to get out of the light. I find a narrow alley, squeeze among heaps of garbage and chunks of ice, and hold my breath.

From where I squat I can see inside the building, I can see them sticking inserts into the newspapers. Their hands move in a rhythm, almost like they're dancing. Tomorrow's newspapers, newly bundled, tied, and stacked and ready to go. And there, outside the building, next to the wall, the stack bound with yellow twine—the newspaper from the day before yesterday. Buy one copy and you buy the whole stack, the man said. And that's the stack he pointed to.

Everyone's busy and no one's going to notice a girl. I move like a cat, quiet and slinky, over to the wall where the old newspapers are stacked. I heft the stack with the yellow twine. It's heavier than I thought, so bulky and heavy I can only take short, clumsy steps. No time for regrets, I have to run. Sorry, guys—I need to check something and then I'll bring them back. I don't have any money but I'll pay you later. I'm moving like a duck, half-running, half-toddling. That twine's going to cut through my fingers.

I stop beneath a streetlight. Sit down on the stack of newspapers and catch my breath. There's sweat on my forehead, twine marks on my fingers. The blood is moving again and my palm tingles. I look around. A clean getaway. Carefully I stand up. The stack of newspapers—how am I supposed to get them undone? I grab the twine, give a lift, then set the stack down again. It's too tight—how can I cut it? There, on the ground, a bent nail. I stab at the twine where it's knotted, stab some more, and *snap*—the plastic comes apart.

I take the copy on top—I want to make sure it's the right date. "Ow!" A paper cut on the inside of my arm. Then I notice the date, but before the numbers register, I see my father. A photo of my father, right above the crease on the first page. It really is him. I unfold the paper.

"Doctor Torture in Hiding."

An—my father. *In Hiding.*

It's Father's face for sure, the same photo that's on his citizen ID. Plump cheeks, corners of his mouth slanted upward. Bushy eyebrows just like mine. My father—no doubt in my mind. *An—Doctor Torture. Master of Waterboarding, Electric Shock, Dislocation of Bones. In Hiding. Torture Victims on His Trail, Offering Reward.*

I hear a voice in my head: *Where did your father hide? Where's he hiding— where!* The voice is getting louder. Scary loud—it's shaking me by the shoulders. *Where did your father hide himself? Your father, Doctor Torture.*

My soul is freezing. My blood is ice cold, my tongue is hard, my heart no longer beats.

Crack! The ice is breaking.

CHAPTER 3

"My apologies, sir," Paek mumbles. "This is the best we could do. Times are tough. Try to hang in there—"

"You don't have to apologize. How long did they say?"

"Just for the time being. They'll come up with a plan."

"Pak knows?"

"He's the one who arranged it."

"Figures. He wouldn't leave me out to dry. So when's the hearing?"

"End of the month at the earliest, that's what I think. They're trying to corner us. And with Pak having to do damage control, it's complicated. Even our analysts are vulnerable—they got involved in something out of our jurisdiction. But right now your safety is our main priority. Rest assured, sir, we'll be all right."

Paek makes a fist and gives me a determined look. That's what he does when he's anxious or lacks confidence. His bravado is a defense mechanism, it's how he deals with his weaknesses, and he knows it. Whenever I see him I feel like I'm watching a defective eldest son. The good news is that he knows exactly what his shortcomings are, and that a son with shortcomings must obey his father unconditionally if he's to be accepted by that father. It saddens me when he goes overboard, when he's vicious and cruel, but I give him full credit and in turn he's loyal to the bone. He's the only one of my offspring that I trust wholeheartedly. And I trained him.

"How's my family?"

"They're well, sir."

"Did you tell them where I am?"

"No sir. We think it's better that they not know."

"Agreed. Well done."

"Your daughter got admitted to the department she wanted—your good wife asked me to be sure to tell you."

"Could you have something sent to her?" I go through my pockets and offer him money. He waves it off and takes a step back.

"That's all right, sir—I'll take care of it."

"No, it's something *I* have to do."

Paek reluctantly accepts the money, and off he goes with his briefcase. I follow at my own pace.

Is the Rehabilitation Center the best the organization could come up with? Rehab center? It's more like a garbage dump, its mission to rehabilitate the homeless, the vagrants, people ruled incompetent by the courts. Originally it was where we kept the people we'd worked over in the College of Education—the guys who couldn't turn over a new leaf and never graduated. This dumpster was their final stop.

There's no sign, just a rusty iron gate, a low cement-block wall, and prefab buildings. The yard is large enough, but still it's oppressive here. Out back are thick woods and tangles of scrub. The compound doesn't try to hide itself, nor does it stand out. But its mere existence hints of intimidation.

Three years. That's how long they have to file charges. I have to stick it out three whole years and not get caught—those are my instructions from the organization.

I pass through the main gate. A pair of dogs are barking fiercely, teeth bared, foaming at the mouth—not happy being tied up, I guess. Paek brandishes his briefcase, riling them all the more. A man with a riot policeman's baton emerges from a building. He swishes the instrument back and forth and the dogs fall silent. Then he leads us off.

Dogs don't bark at their masters, they bark at strangers. They don't feel safe with people they don't know and so they try to scare them off. They try to sense if people wish them harm, and if they do, how much fight those people have in them. When they're sure there's no intent to attack, or if they realize their counterpart is stronger, they stop barking. Whether they wag their tail or tuck it between their legs depends on the opponent's power. To those dogs, the baton is absolute.

The office is in the building farthest back. That pathetic excuse for a director knew we were coming, but apart from a quick glance he keeps his eyes on the papers in front of him. He reeks of scorn and arrogance but he has the pointy face of a rat that would scurry for its hole at the first sign of trouble. The lines of annoyance on his forehead and the thin wrinkles at the corners of his mouth give him a servile, gutless look. This guy is not to be trusted.

"Look at all the fallout I get from the College of Education or the Hearing Committee or whatever you people call it. I take in these broken-down items and feed them and give them a bed. Does anyone bother saying thank-you? No, I'm supposed to empty my pockets for them. Hell! Do you happen to know how much supplementary money I get?"

He slaps a handful of papers onto his desk and gets up. Which is a mistake, because now you can see how small he is. He waddles to his couch and sprawls out on it.

"You received the instructions, sir?" Paek asks.

"Yes, I received the instructions. Of course I received the instructions. Your instructions have caused me a great deal of trouble. Do you not recall, good sir, all the headaches you've sent my way? And now I have the pleasure of hosting this distinguished gentleman. I have prepared for him our largest room, normally it sleeps four, but just for him. . . . And with no supplementary money, mind you. . . . "

His mouth runs like a sewer.

"This will supplement you for a few months," says Paek as he tosses the director a bundle wrapped in black plastic. His voice is ominous and he's gritting his teeth. "If I were you, sir, I wouldn't be too greedy. This *facility* of yours could go under in a day. . . ."

"Greedy? No sir, I just—"

"I understand your esteemed daughter plays the violin. In Berlin, no less. The perfect breeding ground for a Commie."

That's my boy. That's the kid I trained. Guy wants to shadow-box, then deck him. Guy that's sarcastic and looks down his nose at you, you show him who's boss. He doesn't know how to play with fire, burn him. He wants to play a cheap trick, teach him an expensive lesson. You find his weak spots and exploit them. Do that and I'll call you my very own son.

"Now don't get me wrong . . . I only thought. . . ." Already the guy's talking more respectfully. "I mean, with the current situation we need to be careful with each other . . . and there's the fact that we're harboring a fugitive. That makes it dangerous for both of us—"

"All right," I interrupt, "so where's my room?" It's bad enough watching him with his nose in the air but it's worse when he's fawning at our feet. Got him boxed it, the pointy-faced rat. Look at his eyes dance as he tries to figure out what he's in for. Look at him smile, hands gathered in his lap, pretending nothing's happened. My warning light goes on. He's a creepy bastard all right.

"Oh, shall we have a look? I told them to get it ready. . . ."

The guy shifts into gear. As soon as he's locked the bundle of money in a drawer he's out the door and shouting instructions in a voice full of irritation. And, the finishing touch, he turns back with a bow to let us know we're blameless.

"The five buildings over this way are for the ambulatory. Most are vagrants who were found sick on the streets and have no known relatives. We also have senior citizens who were abandoned, even parents dumped here by their children—God only knows how they found us. What's the world is coming to? And those five buildings over there are for our special-needs residents—alcoholics, the mentally ill, they're a pain in the ass, all of them. Still, we try to be consistent in our awareness and our treatment. . . ."

On he goes, one excuse after another. He's working up a sweat making sure everything looks good on paper—accommodations, treatment team, medical staff, volunteers—but the proceeds probably go straight to that belly of his.

You're looking to legitimize yourself, aren't you. Wanting to dress yourself up as a honeybee instead of a shitfly. Help yourself, but you were born a shitfly in a dump and that's all you'll ever be. You probably inflated the number of patients so you get more of the government tit to suck on, but it's still not enough and so you're sticking your pointy snout into every possible opportunity. You found a pipeline that guarantees you a stream of weak and powerless people, and that's where you hatch your eggs and expand your power, you shitfly son of a bitch.

I knew there were places like this, but not that they're run by human trash. Is it any wonder that shitflies breed in garbage?

He stops with an exultant expression—he's just found the object of his search. "I wonder if you know this item. I think he might be one of your graduates. . . . "

He gestures with his chin toward a window and steps aside. Paek takes a quick look in and scowls.

"His mind was gone when they brought him in. We barely managed to save him.

Care to have a look, sir?"

The guy gives me a *gotcha* grin.

I look, but the first thing I notice is the smell—like that of pus from an infection, or mushy, decomposing flesh. Through the window I see a naked man sitting on the floor, his back to the wall. He's so emaciated the fine bone structure of his rib cage is visible.

He's scratching himself all over, his hands moving with difficulty. He scratches his crotch, takes his testicles in hand and pulls on them, then scratches his neck. He stops to gape at himself. Blood oozes from scabs. He looks up, moving in slow motion as if gravity works differently there. He rotates his head and gazes in my direction, his line of sight going past me into the far distance.

"You know this item, don't you?"

An item. And that's what he is, a broken-down item, a lump of skin and lard, garbage to be collected and dumped.

Do I know that item? Well, he is an item, but it takes skill to increase an item's usefulness. No matter how strong an item may look, once you take it in your hands and shake it, it's easy to break down. But you can't leave scars. You can empty the inside, but the outside has to remain intact. An item that's cracked spells disaster. That's what happens when the rookies run wild, and this is where you remove the ruins from sight. That man wasn't manufactured by me. I don't know that item.

***

Set apart from the ten connected prefab buildings for the residents, the office building includes treatment rooms, a cafeteria, and classrooms. But among these facilities, only the cafeteria fulfills its intended use. And guess what—each resident's room is locked from the outside, and when they're let out the residents don't stray far, only making the rounds of the compound grounds.

Daytime is peaceful enough, but only on the surface, the result of oppressive rules and punishment. You don't see the trivial quarrels that usually break out when people are at close quarters. Instead of making eye contact the residents look off in the distance, each inhabiting his own world. Even at mealtime, when they're all gathered together, you hear only the clink and clatter of utensils and dishes. The stubborn silence and the tedious calm are eerie.

Nighttime is a different story. The place fills with noise—the painful moans of the ill, spasms of cackling, long drawn-out screams, bellowing that continues into the night. And when the din finally recedes, there's always stifled weeping. The weeping reminds me of the naked man, of the labored movements of his hands as he scratches himself until he draws blood. I can see his prominent rib cage and his wasted arms, I can picture his unfocused eyes and his slack jaw. His sobbing lasts until dawn.

It's been only a few days but it feels much longer. My room is too large for one person, and it features a fleecy new faux-mink blanket with a rose pattern. The door has no lock and there's no one to stop me from leaving. So why do I feel so frustrated and uncomfortable?

The lights go off, as they're programmed to do. Soon the

howling will start, and then the man's sobbing, which gives me the creeps. I close my eyes and hope for sleep.

An image of a shredded face flits through my mind, a messed-up face like a battered boxer's. And a quivering fist dripping blood. The face is stubborn in spite of the cuts and the eyes swollen shut, the face of a boxer who won't spit out his mouthpiece or let his corner throw in the towel. The face of humiliation I created the one time I lost my head.

I think of the naked man's hands. Something's not right the way they move. I have a fleeting thought of a pair of soft and lovely hands. Could they be the same?

I hear plaintive weeping and curl up against the wall bordering my bed. No shouting, no screaming, just bitter sobs both sorrowful and chilling. I imagine the man's fingernails digging into his flesh. I see the blood flowing. How long before he's flayed himself?

Feet storm down the hall. Two men? Three? A baton bangs on the steel door and the door creaks open. "Hey—go to sleep, you fucking idiot, you're driving everybody crazy, yowling like a cat, howling like a ghost, every damn night. Shut up and get some sleep." And then they kick him. I hear them panting like dogs in heat. So, the dogs are out hunting. *Stop it or you'll kill the kid.* The kicking stops, along with the sobbing. A moment's silence is followed by the slosh of water, and a bucket clanks onto the floor.

The door slams shut, the lock clicks, and triumphant footsteps trail off.

I move my chair to a sunny spot. The breeze is cool but the sun is warm on my skin. It's been a week since the scumbag director's last appearance. And yet the operation rolls along without a hitch. If you've got minions to do the work, who needs the master? Here at the Rehab Center the people responsible for the daily operation are a select few residents. They go around sporting armbands and are absolutely loyal, keeping tabs on the other residents and displaying their authority. They bark and they bully, even with the meek and the docile.

I can't quite pinpoint their attitude toward me. They don't wag their tails and they don't bare their teeth. They keep their distance but they're always watching me. I don't mix with them.

One of the loyal dogs likes to heft his baton as he makes his rounds. But he looks more like a weasel the way he taps on the residents' doors. After lunch I saw him nodding off on the couch in the office, and now he's hanging around out here. Looks like he can't wait for his next opportunity to lord it over the residents.

I spread out my newspaper. Here we go again, another article about me. Well, sakes alive, I've been terminated. Desertion of workplace and unexcused absence—two pathetic excuses for cause. One thing is for sure—the situation back there is punk. If they've charged Hyŏn as well as Paek and Ŭn, then the bad guys are applying the pressure for real. Well, it's only the superior court prosecutors who are bringing the charges—it could be worse.

"Find something interesting?"

A shadow falls over the newspaper—the scumbag director has planted himself in front of me, his thin lips twitching like he's dying to ask questions. I snap open the next spread.

"How did that student of yours end up dead anyway?"

No preliminaries. This shithead has some nerve.

"Way I hear it, he just croaked. I don't get it. Here we work them over till they shit blood but nobody dies on us—people don't die easy, you know."

"You heard wrong—and it wasn't *my* student."

I snap the newspaper together and get up. The scumbag sits down in the chair I've just vacated and starts muttering. "Fucking bastard, arrogant butcher asshole." I feel like I've been clubbed over the head. My hands tremble, and I have to make a fist to control my rage.

I cross the yard and go into my musty building. At the naked man's room I bend over to look through the window. He's lying down, curled against the wall, his back black and blue, the backbone showing. I try the door. Metal clinks against metal—it's locked—but there's no reaction from the naked man.

"Appreciating your artistry? What's it like seeing a ruined item firsthand?"

The scumbag has sneaked up behind me and is looking over my

shoulder. He nudges me with a sly grin.

"We don't make items like this," I say in an icy tone, not looking at him.

The man still isn't moving. He looks too stiff to have dropped off to sleep. And why isn't he scratching himself?

"Why don't you put this one out of his misery too? He raises hell every night—the residents can't stand it."

I stick my hands in my pockets and move off. But the shitfly keeps buzzing around my ear.

"I hear your artistry is splendid, good sir. Number Two Man at the Funeral Home, that's a great moniker. Like they say, number two is scarier than number one. And you designed that whatchamacallit, the Board of Death? The gentleman who makes kids wet their pants with a single glare? How about giving our boys the benefit of your expertise? Then we can rid of some of these pieces of shit. And where in God's name did you learn to pull a guy's arm out of its socket and stick it back in again?"

"How about I get rid of you first, you piece of garbage. You want a taste of Number Two?"

If you want my attention you can start by losing the scorn and vulgarity. How can scum like you talk about my beautiful technique. How dare you nudge my shoulder. I turn and grab the guy by the scruff of the neck, knee him in the crotch, and shove him against the prefab's metal wall. Then I take his wrist. I can dislocate your lousy shoulder, no problem.

"You know what the Funeral Home is for? It's for getting rid of shit like you."

It's a place for eradicating parasitic insects, for snipping off the buds of evil, eliminating all that's foul, impure, and disturbing. Funeral work involves ethics and standards, just like any other profession, even the dumpster business. We can't clean up the world until scumbags like you disappear.

He tries to wiggle his arm free, squirming and squeaking like he's out of breath. His face is blood red and his tongue hangs out. What are you going to do now, try a quick fix to avoid pain, or slink out and wait for an opportunity to strike back? What you really need to do is give up—unconditional surrender. Subtly and steadily I press down on his shoulder—pop. His moans turn to screams, and tears ooze from his bloodshot eyes. I pop his shoulder back in place and give him a shove. Down he goes.

"Maggot!"

He's holding his neck and making a funny little croaking sound. One of the baton-wielding dogs scampers over, but it's too late. He helps the scumbag to his feet. The guy shakes off the dog and spits on the floor. He looks up at me with teary eyes full of fear and keen with hatred. He's breathing hard, nostrils flaring as he tries to digest his anger.

But once my triumph has had its day, contempt sets in. That's the awful part, because I've just set myself up for a terrible downfall. You can't think about triumph when you're dealing with shitflies. This is his territory and I'm sure the scumbag is full of dirty tricks. For the time being I'm on his leash. I've been reckless.

The air feels different, fresh, that's the only sensation. And when the weight presses down on me it's already too late. I didn't hear the door open, or the tiptoeing, or the approaching sound of breathing.

A sack goes over my head, smelling of fuel. They pin me by the arms and legs. And here we ago—clubbing, kicking, hissed curses, the clink of metal. The cowardly master's loyal dogs have arrived, dirty slobbering animals with bared teeth, avid to tear flesh, gobble intestines, rip out hair by the roots. One of them plants his heel on the back of my hand and grinds it. Another one gets into a rhythm: Kick. "Fucking bastard!" Kick. "Fucking bastard." I hear the panting of spineless men. Fists rain down on my face.

"Do you know where you are? You think you run this place? You think you're the boss? Let me tell you who the boss is. It's me—understand? Why do you think the organization sent you here anyway? You could disappear and that would solve everything. And guess who would take the most joy from that, you asshole. Who do you think you are, you fucking bastard? You butcher son of a bitch, you think you've got something to teach us? How about we send you over to the dissection table? Or bury you alive? If you don't want to die, then keep out of trouble, understand? Lay low, butcher son of a bitch."

What is it you're stomping, me or something *about* me? Do I scare you? Is it your hidden fears you're fighting? It's yourselves you're kicking, and the more you kick, the weaker you get. You're out of control—you won't get me to submit by panicking. Guess what? The loser isn't me, it's you. What you'll get from me isn't surrender, it's contempt.

This is violence at its ugliest—lousy, pathetic violence. Go ahead, work me over. Do you know who I am? I'm a warrior, an agent of good who stands up to the forces of evil. Evil must be eliminated, and I won't submit to it. I won't moan—that would only encourage you, make you kick me more. You think I'll kneel down to your stupid kicking?

I feel a dull thud against my head, hear a swarm of cicadas, taste blood. My ears must be swelling like balloons. I smell disinfectant, and something faintly metallic. My bones are screaming, my ears are plugged. My ribs ache, my jaw feels broken.

Everything's a blur.

I awake to whistling—it must be coming from the woods. And to the musical jingle that signals breakfast. I hear marching and a "Hut-two-three-four" cadence. Lunchtime arrives—there's no music at lunch. Someone looks in through the window and vanishes. The light coming through the window fades and night settles in. Lights out. My mind is clear but my body won't move. I smell rice, fresh from the cooker. I'm hungry.

I open my eyes. What time is it? There's silence all around, none of the screams and shouts I always hear at night, no hacking from the old men. I hoist myself up and pass my hands across my face. A lip cracks open, blood seeps out, flakes of crusted blood come off. I wipe down my face with a towel, clear my throat, and spit bloody mucus along with a chip from a tooth.

In the eerie stillness I hear guarded footsteps and the creak of a door. There's a pause, and then movement, the hum of muffled voices, a weight being dragged across the floor. It sounds like that weight is wearing sneakers.

I ease open my door and go out. Every step I take forces a groan, reminding me how sore I am. The moon is bright and it's crystal clear, a perfect night for an evil crime. I see a pull-cart rolling across the grounds, headed for the hill in back of the complex.

Everywhere else it's still.

I wait, then follow. The cart is empty now, sitting unattended at the edge of the grounds. The gate to the uphill path is open—these guys are careless. The woods are dense and I can't make out the trail. Using the moon as a beacon I forge my way up through the trees, branches crackling and snapping beneath my feet. I stop and listen, hear a shovel crunching into soil. That's evidence enough. What needs burying so urgently that they're digging into frozen ground? I retrace my steps, and next to the cart I crouch down and have a smoke. Here come the dogs with their shovels. As they pass through the gate they flinch. I toss my cigarette aside.

"Evening, gentlemen, is that a dog you slaughtered? How kind of you to bury the poor creature instead of roasting it."

I head for my room, followed by muttered curses. At the corner of the prefab I glance back. They're still beside the cart. Back in my room I take my Smith and Wesson from the pack and put it under my pillow. You sons of bitches want to jump me, go ahead. I'll be ready.

"I'm sorry to hear you had an unfortunate encounter, sir. It seems my boys went to the wrong room. Well, think of them as your welcoming party."

"Yeah, I got welcomed all right. Your boys are too rambunctious—they need to learn some manners."

"Which is why you need to be on your good behavior, sir. In a proper family the boys take care of their old pop—as your good self should know, having worked in an organization. Think of them as welcoming you into our happy family. Well, so much for pleasantries. . . . Goodness gracious, your poor face—I'll have the boys fetch you some ointment."

"Before you do that perhaps you should tend to those holes out back. It seems quite a few dogs are buried there. Granted this is a garbage dump, but you're in no position to be—"

"I'm not sure, my good man, that *you're* in a position to be running off at the mouth. You seem to think you've stumbled onto a gold mine. Now suppose we go check on those holes—that puts both of us in a fix, your side and my side, am I right?"

I wait to hear what he says next.

"I think we've talked enough about holes. But speaking of dogs, we actually did slaughter one. Why don't you try it?"

The scumbag spreads out a newspaper on my table, then signals the three loyal dogs arrayed behind him. They produce a table-top butane stove and a big pot, and in no time the greasy dark-red stew is bubbling away.

"I should tell you this isn't some stray mutt—it's a fighting dog. And not just any fighting dog, but the champion, the top dog. The texture of the meat is heavenly—you won't taste dog like this anywhere else. I think you know how it works. A bunch of men slaughter a dog, hunker down around it and dig in, then they get naked and sweat it out in a sauna, and then they get their pipes cleaned—togetherness, you know—and then you have yourself a team. But you're not in a position to get naked, much less get your pipes cleaned, so let's make do with the dog stew."

And the spiel concludes with the guy setting a bowl of stew before me. Well, why not—until the organization finds me a new hideout. I have to admit, my mouth is watering. But then my hand holding the spoon comes to a stop. There, where the dark-red broth has spattered the newspaper, is my face. "Torture Specialist An Vanishes. Police Reticent or Incapable? Victims Offer Reward, Stir Pot." This is no coincidence—he wanted to make sure I noticed. I look up. The scumbag is wearing a sly grin. Shitfly son of a bitch, he's laid one more egg on the rotten meat.

"Looks like the gentleman's stock has gone up."

All is dark except the office. A man dozes inside, legs skinny as chopsticks up on his desk. I take a folding chair from beside the door and before he can react, I slam it over his head. Blood splatters against the wall and he crumples to the floor.

I haul him up, sit him back in his chair, then gag and tie him. He's still bleeding. I find the keys in his pocket and look outside—where's the vehicle? There it is, parked next to the wall, a pickup with a double cab. No time to lose. I kick open the director's locked desk. The black bundle from the organization is gone. But there are documents. I flip through them and stuff them in my pack.

The grounds are ghostly still. I get in the pickup, turn on the dome light, and adjust the mirrors. Is that my face I see, that grotesque, scabbed-over gnarly mess that looks like a toad's back? I check the backs of my hands. They're a rainbow of bruises, the fingers swollen and puffy.

I fire the ignition. The ancient engine coughs, sputters, and rumbles in the gloom.

Time to go get myself lost.

CHAPTER 4

I don't go out till sundown. Keeping to the sides of the street, I pass the shoe shop and the butcher's and arrive at the porridge shop. Quite a jaunt for a bowl of red-bean porridge.

"Please could I get it with a couple extra rice balls," I squeak. "That's how my mom likes it."

No reaction from the auntie as she ladles the porridge. But then she slips a small mung-bean pancake into the bag. I thank her and leave.

I rub my arm, a nervous gesture, and look behind me just in time to see an outline disappear into the alley. A stray cat? No, a person. I hear the shadow in the alley take a cautious step, like it wants to play peekaboo. I take measured steps—*steady, don't look back*—though I want to go faster. Around the next corner and into our alley and I'm safe. I take the last step up, open our door, dart in, and draw the bolt. I steady my breathing.

Was it all in my imagination? A long breath leaks out of me. My forehead resting against the door feels cool.

"Mom, I got the porridge, with plenty of rice balls. And guess what, auntie tossed in a pancake—"

Mom's face—it's pale and frightened. She's surrounded by men who look uneasy and embarrassed at the fact they're uneasy. An edgy oppressiveness hangs heavy in the air. I wish I could disappear. *Who are you guys, anyway?*

Four men, I have no idea who. One at either end of the couch, another standing beside the shoe cabinet near the door, the last man leaning against the living room wall. Mom is sitting between the two men on the couch, hands gathered in her lap, a nice little lamb. She beckons me with her chin. I dawdle to her side, feeling the gazes of the men. Mom makes room for me beside her. I set down the bag of porridge and sit, taking Mom's arm in my hands. She rests a hand on my knee.

"You the college girl, little miss?" drawls one of the men on the couch. His tone is insolent. I notice the sharp outline of his jaw. Try a little tenderness? Forget it.

I stick out my chin and shoot Razor Jaw a look. I don't like you and I'm not going to answer. I don't know you guys and I'm not saying anything. I have no clue where my dad's hiding. You want to find him, be my guest.

"She just started—she got into the Korean literature department."

Mom! My head whips around and I glare at her. What are you *doing!* Who are these men and why do you sit there like a little angel?

Mom draws near and whispers that they're on our side.

Our side? I feel like a snake's tongue is licking me. Dad, Mom, these strange men—all on the same side? I feel goose bumps all over. My blood is freezing, my body is hardening, I feel cold. What's left of Dad inside me, my freezing blood is pushing out. Or is it me that's being pushed. *Our side.* But I'm not on anybody's side, and no one's on my side—not Mom, not Dad, not these strange men, not those shadows hovering around outside.

"Let's call it a day," says Razor Jaw to the man beside the shoe cabinet.

The man nods reluctantly. "Once the special unit gets rolling," he says to Mom, "there's not much we can do. And now that the media hounds have sniffed you out, maybe you should consider moving, don't you think?"

Mom straightens and shoots each of the men a look. "Move? Why should we—we haven't done anything wrong," she says, her jaw clenched. "No—we put a lot of work into this place. I don't want to move. Let's face it—you guys are the ones with the problem, and it makes you uncomfortable. It's not our fault we're under your jurisdiction. If somebody has to move, why not you guys? I'm not going to budge."

She looks like she's about to cry. The man near the shoe cabinet stares off into space. He looks like he wants to get rid of an insufferable pest. And these guys are on *our* side?

"Am I wrong? What did this girl's dad do wrong? Besides being guilty of patriotism. Is it a crime to go after Reds? You know as well as I do he's devoted half his life to catching those damned Reds. We're lucky if we see his face three or four times a year. You know what he told the girl when I was in the hospital with appendicitis? He was busy chasing Commies and don't disturb him unless I die."

By now she's in the face of the man on the other side of her. When she says "the girl" she gives me a shove as if I'm a piece of evidence that's served its purpose. There's meanness in her hands. Her shove sends me toward the man beside me, and I brace myself against the coffee table to keep my distance. I won't soon forget the fierceness of Mom's hand on my back.

The shove is unnerving enough, but what really throws me is Mom's appearance.

The mom I know—neatly upswept hair and a slender, graceful neckline, who glides about with comb and scissors singing in a voice both sweet and gentle—has been replaced by a profane woman who shoves me and barks spitefully.

"You people got your use out of him, you sucked him dry, and now that the wind's blowing in your face you're going to get rid of him?" she growls. "Are you *men* going to feel safe once he's nabbed? You think I don't know anything? What I *do* know is that you put him up to everything he did—didn't you?"

Not even a cough, no movement to break the deathly stillness, only Mom's uneven breathing. Finally Razor Jaw grunts and hauls himself to his feet, and the four of them prepare to leave.

"Sŏna," Mom calls out. "Lock the door behind them."

I'm still clutching the coffee table for dear life.

"What's the matter with you—don't you want to lock the door?"

All right. I get up and follow the men to the door. The last one turns back toward me. Our eyes meet—until I slam the door. I draw the bolt, then look back at Mom. She's gnawing anxiously at her fingernails, and can't sit still.

"I need to clean up the loft," she mumbles to herself, not looking at me. "Put away those piles of books and whatnot. And get rid of the boxes—I don't know why we keep them in the first place, they just get in the way. And—"

"Why the loft? And what are the boxes getting in the way of? You never said anything before about cleaning up the loft—why now?"

"Just do as I say. And something tells me you haven't been going to school—why not? After all that work you put into getting accepted, you need to apply yourself."

"No. I'm not cleaning the loft and I'm not going to school."

"I don't believe this—not from you. What's wrong with you?"

"*You're* asking what's wrong with *me?* Dad did something illegal and ran off, and you're hiding here at home—you're both in hiding! How come I'm the only one who's not supposed to hide? How much longer do we have to live like this? You said he slapped someone around. You said it was a mistake. What about waterboarding? What about electric shock? Was that a mistake too? You think I don't know? Are we still living under the Japanese—is that what Dad is, an errand boy for the Japanese? You said he didn't do anything wrong—then why does he have to hide? If he broke the law, he has to pay the consequences. Remember who taught me that? It was Dad."

"Yes, your dad!"

I don't say anything. "Your *father.*"

I remain silent.

"We're a family. And family members take care of each other, crime or no crime, wherever they are. That's what a family is."

"Mom . . . I'm scared."

A shadow flits past Mom's eyes. Those eyes are heaving a long sigh. And just like a shudder can follow a sigh, her eyelashes are quivering.

"I am too."

***

This is it. I'm at the university I dreamed of, a place of freedom, a campus overflowing with vitality. I'm in a terraced lecture hall that holds hundreds of students. The desks have folding seats and are covered with graffiti. I need to sit up here where the steps end, way off to the side, where I can look down on everybody, where everyone's back is toward me. I'm in the very last row, where *my* back is not exposed. This is my seat.

I didn't go to orientation, or to the assembly for the new students. The university is a good distance from home. One day I stayed home, oppressed by thoughts of Father, and another day I turned back halfway here. I use my loft to escape from the voices of people looking for him. Another day all I did was wander back and forth from home to the train station. And then there was the day I tramped around in the vicinity of the school, past the market and the hospital. I tried to hypnotize myself—*nothing is going to happen, nothing is going to happen*—I tried to steel my heart, but once I arrived at the gate to the school the facade crumbled.

That man didn't reappear but others did. They kept an eye on us, dogging our every movement, reporters opening our windows and peeping in, and policemen with walkie-talkies making the rounds of the neighborhood. And I never did identify the people who kept to the dark alleys, standing like statues for the longest time before giving up the ghost. My nose smelled tidings of spring but for the rest of me it was midwinter. A nasty chill stayed with me throughout, the effect of being under surveillance, spied on, the object of murderous resentment. Every word and action I heard or witnessed was laden with suspicion.

The professor's drone is like a lullaby. My notebook is full of doodling, the pages crammed with heads—pairs of heads almost touching as students work together; heads nodding off; heads seeking relief from boredom—and with hands undoing hair and putting it up again. The backs of some of the heads come complete with expressions—heads tedious, antsy, full of sound and fury, confident, timid. And alone among them, at the top of the page, the front of the old professor's stick-in-the-mud head. He sits and reads from a yellow clump of manuscript, glasses perched on the end of his nose. I add a fly to his receding forehead, and another orbiting in the vicinity, and then another and another. Their buzzing is like the professor's drone, no variation in pitch, no dynamics.

The class is about to end. When it's over, and until the last of the heads below me has left, I'll remain bent down, moving in slow motion as I load my daypack. When the end-of-class commotion dies down and the lecture hall is quiet, only then will I go down the steps, my gaze fixed on my toes, to find an out-of-the-way place to sit until my next class.

The bustle from below tells me the heads are starting to move—seats clacking against seatbacks, a voice calling to someone, laughter and gabbing. The lecture hall empties out and the commotion dies down. It's two hours till my next class, the lunch hours, the busiest and noisiest time of the day. I think I'll stay where I am and have a nice lazy nap.

The monotony is relieved only by faint stirrings from outside, and before long my eyes close of their own accord. *What's that?* A tap on my shoulder, like someone knocking uncertainly on a door, but enough to bring me wide awake.

A guy stands there, framed in sunlight that prevents me from seeing him. I shade my eyes and my hair falls down over my face. He perches himself on the edge of the seat next to me.

"You must be Sŏn. I'm the guy who takes attendance but I don't think I've seen you before. You never answer so I always call your name twice just to make sure. And my name comes right after yours so I can't help but remember. And today you *answered*—I was so surprised I forgot to mark myself present."

Elbow propped on the desk, chin cupped in his palm, he regards me. He drums his fingers on the desk, like he's playing the piano. *Tat tat tat tat*—a steady rhythm.

"Did you do that? Wow, you could be a cartoonist."

I slip the notebook into my bag, sling the bag over my shoulder, and get up. The seat bangs against the seatback.

"I have a class."

He takes me by the wrist. His hand is warm and moist, his grip not too strong, not too weak, just enough to keep me from getting free.

"No, you don't. You never signed up for classes, so I did it for you—I put you in the same classes I'm taking. And this afternoon's class is canceled—the instructor's at a conference. Lucky you— aren't you going to thank me? I won't say no if you want to buy me lunch."

"What's this all about? Let go."

"You make it sound like I'm coming on to you. But I'm the student rep in our department, see? So I'm responsible for my classmates. And even though I'm older you don't have to call me *oppa*, or talk polite to me either. In fact, I'm going to make your day—*I'll* treat *you* to lunch."

He gets up, still holding my wrist, and down the steps he prances with me in tow. He talks too much, he's too forward, and he makes me uncomfortable. So why am I not trying to get away? I try to keep up even though I'm only half a step behind. Outside he weaves his way confidently among the tide of people, occasionally stopping to wave to someone off in the distance.

"Would you please tell me where we're going?"

"I told you not to talk so polite. I've lived twenty years in this area and so I know my way around. We're going to a dumpling place, all right? Trust me, it's awesome."

His smile is warm and thoughtful and it dissipates my suspicions. He's marching proudly, the strong set of his shoulders eliminating my apprehension. And the hand that secures mine is so handsome. That hand has set me aflutter and driven out the coward inside me.

The lid opens and steam rushes out, hot and moist, to join the salty smell of our dumplings and the sweet aroma of steamed bean-jam buns. I'm melting in the warm, humid air, my frozen blood is circulating again, my hardened flesh feels more tender now. And then the warmth vanishes and I can almost feel my body temperature drop. I shudder, but it's a pleasant shudder, like from a sudden chill. I close my eyes, wanting to repeat the experience.

When I open them again he's smiling at me.

"Auntie, one more order of dumplings, please."

The lid opens again, there's another rush of steam, and again I shudder. Auntie calls out an order that's ready.

I feel warm and loose, more so by the minute.

"Good we got here when we did—she's going to run out before long," he says. "Let's wait outside for a minute."

He takes my hand and out we go. We wait for more customers, and when they arrive, the lid on the big pot opens and we're back in front of it. When it closes we back off—until the lid opens with the next blast of steam. The lid opens and closes, we march up to the counter and back. We're more eager for customers than Auntie. She's not so quick to put the lid back on the pot now. And now I'm warm.

The next I know I have a bag of dumplings in each hand and we're heading off. I follow obediently, wondering where the hand went that was holding my wrist? If I stop, will that hand come back?

"Where are we going?" I falter.

"Well, there's too much for just the two of us, right?"

He gives me a wink and strides on ahead. We retrace our steps to school and arrive at the student union building—a place I've never been. Up a flight of stairs we go and down a hall past a girl prone on the floor lettering a placard. A boy dashes by us, a spool of paper tucked beneath his arm. Students are hurrying about hollering to one another before they disperse, or else their heads are together in concentration.

He opens a door and I find myself in a room full of cigarette smoke and smelling faintly of paint. A desk is strewn with piles of paper and sections of colored fabric. Looks of greeting are exchanged, work comes to a halt, and then secretive hands get busy again. What are all these people doing inside a closed room? I tiptoe backward until I bump into him. He's installed himself at the door, a hand on each side of the frame—no exit.

"Hey guys, didn't I promise some heavenly dumplings? Well, thanks to Sŏn, here they are. Oh yeah, Sŏn's one of the new students. She's got stuff going on at home and missed some classes, so you probably haven't seen her. Sŏna, this fine gentleman's in charge of academic affairs, and this one. . . ."

As he's doing the introductions he makes space on the desk and sets down the dumplings. I'm hit with a quick volley of gazes.

"All done?" he asks a girl wearing a modified *hanbok*. The girl pops a dumpling into her mouth and chews as she answers. "Except for the picture. Maybe we should use one from last year's yearbook." "How about a graph?" he says. "That way the other schools can relate to it. Maybe we can ask someone in the cartoon club to draw it for us." "Are you kidding?" the girl says. "They won't give me the time of day—they're too busy." "Well," he says, "we're the Student Association and we're calling a vote to boycott classes, so we need to get the attention of as many students as possible. And the ones who want to come will come, picture or not."

Shut out of the ping-pong conversation, I focus on untying the small plastic bag of soy-sauce garnish. As I'm pouring it into a paper cup someone bumps me as he reaches for a dumpling, and the liquid splashes on my hand. I sneak a section of fabric and use the corner to wipe it off. Some of the students go back to reading the stuff they've printed, some are eating dumplings, some are chattering away, and no one's paying me any attention. "Now I know why my parents work their butts off to send me here," says someone. "Did you know the university foundation built a hotel in Ch'ungju?" says someone else. "Yeah, that's where our tuition goes, it sure as hell doesn't stay here. Everyone knows the guy who runs the foundation is making his family rich." And then he's gone, called out to the hall, and I still feel all alone in this beehive of activity.

All the dumplings are gone except for a scattering of crumbs, which I dispose of. I notice a white sheet of paper with spatters of soy sauce. Chin cupped in my hand, I stare at the pattern, three drops that form a squat triangle. With my pen I transform the three spots into a man's fleshy face. I make the cheeks droop and give the thick lips an oily shine. The red pepper powder in the garnish makes the face look like an apoplectic toad.

"Back in the day a family would sell a cow to put a kid through college. But all a cow gets you now is one semester. Next year I bet a semester will cost two cows. So to graduate, how many cows would you need? Or how many chickens? That kind of a graph would make the situation real, it catches the eye, it's simple. What do you think?"

As the words flow by I doodle and scrawl. Here's the greedy foundation director, belt unbuckled, legs spread, wearing a suit but with his underwear showing. I draw a trapdoor hanging open between his widespread legs—and then a cow trudging toward it. He brought me here and now he's gone off somewhere. Should I wait? Should I leave? First I'll draw a calf—more precisely, the rear end of a calf, its tail swishing as it follows the cow. But now I need to add a farmer holding on to the calf's tail. Cow, calf, farmer, all in a row. I give the farmer a wrinkled face, a bent waist, and a bare foot with a shoe off to the side. Good enough? Should I say goodbye? I'll just sneak out, they're not going to notice. Oh shoot, I can wait a little longer. I add grass and flowers trailing from the farmer's bare foot. How about more grass and another cow over there, grazing? Aha, another soy-sauce spatter—that can be the cow enjoying its grassy meal, not knowing it's going to be led away—

Suddenly everything's quiet, only a faint stir. I look up to see everyone's gaze directed at my fingertips. I shield my drawing.

"Sorry, I was just—I didn't think you'd need this paper."

One of them eases my hand aside, picks up the drawing and inspects it. Heads gather. "Wow—looks just like the director, doesn't it?" says someone. "Catch the bow tie—you know how he's always bragging about being trained as a singer—and of course he had to sing the national anthem at the assembly for the new students, right?" "Look at the way the farmer's holding the tail—reminds me of my father—my father's a farmer, you know." "Hey, Min, you should see this—come here, look—not bad, eh? What did you say her name is? Why don't we use *this*. Min, ask her."

I sit with my hands in my lap and look about, not sure what to make of it all. They're looking at me, wanting to know my name, asking my consent.

"Sŏna, it's okay if we use this, right?"

I swallow heavily and nod, careful not to seem arrogant.

"All right! Min, where did you come up with her—she's a treasure!" Someone takes my drawing, and someone else gets back to sorting out what they've all printed—once again the room is buzzing. Min sits down beside me. *Min*—I silently pronounce his name. Min. Min and Sŏn. Sŏn and Min. Not bad.

I feel a touch beneath the desk. It's Min's fingers, two of them, gently feeling my thumb. It's like I've been stung. My fingertips are numb and then one by one the fingers begin to tingle—an electric current passing through my palm. And now his fingers are passing through the spaces between mine and gently stroking the back of my hand. My wrist feels hot, and the next moment the current shoots through me. I can't move. Then quick, his fingers spread and lock with mine.

A faint sigh escapes me, and then a delicious shudder. It's the sensation I had when my ears were pierced and when my face was hit with the steam from the dumplings. It's like the sweet trembling of a baby feeding hard on its mother's breast and suddenly dropping off to sleep. It's the faint tremor and the soft breath I make when I'm whistling, it's coming from all of me and not just my mouth, it's my body that's whistling.

I feel the *thump-thump thump-thump* of my heart. How can it beat so fast? I look up at Min, his chin in his palm, his head askew as he observes me—just like in the lecture hall. Beneath the table his other hand moves gently over the back of my hand.

My navel prickles, and then my chest. Something's moving inside me, quivering the way my chin does when I'm about to burst into tears. Others aren't aware of it.

"We're having a retreat this weekend. How about joining us? Everyone all right with that?"

Though Min is talking to the others, his voice loud and clear, his eyes remain on me.

"Sure, she deserves a big welcome."

"Yeah, why don't you come along."

Min feigns a frown, then smiles. Everyone's eyes are telling me they're hoping, really hoping, I'll say yes. Beneath the desk Min's fingers give mine a squeeze and then relax. My fingers respond, and then my voice.

"All right."

I'll go. You and me, and all of us. *Us*. It's a cozy feeling, the promise of flesh touching flesh, of one body warming another, of breathing, talking, and watching as one, encouraging, welcoming, and supporting one another. I feel their warm gazes and *our* two joined hands.

I'm tiptoeing over a soft expanse of sand, my toes sinking in. I can hear my body, alive and moving. My heart beats, my blood flows, my flesh trembles—I'm alive.

And then sound no longer registers in my ears, or movement in my eyes. My every sense is directed toward one object—Min's hand. My body moves in rhythm with that hand. It moves, my hand twitches. It grows still, I swallow. He links his fingers with mine, the sole of my foot tickles. He releases my fingers, my ears ring. His hand retreats, I can't breathe.

Barely moving my lips I call Min's name. I feel warmer. Drawing his name to my bosom, I feel his body heat, almost as if we're touching. Slowly, tenderly, he warms me and I warm him, we inhale, exhale, breathe in and out, our hearts beating as one.

Everything is gentle. I'm being lulled to sleep by a rocking cradle—it's so sweet. I'm smiling a dreamy smile in response to his wondrous gaze. A moan escapes me and segues into humming.

That first instant when his fingers spread mine apart and linked with them, the current that shot through me, the sigh that leaked out of me like air issuing from a pump, sounding like the faint release of air that comes just before a grin, or the whoosh of steaming breath when you're rubbing life back into frozen hands. Just thinking about these sensations turns on the current and gets my navel prickling again. And that place deepest inside me never fails to twitch.

Lying in my loft I touch that place ever so lightly. It moves, it really does. Twitch twitch. Twitch, still, twitch, still—again and again, a regular rhythm. In go my fingertips. I never realized there existed within me such a marvelous place, so moist, soft, and dozy. It's like a forest at daybreak—wings fluttering, flower buds blossoming, dewdrops gathering. It's like an endless expanse of tidal flats, a place of living creatures that glide on their bellies, suckers contracting and then expanding. It's a universe, where the world bursts into light and a new world draws that life into itself.

My body is a festival, puffy as whipped cream, hot as a curling iron, tangy as an apple. Starting from this core a shudder shoots through my navel, into my breastbone, up my throat. Ahh . . . what a feeling!

I sit up, startled and still quivering. A giggle escapes me.

I have to call Chini. I have to announce to her there's someone I love, that I'm part of a Campus Couple, that something meaningful has gotten my heart to pound.

I fly down the steps of the loft. I haven't been in touch with Chini for a while. Every time I call I get her mom, who puts me off—Chini's out somewhere, she's not back yet. I pick up the receiver and punch in the number I know by heart. I hear the ringing. Chini absolutely has to answer. If it's her mom I'll hang up.

"Hello."

It's Chini—yay!

"Chini, it's me. How come you're so busy? You haven't called. And when I call, you're never there. Chini, guess what? I was at school doing a drawing, and you know that protest over tuition? Anyway, my drawing is going to be posted all over campus—they like it. Chini, are you there? And you know how it started? I was sitting in the lecture hall and this guy took me to a dumpling shop, he just takes me by the wrist and off we go, and there's so many dumplings, and—oh, I need to see you so I can tell you all about it—and me and this guy, we just might . . . Chini, are you there? I'm sorry I'm blabbing so much—Chini, why don't you come over? Chini?"

"My mom's after me about being on the phone too long—let's talk later."

The phone goes dead. No goodbye—she just hung up. I didn't get to say what I really wanted, not a word. I stand there listening to the dial tone. What's going on? Chini and I have jabbered on the phone for hours on end and her mom's never said anything about it. And didn't Chini carry on for an hour or two about her orientation and all the clubs she joined? So why now? Was I chattering too much? Is she mad because I was only talking about myself? I wonder if she found out I stole her lines. What's going on? I feel a chill come over me. Chini's weird.

CHAPTER 5

The dogs are barking and they're getting closer. Do I rate trackers now that my stock has gone up? But who the hell would come way out here except maybe a spy from up north?

I'm strong, stronger than anyone else, stronger than any dog. I see in the dark, I penetrate darkness, I ferret out the power that's hidden in darkness. I can make a rock cry, I can *be* a rock if I want, or I can be the tears of a rock. No mutt, dog, or canine can faze me.

So what am I doing in an abandoned house up in the hills where the roads are overgrown and it's damp and dark because the sun hides out west of the ridge? My ears perk up at a breath of wind, I tremble at every sound I hear in the distance. Why?

Because of those other dogs, the mad ones.

It's late at night and even the wind is holding its breath. The barking has stopped but my ears keep manufacturing noises—tiptoeing feet stepping on a dead branch, the baying of hunting dogs, the horns that spur them on. Did that man near the town make me? Did he linger beneath the shrine tree to see where I was headed? Maybe I should have dumped the truck outside of town. Come on, there was no sign of anyone following me, not even the grass was moving. Plus, I walked a good half day, altering my pace along the way. None of those sons of bitches would slink all the way up here.

The problem is, noises get blown up in the dark and you don't know where they come from. You can't see and so you don't know what makes them. Not knowing breeds fear, and fear breeds terror. You can't submit to terror. You can't let the dark play tricks on you.

Suddenly I notice everything is dead still. There's tension in the air, like at night before a storm. I feel like a bow at full draw. Now I miss the barking. I ease the door open. Why is it so bright out there? I open it more, and great thick flakes of snow fly in. It's piling up in the yard and the hills beyond. Maybe that's why the dogs were making a racket. I shouldn't have let it get to me. Out to the veranda I go. A snowflake lands on my cheek, giving me a shot of cold, then warmth when it melts. Virgin snow always makes me want to relieve myself. Pecker in hand, I tense my rear end, stick out my belly, and send a stream as far as it will go. And then a belch escapes me.

My snow-covered hideout is perfect. The most experienced tracker will give himself away the moment I see his tracks. But the same holds for the most elusive quarry. So is it the perfect hideout or the perfect lockup?

I open my eyes. The only sound is the occasional *whump* of snow falling to earth from a tree branch. I'm in a dirty room where the paper is coming off the cement walls. The ceiling is speckled with mold and with rat urine the color of mustard. Scattered everywhere are odds and ends of clothing and all manner of household items. I pull my pack close. In it are canned food, pastries, a carton of cigarettes, ramen, soft drinks, and *soju*, items I picked up at the market near the bus station. They'll last me a week. I could have stocked up more, but I didn't want to draw attention to myself in a small town where word gets around. A day or two of hunger won't kill me. And the cold I can put up with.

I rip the cellophane from a pastry. The crinkle annoys me. I listen—all is quiet. I bite into the pastry and sour saliva rushes into my dry mouth. My jaws feel creaky and suddenly I'm starving. I devour the rest of the pastry and open a second one.

The cawing of a crow breaks the silence. Pastry half-in and half-out of my mouth, I crack the door and look out. Still cawing, the crow takes flight from the top of the collapsing wall that encloses the house—the cawing of crows always gives me a bad feeling.

Other crows are perched where the wall still stands, and still more are scattered about the yard. Clad in their black robes, they wait like messengers from Hades.

What the hell are you waiting for? Do I smell like a dead man?

I open the door the rest of the way, step down to the yard, and throw the remainder of my pastry at the crows. One of them takes it in its beak and flies off. I pick up a rock and hurl it at them. All they do is hop a short distance away. Lousy bunch of crows. Rocks don't scare them and I guess I don't either.

Eyes closed, they look like they're meditating. Black feathers shining in the sunlight, shapely beaks opening almost imperceptibly—how languid they look. No greedy pecking at food, no flapping of wings in alarm. No signs of suspicion, no jealous looks among them. Heads in the breeze, taking in the fresh air, they're basking in the sun.

They're full enough not to be desperately reliant on food, and tough enough not to be intimidated by a thrown rock. And here I am, wishing I was one of those crows warming themselves in the sun, and yet so anxious they spook me. I go back in and close the door.

I lie down with darkness. Darkness summons sleep, sleep summons hunger, and hunger in turn summons sleep. The crows caw and morning arrives. It seems I've had visitors during the night—there are paw prints in the snow, leading across the yard, toward the kitchen, and around to the back. A thin film of sleep clings to me. Night falls and the wind comes up, the moon rises, and the dogs bark. The night is long and the barking doesn't stop.

Should I clean out the firebox, lay in some pine boughs, get a fire going? But then in town they'd see the smoke. Better to buy a camping stove instead. How about jumping on a bus to the station and having myself a hot bowl of soup and rice? Or else go up in the hills and hunt? Or maybe set a trap in the yard?

My mind is in overdrive but I can't lift a finger. Why bother? I can reach everything from my sleeping bag while the lower half of me stays warm.

I take my Smith and Wesson from between my legs. Warmed by my body heat, it's my only source of warmth. We're doing a heat exchange, the gun and I. The one thing I absolutely need right now is warmth—body heat, a warm breeze on the tingling cold tip of my nose, a hot bath, a spicy bowl of my wife's soup and rice. I miss her with her thumbs down inside the bowl to get a better grip, and I miss her giving me a thumbs-up to show she adores her man and the work he does.

I've burrowed into my sleeping bag but questions are flooding my brain. What is the organization doing? By now they'll know I've flown the Rehab Center. Maybe that scumbag director is keeping quiet now that he's been exposed. Maybe I should have contacted Paek. Hell, I can't be sure of anything at this point. *Go lose yourself somewhere.* I can hear Pak's voice. I wonder if he knew all along how my stint at the Rehab Center would end. I wonder if they're arranging a new hideout. And what did that shitfly mean: *Why do you think the organization sent you here? You could simply disappear and that would solve everything.* Am I a scapegoat for the organization?

Before long that tiny seed of suspicion takes root, sending a tendril of doubt to my feet. From that tendril a network of tiny roots digs into me, infesting me with biting bugs. But I've never been one to harbor suspicion, and now is not the time to start doubting the organization.

I need a newspaper to see if they've sent me a message. I can't hide here forever, laid up in a sleeping bag. And some fresh air and warm sun wouldn't hurt.

The snow is melting. Where the sun has lingered longest a path has appeared. It's time to leave. But one order of business remains. For which I need a pastry, a packet of ramen, a can of pike mackerel, and then the basket and length of cord lying in the corner.

On the veranda I cut the rock-hard pastry into four hunks and toss them into the yard. The crows scatter and then one of them, the biggest, hops back and lunges at one of the hunks. When it comes to food, the strong have good instincts. Another bird snatches the second hunk, two of them share the third, and Big Crow gets number four. And then the crows on the wall gang up, and by the time they finish pecking, the pastry hunks are reduced to crumbs. The crows who missed out squawk in displeasure and scurry around helplessly. Next, the ones in the treetops drop down to join the party. Such is the effect of a hunk of pastry, more powerful than a thrown rock.

I place the packet of ramen on the veranda's wooden floor and punch down, rip it open, and scatter the noodle fragments all over the yard. The crows hop, spread their wings, and charge. Beaks clash and wings thrash as they jockey for position. All that matters is the food for which they're so ferocious. That, and who gets the biggest share. They scurry and rush, they push and shove, they attack and fret. How tenuous your peace. You get dislodged; you clash beaks; you're so close you can sense one another's warmth, but how much trust do you have?

I open the can of pike mackerel, releasing its fishy smell. A crow has staked itself six feet in front of me. Are you the bravest of the bunch? The head honcho? Got your eye on this mackerel? I drop a chunk of it into the yard. Just when it looks like he'll maintain a respectful distance, his hard beak shoots out and it's gone. Yes, you're the head honcho all right. Takes more than a ramen cluster to satisfy you. I get to my feet. Hang on, don't go anywhere—I'm going to teach you what it's like to be the king.

What's left in the can I dump on the ground, and then I retrieve a single chunk of it. I find a stick, loop the cord around it, then prop the basket over the mackerel high enough for the crow to enter. Finally I crush the last chunk and make a trail out of it, leading from the basket.

All right, we're ready. Come on, no more pastry, no more ramen bits, you're in the big leagues now. Pike mackerel—you know the taste of mackerel, right? Come and get it. The crow takes one calculated step, then another. I'm waiting. He draws ever near, one step and then another. He stops at the basket, in goes his head, then it jerks back out. Then he goes all the way under. Not just yet—I have to wait till he bites into it. Go on, take that mackerel, get a taste of that fish. Triumph is at your beak. There—got him! I pull the cord and jump for the basket. I can feel his wings thrashing inside. The more agitated he gets, the calmer I feel. I close my eyes and feel him writhing, feel the *whap* of his wings.

To lead his flock, a king needs to bait them with a steady supply of food. A king's first duty is to protect his flock from danger and rid them of worries about food. But bait alone is no guarantee, and they also need a taste of fear. Those who oppose the king are eliminated. A world without a king, a world away from the flock is dangerous. So they listen to the king and take cover beneath his wing. That's how a king stays in power.

Until now your tough beak and strong body were sufficient to intimidate and provide for your flock. You were the fearless king. And here you are trapped under a basket. But guess what—I'm going to make you the *real* king of your flock.

If a king has to decide between giving bait and instilling fear, he'll strike fear.

Your death will teach your flock the meaning of danger. It will teach them never to show off their bravery, and never to get close to people. It will teach them fear they can feel in the depths of their being. And that's how you'll save your flock. Your death will make you a genuine king.

I take the crow in my hands, feel the firmness and strength of muscle and bone nourished on meat, its fine bone structure from the neck down. The crow's head is dead still, it's given itself up to me. I feel the ribs; its desperate heartbeat seems to be easing, the *thump-thump thump-thump* ever more faint. Is that resignation I feel, or resistance, or a ploy? Perhaps it's a defense mechanism that comes with extreme terror. I take its head in my hand and gently close its eyes, as if placing a hood on a condemned prisoner.

Your end will be painless. Your crime is that you weren't afraid of people; you scorned them. You're guilty of being valiant and showing it. You were born in garbage and lived a life of garbage. And now you need to show respect. This is what fear is all about. If you want to be a true king, then look me in the eye. Now you see— you're a mere crow, a shitfly.

I twist my wrist hard to the right. *Crick-crack*, there goes its neck. I hear a faint breath. The neck goes limp, the head droops, but the body is still warm. Its heart still beats—no, that's my pulse.

You're dead and I'm alive. So why am I still holding you? I don't want my blood to revive you. I launch the crow toward its flock. Behold your king, fearless and brave, king of all you cowards.

The dead crow thuds to the ground. The crows on the wall take flight, a single feather drops at my feet, a shiny black tail feather. Now you know who the real king is, who the strong man is. The king is me.

***

"Courier wanted, fast and reliable, for demanding work; Kohŭng City Terminal lots for sale; Namyŏng-dong General Construction Company; contact Department Head Pak" the same ad, four days running. Namyŏng-dong—the organization is trying to find me. I read the fake help-wanted ad over and over. One thing's for sure—the organization knows about the Rehab Center. But it's also clear that the scumbag director put a nice spin on what happened there. Will my next shelter be fancier than the Rehab Center? Fat chance.

I check my watch. Granny should be back any moment. I peek outside—no one in sight. It's good and isolated here, along the river but beyond where the houses end.

Before I found this place I tried a storage room, a mud hut, other abandoned structures. The clincher here was the small sign posted outside—"Room for Lent."

My first thought was simply to correct the spelling. It wasn't much of a place, and I wouldn't feel safe living with others. So I got out my pen and was changing Lent to Rent when out came Granny. Even for an old woman her back was awfully bent. She beckoned me inside and I wondered if she'd been waiting, if she'd made that spelling mistake to catch my eye. Whatever, her spell worked and in I went. I was accepted with no questions asked.

Here she comes, a great big basin on her head, one hand steadying it and the other swinging alongside. I greet her just outside the door—if I go out to meet her she might feel obliged. I relieve her of the basin and set it on the ground. There's a tinge of fulfillment in her face—she accomplished what she set out to do and now she's back.

"How's business?"

"Not bad. My barley malt and dried squash were a big hit."

With a smile she flourishes her purse, and I hear the tinkle of coins. Always the same answer, always the same flourish—though in fact the basin is just as full as it was when she left. There's no one to buy her goods. Regardless, day in and day out, back and forth she goes, toting that basin on her head and displaying her produce at the station in this small town that's served only by the slow train that arrives six times a day. Maybe she doesn't really mean to sell but goes just to be there, Granny and her goods. Or is she waiting for someone who never comes?

She puts her purse back in her pocket and taps it a few times, pleased to know it's secure. Then she squats and uncovers the basin, takes out a newspaper and a pack of cigarettes, and hands them to me. All of it matter-of-factly, part of her daily routine.

Discreetly I place a few bills in the basin, and she grins.

She stands up, this time straight, and heads for the kitchen. But no sooner is her back turned to me than it's bent over again. I go to my room and read the paper. It's full of dogs barking about what they're going to do to me. Swell. No fake ad either. Not a good sign. It's time to hit the road. I put down the newspaper and from the kitchen I hear the muted clatter of dishes as Granny prepares dinner, the sound of running water, the chop-chop of knife against cutting board.

And now she's knocking on my door. Enter Granny with the dinner tray. I receive it and she sits down across from me. She wets her spoon in her soup before taking her first mouthful of rice, then follows with a spoonful of soup. She uses her spoon only, no chopsticks. It's not that she's lost her teeth and that soup and steamed rice are all she can eat. It's just that with whatever she eats—greens, kimchi, or whatnot—all she does is dip her spoon into the juice. All the solid stuff is left for me. And I make quick work of it, pretending I'm not aware she's doing this for my sake. But with every mouthful that comes off my chopsticks I hear her refrain:

"Take your time, young man, and chew nice and slow."

In the presence of Granny and the meal tray I've become a

child who needs constant reminding about how to eat. A child who, through no effort on his part, is perched on Granny's knee. Couldn't I remain Granny's little boy forever? I realize the soup I've just swallowed is too hot. Or maybe Granny's constant reminder is heating up my innards.

"Granny, where is your family anyway?"

She doesn't say a word. But there's no note of sadness in her expression, no sign of wistfulness, just that gentle smile. I wonder if she was born with it.

"How could your good husband go off and leave such a pretty wife? And what happened to your children?"

She sets down her spoon, swishes a mouthful of water, then turns on the television and hunkers down in front of it, arms clasped about upraised knees. The smile remains but she can't conceal the look of solemn reflection that's come to her eyes. Her small, rounded back resembles a sow bug, an insect that's been hiding in the dark, dank space beneath a rock when, suddenly exposed to bright light, it rolls into a ball and plays dead. A forlorn chill emanates from that bony back.

"Don't mind the tray. I'll clear it when the show's over. This program is a kick, I tell you."

She says this without removing her eyes from the screen. Why did I have to bring up her family? In a home where old folks live you'd expect to see a venerable family photograph framed like a presidential medal. Nothing of that sort here. I've wondered about Granny's past, why she maintains this forlorn household all by herself. And where are the neighbors? But all my wondering has done is make Granny tense. I quietly remove the tray and myself, put the dirty dishes in the sink and the leftovers in the fridge, and head outside.

The nighttime air is a nice refresher. I might as well have a walk along the river. I stop now and then and take a deep breath. The air has a fragrance to it. I've enjoyed my brief respite in Granny's embrace, my short sweet nap, and it's time to move on. Okay, let's do it.

I find a cardboard box and cut it into rectangles that I carefully label, leaving a bit of my heart in each one: "Barley Malt," "Dried

Radish," "Dried Squash," "Millet," "Toasted-Grain Flour," "Acorn Jelly." And finally a sign, larger than the one I first saw: "Room for Lent." A sign I hope will catch someone's eye.

I hang the larger sign from the gate and go in. Granny's asleep, head resting on a roll of toilet paper. The television's been turned down, and the light from the screen flickers across her drawn face. I replace the roll of toilet paper with a pillow. Granny's mouth is drawn in a smile, even in her sleep. Maybe that smile comes from the wrinkles of adversity—a tough life she's survived only by smiling. I leave the smaller signs on top of the television, along with a wad of money. I say goodbye to her smiling face and prepare to depart.

"Make sure you have a hot bite to eat before you leave, eh?"

Her voice is like a hand grabbing the scruff of my neck. I don't look back. A nice hot meal. Rice just cooked. What a warm feeling in my throat.

"Even heroes need their energy if they're going to save the country. Have a bite before you go."

***

The alley lies beyond the reach of the streetlights. A man lingers there, then disappears. A woman with a ponytail bound high on her head exits the alley, high heels snapping against the pavement. A pair of night guards pass silently on their rounds. Their booth is a hundred yards off. A cat creeps down the near wall and climbs the wall opposite.

Everything that moves draws my suspicion. Even the piled-up bags of garbage feel hostile. I shift my gaze from one building to the next, from one patch of darkness to another. I don't trust anything, and I can't tell the difference between what I need to be suspicious of and what I can trust.

My homing instinct led me here, I was controlled by a spirit not my own. Was I rash? To avoid danger I've come to the heart of danger. I'm hiding between buildings but feel I've been deposited smack dab in the middle of a plaza.

The people are gone. I wait a little longer just to be sure, then steal out of this alley with its urine stink. Moving quickly and hugging the walls, I arrive at the entry to our building; it's plastered with posters and notices. I feel behind the letter box. Nothing. Damn. What next? I go up the steps, careful not to make a sound, and put my ear to the metal door. Nothing. I knock gently four times, afraid the sound will carry up the steps and through the building.

Next I try the side of the building. I pass a row of LP tanks and find the window; it's covered with security bars. I reach through and try pushing the window open. No good, it's locked. I tap on the pane. My heart starts pounding. No response from inside. Again I tap, this time more forcefully. A shadow approaches from within, and I tap once more. The silhouette vanishes. She's been looking out but she senses danger too. There's no way I can indicate my presence without making noise. *Quick, do it.* I put my mouth to the security bars.

"Honey!" Was it loud enough? "Honey, it's me!" This time louder.

I don't think I've ever said *Honey* so desperately. I feel like a boy who's looking for his mommy. Finally the window opens and I see my wife's face. I reach out for her. She pulls back and disappears.

Not a minute passes before she comes out, but it feels like an eternity. In that short interval there skims through my mind a procession of every possible catastrophe. I feel the despair of a man who has just been handed a death sentence.

She stops at the corner of the building to make sure who it is, looks about her, then rushes up to me. You might think she's a fragile sort who scares easily, but she's a strong woman, a woman who glides through her beauty parlor styling hair to the accompaniment of soft music, but a righteous woman who is outraged by the social ills that make me so indignant. The first woman I could trust, and the last.

"What happened to your face?" she blubbers.

At the sound of her voice I feel the big hurt in my chest dissolve. She reaches tentatively for my face. The warmth of her hand on my cheek feels strange. I rest my hand on hers. She quickly turns away, looks up and down the alley, then takes my hand.

"Let's go, it's no good being out here. I know a place."

She releases my hand and sets off. I follow her, keeping close to the wall. I feel like I'm toting a huge load. She arrives at the beauty parlor, opens the door, looks around, then signals me. I steal inside, gaping in amazement at her breathless movements— lock the door, look out through the window, check the lock again, close the blinds then peek out through them. She takes me by the hand and leads me to the back room. She closes and locks the door but leaves the light off. I can see her trembling and yet she hasn't missed a beat. I wonder if she's been preparing for this moment ever since I went and got lost.

All I want is to sprawl out and go to sleep, with the feathery touch of her fingers passing through my hair. I feel like I'm sinking into the floor.

She opens wide the door to the loft and gives me a meaningful look. She's more determined than I am now.

Up the steep wooden steps I go. Steps leading up to heaven, steps leading down to hell, steps leading up to a low profile. At the top I look back down.

My wife is waving up at me. Just like Granny on the highway waving as if to a child who might never return. The door to the loft closes.

CHAPTER 6

My blown-up drawing hangs tall from the front of the Student Union. When the wind blows, my drawing flutters and flaps and bangs and snaps. That wind is so refreshing, like a sudden rush of warm air, feverish, liberating, light but not lightweight. In my dreams it's the wind I always associated with college. I drink in the moving air.

I'm at the retreat, my very first. We're individual and yet several, we're several and yet united as one *us*. And I belong to *us*, I've become important to *us*. This I know from the look on Min's face. There's no campfire, but that's all right. I'll take Min over a campfire any night.

Min has laid out my bedding next to the wall and is lying beside me like a second, protective wall. I listen for his breathing. On the far side of the room they're still singing, but it sounds like the drinking is coming to an end. Someone turns out the lights, and all I can hear now are steady breathing and snoring.

Are you really asleep? Not me. I can't get to sleep—is that normal? I can hear you breathing. I let out the breath I've been holding. I want to feel your gentle hand again, I want your slender fingers to link with mine. I wish I could go to sleep with our fingers locked together. I want us to inhale and exhale, to breathe in and out together.

Good for you that you're asleep. It's fortunate you don't know the riot of my heartbeat, that you can't see me lying motionless except for my heavy swallowing, because I'm afraid of making my quilt rustle. I pulled the quilt close wishing it was you. The quilt smells of you—it smells of freshly cut grass, of buns filled with sweet red-bean jam. Your face is visible in the darkness. You're within reach of my hand, I wish I could touch your eyes, your nose, your mouth. . . .

It's the middle of the night when I arrive home, and I'm dog tired from tossing and turning all the previous night. First thing to do is check on Mom. I enter our building and run up the steps toward our unit. Until I come across a man with a camera, a woman sitting on a spread-out newspaper, and a man drinking canned coffee.

The woman rises. "You live here?"

"No, ma'am."

"Ever seen the man who lives in this unit? He's super famous. Maybe you've seen some strange people coming and going?"

"I don't know who you're talking about."

I turn, trying not to rush, and go back down the steps. "You live here, don't you? He's your father, right?" The woman grabs my arm.

"I said I don't know."

"Haven't you had contact with him? Is it accurate to say that half a year's gone by and you've had no word from him? Is it true he took off overseas?"

"I *told* you I don't *know!* I don't know who you're talking about. I don't have anything to do with this."

That's not my father. I don't know him. Whatever he did, I don't want to know about it. My dad is far away from here. No, actually he died a long time ago. With a get-out-of-here gesture I run off. Why won't you pests leave me alone? Why do you always show up just when I'm happy, why do you interfere with my life? Get lost, all of you.

I arrive, panting, at the beauty parlor and go to my room, then open the small door to the loft. There in the flood of darkness, a pair of eyes, the eyes of a scared animal. As my own eyes adjust, those two eyes fill out to a crouching body, neck stretched out, ready to spring forth.

Father puts a finger to his lips—"Sshh."

I suck in my breath.

No, that's not him. That's not the dad I remember, who took out my tooth with his Monami pen, who hooked up my light. That's not a man, it's an animal with gummy, fear-ridden eyes that looks like it's starving, a riled-up animal that wants to charge.

That animal is not my dad. What's it doing there? Why is it hiding so close to our home? Reporters swarming around, police turning our home inside out, people I don't know grabbing me, shouting at me, telling me to find my father, and while we put up with the hassle this animal hides like a rat in the loft? My loft? How long has it been there anyway?

"Sŏna."

Don't you call my name. I don't know you. Whatever you did, I don't want to know. Just leave me alone. I shut the door, holding the knob as I catch my breath.

"Sŏna."

This voice is coming from behind me. It's Mom. My hand clutching the doorknob goes limp.

"Did you say hello to your father?"

She's smiling, little folds at the corners of her eyes. She takes my hand the way girls do when they lead you off to make a confession. She looks at me, lips twitching and eyes sparkling, then puts her mouth to my ear and makes *her* confession, half-proud and half-sheepish, like a girl who rounds up her girlfriends to hush-hush about her first period.

"Your father's back."

Your father's back. You mean, *Your father's risen from the dead*? Or, *His majesty has returned to the palace—bow down before him!* The voice coming from her bright, smiling face sounds like a chorus of angels. She's a holy woman delivering word from on high. But the news is unholy, I can struggle all I want but it's going to strangle me. *Your father's back.*

Father opens the loft door from inside. A humble foot appears first, and down the slanting wooden steps he comes, hunched over and unsteady. This exalted personage who has descended to my lowly room has the impoverished appearance of the persecuted and wounded, the face of a frightened animal, and the posture of the basest guest at a sumptuous feast conjured by the holy woman.

"Here's your butterfish sashimi, dear. This is the season for butterfish, and you won't believe how fresh it is. Look at the silver color—it's almost alive. Come, dig in."

Mom pushes the platter of sashimi toward him across the portable meal table—a maidservant fussing over her master. Thin ovals of butterfish are arranged in an elegant curve to resemble a whole fish, and they're accompanied by pan-fried zucchini slices garnished with slivered red pepper and a block of beltfish grilled to a golden brown. The presentation is lavish and beautiful. Father stuffs his mouth with clumps of butterfish.

And then with her chopsticks Mom debones the beltfish and places chunks of it atop his rice bowl, all the while shuttling side dishes in and out of his reach and urging him to partake. Ravenous, utterly absorbed in the act of eating, Father finishes the entire plate of butterfish and then the heaping bowl of rice and beltfish. He pays no attention to me hunched up across the table.

He slurps and licks his lips, his chopsticks darting and pincering, his eyes focused on the food he's wolfing down. Disgusted, I fix my gaze on the edge of the table but I can't block out the smacking of his lips. It makes my flesh crawl and my stomach churn.

"I'm going to re-open the shop—it's been idle too long. Good idea, don't you think, dear? Who would ever think of looking for you in a busy beauty parlor? With you close by I'll have peace of mind. I'll be right here, the gatekeeper. But you never know—we should add a lock inside the door to the loft. Oh, and what about new wallpaper to camouflage the door? Hmm . . . do you think that would attract attention?"

Mom's endless plans—new wallpaper, necessities for the loft, ways to sniff out danger. She's a general strategizing for battle. From holy woman to maidservant to interior decorator to military strategist, Mom is transforming, all in the service of Father. It's going to be a long, drawn-out war.

"And Sŏna! As for you. . . ."

As for me. Why me, invisible till now?

"Why don't you stay here, and not at home. If I'm here all the time I'll draw suspicion. At night you can look after your father—bring him what he needs, take care of his meals, make him comfortable. All right?"

"What? That's ridiculous."

Mom gives me an uncomprehending look. "Ridiculous—how?"

"Dad stays up there and I stay down here? You don't see anything strange about that?"

"No, why? Can you think of a safer place? Tell me."

***

And sure enough, the Greenfields Beauty Parlor is back in business. Mom has whisked away the layer of dust, mopped the floor, and polished the windows to a shine. But where are all the customers? The rumors about Father haven't helped, and mostly we see elderly women wanting a long-lasting perm at a cheap price, and longtime customers who have left the area but return for the curling irons. As before, Mom turns on the radio and sits in her chair, reading a book or drinking coffee, but now she's waiting for customers. Once in a while a gaggle of women with nothing better to do peep at Mom in her misfortune.

Mom gets in the first punch, groaning to them, "Well, someone has to make money." Customers or no, while the beauty parlor is open for business she never casts a backward glance toward the loft. She's carrying out to perfection the role of a woman surviving the absence of her husband.

And I'm the Catcher in the Loft. After the milkman and the paperboy have come and gone I bring in the milk and newspaper, set them outside the door to the loft, and take off, not to return till midnight. Father retrieves these items when I'm gone. Father in the loft never reveals himself to me, and that suits me just fine. To keep the loft at arm's length I force myself to go to school, where I have Min, and *us*. Back from school I linger in the unlit beauty parlor before going to my room, where I bury myself in my quilt and go to sleep with the lights on. I have a nagging suspicion Father's getting into my stuff, but I don't dare fetch any of it.

My first assignment from on high is to take care of Father's pension.

For his 21 years and 8 months of service as a policeman he's accrued a grand total of 35,288,340 *wŏn*. But because he was terminated for absence without cause, he can only receive half of that pension, or less than a million *wŏn* per year of service. That's what he gets for more than two decades in the police force.

With a copy of our family register from the precinct office, and documents given to me by the officers who worked under Father, I'm off to the pension office. An official examines the documents, industriously scribbles on a form, then returns the documents, explaining that he can't release the money until the recipient shows up in person to apply for the pension. The form with Father's stamp designating me to act in his behalf is useless.

I parrot the lie Mom has cooked up—my father is gravely ill and unable to appear in person. And the man parrots back that they can't bend the rules. But I can't go home having failed my mission—I'll be punished for sure. So I make a scene and squawk about having to carry a person here on his deathbed just to get his hard-earned pension, and what if it kills him as a result? My tantrum makes me feel Father actually is on death's doorstep. There's the tingle in my nose—good, it's working. I start crying, and once the tears are dripping I plead like a little girl for the money. I sense all eyes on me, as well as looks that say, *Poor thing*. I hear an elderly woman clucking and feel her stroking my hair. But all the official can do is fidget, and after telling me one last time there's nothing he can do, he sneaks away.

So I have in fact failed my first assignment. All I have to show for my efforts are the family register and the authorization from Father. These documents in hand, I leave the building in tears. But why am I crying my crocodile tears? Because of the sorry ending to my first assignment? Are they tears of pity for my ghost of a father hiding in the loft? Am I mourning the possibility that Father will die a living death? Or do these tears conceal my murderous feelings for him?

The strength drains from my legs and I plop down on the steps. I look at what I'm holding. Family head—An; spouse—Ae-ja; child—Sŏn. Irrefutable, immutable, like it or not, I'm his sole offspring, Sŏn, daughter of An. A tear drops onto his name.

Where do I go from here? Not the beauty parlor—the loft, my last refuge, has been stolen by Father. I have no place to relax, no place where I feel comfortable. I sit at the playground in Chini's apartment complex, waiting for her. This playground used to feel so huge, but now the seesaw's broken and there's a mound of trash at the bottom of the dirty slide. We used to hang out here on midsummer nights eating ice cream. We had to keep licking it before it melted.

Here she comes. I get up from the swing and run to her. "Did something happen?" Her voice is frigid.

"No, I just wanted to see you. It's been a while, I haven't heard from you, so . . . are you really that busy?"

"Kind of."

"Want to get something to eat? I haven't eaten all day."

"It's late and I need to get home."

"Chin, did I do something wrong? What's going on?"

"Why didn't you tell me?"

"Tell you what?"

"I . . . you know what? You're scary. How can you go around as if nothing's happened?"

"Chin, come on."

"I'd kill myself if I were you—I'd be so ashamed."

"You knew?"

"How could I not know? Everyone knows."

"But I'm . . . not part of that, and you know it. Chin, I'm really . . . it's hard . . . and you're a friend. You're my *friend*."

"That's right, I'm your friend and I'm ashamed of it. So I'd appreciate it if you wouldn't come visit me like this."

She turns away from me. I grab her arm but she jerks it free. Such a stiff, hard movement. How can she be so mean?

"Would you do something for me—could you . . . keep this a secret?"

"From who? The whole world knows."

"Just don't mention it to our friends, okay? Please. I did it for you. I didn't tell anyone. Don't you remember?"

"Are you guilt-tripping me? For a mistake I made way back when?"

"No, that's not what I meant—"

"You give me the creeps. A girl like you—I knew it from the start."

Chini grits her teeth. The next moment she's disappeared inside her building. From the start? . . . When was that?

***

Here comes Min, white T-shirt tucked neatly into his pants. He spots me and waves. His arm is wiry, and when I glimpse the hair in his armpit, my face gets hot and I look away. He comes up to me flashing a pair of movie tickets and grinning.

"I had to stand in line for an hour to get these. Let's go. We'll have to walk a ways—are you okay in those shoes?"

And off we go. The wind is up but the sun is hot. We haven't walked far and already my face is flushed and my armpits are sweaty.

The theater district is filled with a human tide of moviegoers. As I'm being bumped and jostled I feel Min's bare arm brush my forearm. The mutual touch of down against skin, the slight rubbing sensation, the feel of bare flesh against my arm, it's all so gentle and refreshing. I can't help but sigh. Min rests a hand on my shoulder and whenever we have to cut across the stream of people he tightens his grip and draws me close. We arrive at Pagoda Park and he releases my shoulder and takes my hand.

"The mothers from the Family Action Council gather here every

Sunday. Let's see if there's anything we can do."

That's Min for you. I'm always thinking it will be just him and me, but when I meet him, others have joined the party or else he's involved in some gathering. Here today slogans are being chanted and placards waved. Min comes to a stop among the chanters, whose slogans I'm oblivious to. But as long as I'm with Min everything's fine. I like his expression, whether he's elated, scowling, or just plain rosy-cheeked. I like doing the drawings he asks me to do, and I like hearing him rave about my drawings. I like it even more when we're walking hand in hand. He alone knows me, strokes me, comforts me. Min and his beautiful hands have melted my frozen heart and brought it, pounding, back to life.

I hear an amplified voice from the far side of the park. I see a mass of people holding signs, and around them knots of senior citizens, arms folded across their chests, taking in the scene. I lag behind and Min turns and draws me forward.

"Are you okay with this? We've got two hours till show time, so we can stay here for a while then get something to eat."

Of course I'm okay. Taking my hand, staying by my side—what could not be okay about that? Hands linked firmly, we make our way into the heart of the crowd. Most of the picketers are elderly and they don't seem able to move well. Min stands me in front of him and rests his hands on my shoulders. I turn and observe his face, even as I ease myself back against him. But when I turn back to the demonstrators I notice the huge face displayed on the signs. My father's face. And above it, in crimson letters, WANTED: TORTURER AN—REWARD OFFERED.

"Shame on the police, shame on torturers, we demand accountability." The chanted slogan is loud and clear through the portable loudspeaker. My feet are planted to the ground. I feel hard as a rock and can't move.

"Why don't we just go," I mewl, my fingers clenched into fists.

Min cranes his neck, looking ahead, wanting to move forward. My shoulders quiver and my ears are ringing. The demonstrators are advancing toward the street. Hands offer flyers to Min and me. Should I take one? Then toss it? I take one and stuff it in my bag.

"Min, can we go, please?"

"Oh come on, let's watch."

The demonstrators form a line, signs held out in front like in a mass game. I feel like I'm at a public execution and the severed head is part of the procession. Only it's my father's bloody head.

"Let's just go, please? I'm getting dizzy. Min, please." By now I'm shouting as I try to backpedal.

"Hey, why so upset? All right, let's go."

Min walks me into a narrow, dirty alley that stinks of fish. We pass a grilled-fish eatery. I stop and turn to him. "Min, can I depend on you—please?"

"What?"

"Can you have my back, no questions asked, even if I did something wrong?"

"How am I supposed to have someone's back if the person did something wrong? I need to hear the story first—"

"No, I mean unconditionally—believing in me, supporting me, telling me I'm right whether I'm right or wrong, patting me on the back. Isn't that what it means to have someone's back? I need someone to have my back, I really do."

Min's forehead creases as he considers this.

"All right, I have your back—unconditionally. And you have my back— unconditionally?"

The furrows in his brow disappear and he puts on a bright smile, but it doesn't feel real. I force myself to believe he means it and isn't just weaseling out of a fix.

"Thank you."

"For what? I have your back now—remember?"

"Right. And I have your back—unconditionally. But Min . . . I . . . I have something to tell you. And if I don't do it now it's going to drive me crazy."

"All right, but let's not be so frantic—you're about to have a heart attack. So what is it?"

"That's my father."

There, I said it. I spilled it. Too late now. And I haven't even said I love him yet.

But I had to come clean before someone else tells him.

"What?"

"That's my *father!*"

"No kidding—where?"

"Where you've got your foot—on that flyer."

Min looks down. His foot is on Father's throat. He lifts his foot a couple of inches, then sets it down again. He looks at me, his mouth hardening for an instant, then relaxing. "That's your father in the flyer? Come on, Sŏna, you're joking, right?"

His voice is so jolly and pleasant. He doesn't understand. With an exaggerated laugh he pats me on the hip. The laughter rings inside my head. The face in the blurry photo in the flyer doesn't look real. It's more like a sketch for a painting of a monster, and it's enhanced by the crimson lettering and the slogans of outrage. If I were Min I wouldn't be able to connect that face either.

"No, I'm not joking—*that* is my father."

"Sŏna!"

"An, the torturer—he's my father."

"Will you stop it! You're saying you know that son of a bitch? That torturer? He's a torturer! Sŏna, you're taking this too far."

"No, he's my father."

"Do you know what torture is? It's something animals do. A young man right here in this country, our country, is *dead* from torture. In a pitch-black room he got water poured into him till he died. You know who those demonstrators are? They're average people who were made into spies by torturers. They were fishermen, fishing for milkfish or whatever they fish for, and the torturers fabricated spies out of them. They were having a drink, minding their own business, they made a slip of the tongue, somebody heard them, they got dragged away, and they turned into spies. How? Torture."

"I wish I was the daughter of a spy—then I could get some sympathy. I never chose a torturer for my father. You said you had my back. Unconditionally! You said so!"

What a stupid mistake. I should have kept my peace. But once you take off downhill, you can't put on the brakes—that's me and my tongue. Just like the first spoon of rice makes you ravenous, like the epiphany of love deepens love's emotions, like a moment of physical pleasure demands rapture, my heart and my soul have quickened in spite of myself. I want to tell Min that those words jumped out of my mouth by mistake. But there's no turning back.

"Why do you keep talking about having your back? How am I supposed to have your back, huh? You wish you were the daughter of a spy? How can you say that? Are you out of your mind?"

He grabs the neck of my blouse and shakes me. My blouse rises up, my bare waist is showing. I struggle in Min's rough grip, trying to pull down my blouse.

"You're an operative, is that it? You've got a hidden scheme, don't you. That's why you came on to us—you had it all planned."

"I'm an . . . operative?"

"If you're the daughter of that son of a bitch—where is he anyway, he took off overseas, right? If you're his daughter you should know!"

"No, I don't know. I don't know anything. I'm not part of it. I didn't—"

"Why are you telling me this? Why *me!*"

"Because . . . I love you."

"You love me?"

"I didn't want to hide anything. You can't hide something from the person you love . . . isn't that right?"

Min glares at me, breathing hard. The hand clutching my blouse relaxes. I want to collapse. And now Min is bellowing and pounding his fist against a wall. I take hold of his white T-shirt. He knocks my hand away. His eyes are bloodshot.

I hear the drumbeat of the hunters. Beautiful green fields of wildflowers in full bloom spread out in the distance, rain showering down upon them like a hail of arrows. In those fields a pitiful beast is dying, crimson pumping from where an arrow has penetrated its heart. Beautiful horns, a long neck, soft fur. And still the arrows whiz through the air, now piercing its dark, lucid eyes and the muscles of its slender neck. That beast bristling with arrows is like a crimson flower. I want that flower. I draw the beautiful, innocent beast to my breast and it takes its last breath. Flies buzz in the black cavity of its mouth, worms wiggle in the dark sockets of its eyes. The belly swells to bursting and the bowels pour out. The flesh decomposes and the bones turn to ash that rides off on the wind. The beautiful beast in my bosom is dead and gone, and now there is only the wind to embrace me as I mourn.

I'll always remember you, your beautiful horns and your soft fur. I'll remember you until the moment you galloped into the green fields. I'll mourn your death each and every day of my life. I'll send you the sweet kiss I tasted with my first pure love.

On that spring day when love first came, I felt the tips of my toes rise from the ground and suddenly I was floating. I can't help giggling at the memory. And now I approach the light, with death crying behind me, I climb a stairway toward heaven, mourning all death as I go. A life is gone and the gates to a world have closed, and a single light appears before me—the Greenfields Beauty Parlor. My own green fields, my paradise, where I'll feed on the grass and drink the water and enjoy the sun and there is no death.

I go into my room and close the door. In the darkness I sit against the wall, desolation cloaking my back, time flowing quiet and still. I put my ear against the wall. *Thumpthump thumpthump.* The rhythm of a heartbeat—spirits must dwells in these walls. Spirits of the green fields, spirits of the woods. I tell stories to those spirits, I speak to their heart about the beautiful beast that died in my bosom, the beast that was my first and my last love, my one and only romance. On this cozy night the spirits and the silence are attentive to my thoughts.

***

I always believed that keeping a secret can solidify a relationship. Joint ownership of that secret is a barometer of your closeness with a person. But I know all too well that secrets can also be harmful. Because if you want to share a secret, you're asking the other person to shoulder a heavy weight. And because it's imposed on her, she feels compelled to carry that baggage whether she wants to or not.

I remember when Chini first whispered it to me: *Don't tell anyone, but in a little while I'm meeting some kids in the arcade—you want to come?* I was happy enough that she'd told me the secret, but thrilled she was asking me to be part of it. Her secretive voice left a tingle. What had I done to deserve this? I was the chosen one, and part of a group, and something good lay ahead. That's what sharing a secret meant to me. I kept my mouth zipped so that the secret I now carried would never leak out. Only later would I learn that sharing a secret means bearing a burden.

There were five of us, and the secret was the hundred-thousand-*wŏn* bank check in Chini's pink plastic wallet. There in the underground shopping arcade she showed us the check and said we weren't going home until we'd blown the whole thing. She told us we could each choose a small gift. Nothing suspicious about a gift. One girl picked out a teddy bear, another a pencil sharpener, and I ended up with a set of stickers. But if the idea was to spend a hundred thousand *wŏn*, items costing two or three thousand weren't going to fill the bill. So off to the food court we went. But by the time we finished stuffing ourselves and traipsing around, by the time the gifts in our pockets were starting to lose their novelty and we wanted to go home, reservations were surfacing. *I wish I'd bought a Walkman,* one of the girls said. *Yeah, a couple of them,* said someone else. *No—no more stuff,* said Chini. When we responded with a chorus of *Why not?* she said *Just because* and then lowered her eyes. That's when we caught a whiff of a stinky fish. *Where'd you get that money anyway?* one of the girls asked. At first Chini wouldn't answer. There was a tense silence. Then—she'd gotten it from a cousin who had just come back from overseas. Her answer confirmed our suspicions. Within the secret lay another secret. But none of us voiced our doubts to Chini. Because each of us now bore evidence of the crime. We were sister conspirators connected by a tainted secret. *I* hadn't stolen the money, it wasn't something *I'd* found on the street and neglected to return to its owner, and yet I couldn't free myself from it. I felt like we were accessories to a murder. Chini was the killer but all of us were involved in dismembering and hiding the corpse, each of us had blood on her hands. We were co-conspirators, accomplices in a crime. And what bound us in this conspiracy was a secret.

To keep a secret a secret you need a new secret. And so Chini planted in each of our palms a 10,000-*wŏn* bill, reminding us to keep mum. It was dark by the time we emerged from the arcade. Like pirates guarding our booty, we were happy to go our separate ways. Back home, before I went inside, I found a chink in the wall and hid my gift and my money. This plunder was the proud proof of the secret Chini and I shared, but it came with a price—the knowledge that we now shared stolen goods as well.

It came to light a few days later that the source of the money was Chini's mom's wallet. Someone else's mom got to wondering about the teddy bear—or was it the pencil sharpener?—someone mentioned Chini's name, which was then passed on to one of the teachers, Chini's mom was notified, and each of us was summoned by our teacher and questioned. I kept my mouth shut, not mentioning a word about the stickers or the money. Spill the secret or tell a lie? It was a choice I couldn't make. I wasn't persuaded by the prospect of avoiding a scolding, and I wasn't intimidated by the threat of my mom being notified. But my efforts at loyalty were in vain. For whatever reason, I was branded a traitor by Chini. The fact that I'd kept the secret was not important to her. Chini in turn was branded a fallen leader by the group she had endangered. And so the traitor and the fallen leader got lumped together.

At every opportunity I checked on the stickers and the money I'd hidden. No longer was it proud proof or a token of accomplishment. This adventure served as a warning: Beware, you who would enter the world of secrecy without fear. Secrets aren't something you dare spill out, nor are they something you listen for. If someone comes up and takes you by the ear and whispers *You're the only one I'm telling*, you have to say *No confessions* or *I have enough sins of my own without sharing someone else's* and remove yourself at once. You have to reject the serpent's treachery.

That was the last secret Chini and I shared. But now I'm wondering if I should have told her that I used her lines at the gathering for the new students. Maybe that's why she's acting so weird. Maybe it has nothing to do with my father. Would confessing to her make a difference?

And what secret was I trying to confess to Min? The love budding in my heart? The loft that's weighing me down? What burden was I wanting to share with him? I should never have asked him to help bear the weight of my crime.

CHAPTER 7

The milkman wheels past on his bicycle. The old woman with the Bible beneath her arm moseys clear of the alley. She comes out of that alley every day like clockwork, always in the same outfit—white canvas slip-ons, knee-length black skirt, jade green blouse. Soon the newspaper will arrive, and then light starts coming in through the window at the base of the wall. Sunup is earlier by the day.

I cover the window, sit up, and pull the plastic container up close. There's only about six inches to the rim—not enough for the contents of my heavy bladder. And if I have to tilt it, there'll be even less room. Which means I can't do it sitting, which is half-assed anyway. So I get up, but to avoid bumping my head against the ceiling I've got to stoop over, half-crouching, half-standing, one hand holding the container, the other my pecker at the ready. And it's hard to control the flow. If I miscalculate, over the side it goes.

Anyway, let her rip. In a blink the container's full, and by the time I cut off the flow it's streaming down the side. Dammit! It's getting on the quilt. Can't she find a container that's got some capacity? I smell piss on my hand. I cap the container and set it at the bottom of the steps.

I push the quilt off my sleeping pad and onto the linoleum floor. Here in the loft I can either sit or lie down. If I lie down, it's either with my feet on the boxes or else curled up on my side. And with the damp quilt off to the side, it feels even more cramped.

Here comes the sun. Soon the loft will be hot and urine-humid. The thought of that heat makes my throat burn with thirst. I reach for the kettle near my head, then realize I drank it dry early last night. My stomach grumbles. Even if I lie absolutely still, in no time I'm hungry and thirsty and need to pee.

I thump my heels on the floor twice. Sŏna, time to get up. No sound of her stirring. I thump twice more. Come on, get ready for school—you need to get moving.

Now I can hear her, the door to her room opening and closing, the scuff of slippers, the *ding-a-ling* of the door to the beauty parlor, and again the scuff of slippers and her door opening. And then my door opens, just wide enough to admit her hand. Without so much as a how-did-you-sleep, she deposits milk and newspaper and removes the urine container. She moves her hands like a bad-tempered little kid. I have half a mind to ask what's wrong but decide not to press the issue.

I move my wall of boxes away from the top step and perch there with my legs dangling. With the tip of my foot I open the door a bit wider then go down and retrieve the carton of milk. I take a mouthful and enjoy the sensation of the cold liquid as it descends. I drink the remainder and swish it around before swallowing.

The hot water heater clicks on and I hear water running. It stays on awhile, which means she's washing her hair. Next I hear the clatter of cosmetics jars, footsteps and scuffling slippers, the hair dryer, drawers opening and closing.

Now she's back in her room. Head down, hair falling over her face, she stubbornly avoids looking my way. I drop the empty milk carton down the stairs and into her room. She ignores it. To keep herself out of my sight she minimizes her range of motion in the small room. All I can see is her feet daintily stepping over the milk carton. With my foot I push the damp quilt down the steps.

"Can you wash it for me?"

She gathers her backpack and clothes, and once she's secured them against her chest she kicks the quilt outside her door. I hear the rustle of shoes being put on and clothes patted down, and then a sigh, and a dozen footsteps later, the *ding-a-ling* of the front door. *Sŏna, don't forget to lock the door.*

It's quiet. Too quiet.

I creep down the steps then turn and re-stack my wall of boxes. Standing on tiptoe at the bottom of the steps, I inspect my handiwork. No reasonable person would suspect someone was living behind those boxes. And I can always hide beneath the quilt. A look-see wouldn't be a problem. People don't see what's right under their nose, they don't bother with the obvious—who would dream of staging a manhunt in a loft? I step through the small door then turn and close it. Thanks to the wallpaper, its outline isn't readily visible. Damn good camouflage for a hideout.

Sitting cross-legged on the floor of her room, I spread out the newspaper—that's the best way to read it. This is when I can relax, before the beauty parlor opens for the day. I scan the help-wanted ads. Nothing. It's been a while since the last message. Well—"FM Music Salon" has a new announcer, Kim Chisuk instead of Son Chihye. Too bad, I like Son's sweet voice. Those student demonstrators are getting life or else 12 years. That makes sense. Like the judge says, when students take to the streets with criminal behavior on their mind, when they start fancying themselves guerrillas, when they protest state power, they're no longer students, they're felons, and they deserve heavy sentences. They wouldn't be involved in these shenanigans if not for the Commies riling them up. *I Love My Wife*. Here's a trashy movie for you. "What better expression for the passion you learn at the ripe age of forty, when you give her your all." Oh, come on, what are you going to give her, the bank? "Kim Chihŭi pours body and soul into nude love scene." Middle-aged men are going to love that! The latest installment of the novel. A visit to a cultural treasure. I turn the page. Okay, the Special Investigation Committee. And there's my name again—now what? "Guidelines needed for imported food products containing carcinogens." What's my name doing in the same article with carcinogens? To hell with that! Why don't they leave me alone? I crumple the newspaper.

Ding-a-ling. It's the time my wife arrives, but there's a moment of tension as I flatten myself against the wall. Yes, those are her footsteps, I don't hear anyone else's. The door to Sŏna's room opens and in pops my wife's head.

"You're up? She left for school already?" She tsk-tsks as she enters, then spreads the legs of the portable meal table and sets on it the breakfast from the cloth bundle she's brought. At the beginning she went out of her way—even soybean-paste stew in a nice earthenware pot—but these days it's only steamed rice and a few dried fixings.

"No soup again?" I grumble as I take up my chopsticks.

"I get nervous leaving home with a big bundle. All kinds of people are watching the place now. And the reporters are still poking around. So you'll have to be patient—I'll make it up to you on Monday, when I'm closed. And this is your lunch."

So saying, she produces two more aluminum lunchboxes from the bundle. My wife tends to be overly cautious. She hands me the lunchboxes with a solemn expression that reminds me of the wives of freedom fighters during the Japanese period who delivered funds to their men. But if this keeps up, it won't be long till I'm down to a measly rice ball. While I'm eating she goes out to fill the kettle and look for anything else I might need. All the while she periodically looks out the window, her ears perked up.

"No news from Paek?"

"Oh, that reminds me—there's a hearing tomorrow. He said he'd give me an update—he's expecting a good outcome, told me not to worry. But . . . they're not going to release your pension. Paek said there's nothing they can do. But if you can't draw your pension, then what? The beauty parlor can't support us all by itself."

"Go see Pak. But don't let him know I'm here."

She looks off to the side and fumbles with the corner of the table. That's what she does when something's on her mind. I scrape my rice bowl clean and swish water around inside my mouth. And after a time my wife gets back to business and extracts several items from her bag.

"I bought you some pajamas and underwear. I don't want to tell you how far I had to go. The shops nearby, they all know who we are, so what am I doing buying guys' underwear when my husband's gone missing? Go ahead, try them on."

With a bashful smile she hands me the clothes. *When my husband's gone* touches a nerve. I understand how she feels, but what's she doing playing the widow when I'm right before her eyes, alive and kicking? It's damn vexing. I strip off my top and my undershirt, noticing they both smell, and try on a new undershirt and the pajama top.

They're soft and cool, not clinging—I like the feel. Next are the new briefs. She removes the labels before handing them to me, then nods, *Don't be shy.* I get to my feet, remove my pajama bottoms, and am lowering my briefs when I hear,

"Honey." Her voice is soft. "I'm. . . not quite sure how to say this, but it's nice to have you here."

There's an ardent look to her eyes as they meet mine. She's still holding the new pair of briefs and she looks down and fusses with them. I feel as if a cool breath of wind has passed through my crotch. She reaches out and takes hold of my instep. Her hand feels hot.

"Isn't it about time for you to open the shop?"

I carefully disengage my foot, bend down, and reach for the briefs. But she snatches them away like a little girl throwing a tantrum. I ignore her and snatch them back, and after I've stuck my legs through them I try on the new pajama bottoms. She's biting down on her lip. Like a clueless idiot I take my lunch and crawl back up to the loft.

I secure the small door, then realign my wall of boxes. I snug myself against the window and listen. The door to my daughter's room closes and I keep still until I hear from the washroom below the loft the clatter of dishes in the sink.

I remove my pajama bottoms and lower my briefs. My testicles lie limp on the bare floor, showing as much life as a dog's balls in the heat of late spring. The actress pouring heart and soul into her nude scene comes to mind—I stroke myself gently.

Shameless son of a bitch—no matter how I caress and sweet-talk it, there's no response. I bring my hand to a stop and look between my legs. My testicles look as mushy as a couple of sea cucumbers that have gone bad. But what's that? A white hair. And there's more. When did my thick black pubic hair start turning gray? I lean over, ferret out the white hairs, and pluck them.

It used to be that as soon as my wife gave me the cue—the downcast look and the I'm-so-bashful body language—I'd be stiff in no time. When she visited me at work with a change of underwear I'd lead her off to the night-duty room and couldn't wait to drop my trousers. I was home only once or twice a month back then, and the first thing I'd seek out were her tits. And at night that announcer's voice coming over the radio brought me standing to attention. Since when did my hand, my sweet words, and my ear stop sending cues?

Oh well, the shrinkage is only temporary, nothing to be ashamed of. Nothing wrong with the big fellow that a good dose of sunshine won't cure. I kick free the briefs from my ankles and sprawl out on my back. That sun is nice. Hands folded behind my head, legs outspread, I'm like a baby waiting to get powdered and changed into a new diaper. I curl up on my side, a useless old fart, all washed up. Then I take off my pajama top and undershirt and lie flat on my stomach, just like a road-killed frog flat on the asphalt. Nothing helps, my mind won't shut down. It's going to be a long day.

I awaken to a noise. I open my eyes and hear from below the cackling of a gaggle of broads. The astringent odor of kimchi stew removes any lingering traces of sleep. My mouth waters but it's a sour taste. I set my two lunchboxes on my cross-legged knees and have a quiet meal. Then I scan the crumpled newspaper, front to back. What next? Let's try paper-folding—even though I only know how to make a boat. I take a sheet of the newspaper and begin, but midway through I recall that I've also made a hat. So my paper boat becomes a paper hat, and with hat on head I lean back against the window and nod off again.

My desultory midday nap is interrupted by loudspeakers from trucks peddling eggs, fish, and vegetables. I lurch up to a sitting position—was that my name I just heard? My paper hat has slid down to my shoulder. My nose picks up the chemical smell of perm solution. I unfold my paper hat and read the print, ads and all, then fold the page back into a boat. The sun goes down. This is how I spend a day in the loft.

I think I've only dropped off for a moment, but the next thing I know, night has fallen. It's hard to keep track of the time. Not infrequently I find myself looking around, feeling I've just now been dumped out in the middle of nowhere. But I'm always here in the loft. I doze off around sunset and I'm always confused when I wake up: Is it early evening, the wee hours of the morning, sunset, daybreak? Am I inside a dream or outside?

I can't hear the radio, or any other noise for that matter, and I don't see any light. She must have closed up for the day and I must have conked out—or am I still dreaming? What's left of my lunch stinks.

I hear the cheery *ding-a-ling*. The front door closes and I hear the scuff of feet. It must be Sŏn. What's that—something getting knocked over? Is my college girl drunk? The scuffing is coming from below the loft now. And then the door to her room opens and closes. She doesn't turn on the light. The silence eats at me, and I put my cheek to the floor and listen. All I hear is the whir of her mini-fridge. Did something happen to her?

At last I hear her voice, a mere murmur, the words muffled. I sense she feels weighed down. I tiptoe down to the landing and put my ear to the door. It makes no difference. But wasn't that "Dad!" she blurted?

***

Look at her pout. *This isn't my idea*, she's announcing. Her eyes are fixed on the bowl of kimchi on the low meal table where we sit. In spite of her cutoffs and a T-shirt there's a touch of the lady about her, though she still has the face of a little girl.

I examine that face. The fleshy earlobes and bushy eyebrows are mine, but the thick lips must have come from her mom. Well look—she's gotten her ears pierced. How did she manage that, she used to spook so easily. I guess that means you're a college girl. Despite my best intentions, the faint impression of nipples against T-shirt catches my eye. That demure look is going to get the boys' tongues hanging, let's hope she's not too innocent. I just wish I could do something for her—after all, men are better than women at judging other men—because she's getting back later each night, and on one of those nights I heard her crying.

"Here I am," my wife singsongs as she enters toting a pot. She's in high spirits, and any moment now she'll start humming. She sets the pot on the table, opens the lid, and out comes a blast of steam and a rich, oily aroma. Slow-cooked chicken stuffed with all the herbal fixings. Hands wet from the washroom, she tears off a thigh and places it in my soup bowl.

"Can you believe there're still places with free-range chickens that they cut up for you? Remember when you could get them at the market? Those days are long gone. I made sure this one came with the gizzard and all—just for you."

So saying, she strips meat from elsewhere on the chicken and offers it to me. I take it, but for my daughter's sake I wish she wouldn't make such a big production out of it. My daughter's posture is the same—head down, eyes downcast, even breathing, not a peep out of her.

"Here, have some," I say, placing the meat from my wife in my bowl and breaking off a chunk of the thigh and placing it in my daughter's bowl. No word of protest, no thank-you. She's ignoring me. All she does is poke at the meat with her chopsticks.

"Go ahead," my wife says to me. "Eat."

"Is there any cold rice? It goes good with chicken broth."

"I knew you'd say that—and the answer is yes. But I want you to try the meat first. Remember that chicken gizzard stew place near your office that you liked so much? One bite was enough for me. I had high hopes you'd take me someplace scrumptious—but *chicken gizzards?*"

There's nothing like eating to stimulate your appetite. Once a nice fat chunk of meat slides down my throat, my starved stomach calls for more. And so I gnaw away at what's left of the thigh, holding it in both hands. At the same time, my wife has been feeding me with strips of meat and now she fills my empty bowl with broth.

"Some of your underlings took up a monthly collection from their paychecks. It's a pretty hefty amount and they've decided to keep doing it every month. Now who was the guy who brought it—he's short, kind of dark—oh, what was his name? We went to his wedding—god, why can't I remember—"

"You mean Paek?"

"Yes, that's it—Paek. He's your point man, right."

"It figures—I did my part for those guys. How about Pak—have you seen him?"

I dip a spoonful of cold rice in the broth and bring it to my mouth. A gamy aroma wafts from the lukewarm soup. *This* is what soup should taste like. To heck with the spoon—I pick up the bowl and drink from it.

"Yes, I have. But he didn't say much—only that we'd have some good news before long. . . . And I didn't say you were here—just like you told me. But it was kind of strange."

"What was?"

"Well, something wasn't quite right. We met in a coffee shop but he was antsy, he kept looking around, it seemed like his mind was somewhere else."

That doesn't sound like Pak. Nothing slides under that man's radar. My wife must have misread him. Anxious minds create ominous scenarios. Her world is the beauty parlor and she's not a quick study when it comes to taking the measure of a man.

Crack! Chopsticks slam down onto the table. "I'm sick of this."

My girl's voice is low-pitched but clear. Her arms hang limp at her sides and her eyes are on the table in front of her. My wife's industrious hands come to a stop and she looks back and forth between us.

"Sweetie . . . what did you say?"

"I'm dropping out."

"What are you talking about?"

"Just what I said—I've had it with school."

She's still looking down, her lips the only part of her that are moving, spitting out the words with no emotion. She picks out a chunk of chicken, stuffs it in her mouth, and chomps into it, and in no time she's stripping more meat, dabbing it in salt, and munching away.

"What?" my wife says, prodding her shoulder. "You worked so hard to get into that university and now you're giving it all up? It doesn't make sense."

My wife keeps prodding and my girl, instead of answering, keeps stuffing her mouth and slurping broth.

"What are you trying to tell us? What's the matter—you were never like this before. Are you afraid we can't afford it now? For heaven's sake—"

I take my wife's arm and lower it before she hits someone with the soup ladle she's brandishing.

"She must have a reason," I say. "If she doesn't want to go, why force her. Hell, show me a school these days where the kids mind their own business and focus on their studies." And then I turn to the girl. "So, do you have a plan? Why not take some time off, you can always go back."

Silence.

"Your father asked you a question," says my wife.

Silence.

"Why would you want to drop out of a school that kids are dying to get into? Now you're—"

Ding-a-ling goes the bell just as my wife pushes the table aside so she can slide next to our daughter. What the hell. *Didn't you lock the door?* I silently mouth the words. My wife's eyes grow wide.

"Anybody home?" A man's voice. "Ms. Nam, Nam Ae-ja, are you here?" A second man. "Anybody here?"

I slide along the floor to the wall and gesture with my head to my wife—*Answer them.*

"Yes, coming," my wife calls out, her voice cracking.

I reach behind me, fumble open the door to the loft, and scoot through it. I haul myself to my feet and am about to start up the steps when my wife whispers furiously, "Dear, your bowl!"

My bowl. Half bent over, I look back at the meal table and see the bowl, spoon, and chopsticks of someone who's not supposed to be here. I reach out and grab them. Holding them to my chest, I grope my way back up the steps. I feel like I weigh a ton. One of the chopsticks falls out the door and back into the room. No time to retrieve it.

And now the bowl turns upside down and the dregs splatter my face. I continue up the steps, sucking in my breath. A soup-swollen grain of rice is inside my nose. Be quick, be quiet, make no sound! I work the grain of rice from my nostril into my throat and swallow it. Finally I'm up. Close the door and I'm good.

The problem is, the door is wide open and how am I supposed to close it from up here? My wife's not there. "Who is it?" Her voice. Chicken bones all over the table. The huge stew pot, two soup bowls, two spoons. And the outline of my bowl with splatters around it, left by a man who's not supposed to be here. And on the floor the chopstick I dropped. My daughter, quiet and motionless, looks down at the table, arms at her sides, as if gravity works differently where she's sitting.

"Sŏna," I hiss. "Close the door!"

Slowly her head comes up. She looks at me with a wooden expression and blinks like someone has just awakened her. Sŏna, it's all right. Don't be afraid, just get up. Then come and close the door, that's all you have to do. Nothing's going to happen. I know you're frightened but don't worry, Dad's not going to get caught. But you need to hurry. It's all right, Sŏna, your dad is here. Will you please get up and close the door.

I wave frantically, trying to get her attention. The door to the loft seems so far away. Ever so slightly she pushes the table aside. "—and the last contact you had with him was—" A fragment of speech from one of the men. My daughter rises unsteadily and moves without haste, with no sense of urgency, toward the loft.

"That's it—good girl. Now close the door quietly and we're all set."

She stands motionless, clutching the door, looking like she's lost her mind. Her eyes are vacant, harboring nothing and reflecting nothing, silent eyes devoid of emotion, black holes of silence.

"Is that a room back there?" The other man's voice.

Sŏna, no time to waste! Stop agonizing and just close the door.

Instead it's her eyes she closes. But then the next moment her gaze jerks upward. Her eyes now hold the cold gleam of determination that precedes a weighty decision. Her forehead furrows then relaxes, she bites down on her lip then releases it.

Her teeth are so white.

"Mind if we have a look?"

"It's my daughter's room, for goodness' sake!" my wife shrieks. "Just because you're the cops you think you can invade someone's room? Go get yourself a search warrant!" Her voice is getting closer. There's no time.

The window. Even if I jimmied it open I'd never fit through. Meet them head-on? We'd end up in a scuffle. Two of them I could handle. But outside, then what, there must be more of them out there. Best to stay put. I flatten myself behind the boxes, then reach over for one of the empty ones I keep just in case, and add it to the stack at the top of the steps.

I can't get caught, not now, not with my wife and girl looking on, it would be too ugly. I take a deep breath, close my eyes, and swallow heavily. The gulp rings in my head like thunder, and then the door to the loft whumps shut, gently rattling the window. I sense movement below and hear the door to the room open. My body tenses, my big toe cramping and then my calf and now the inside of my thigh, followed by a tingle that reaches the tip of my nose. I hold my breath.

"Aha, a feast. You good women polished off a whole chicken, just the two of you? Wow." Sarcastic bastard. I smell something raw, acid surges up my throat, I want to throw up.

"Why not? Is a woman with a missing husband supposed to swear off chicken? Is it against the law to eat what I want? Are we criminals? Then what does that make you, Mister Policeman, barging into a young lady's room? Why aren't you looking for my husband—I'd like to know where he is too. Have you seen enough, or do you want to check out her wardrobe, have a peek at her underwear!"

She's hysterical. Dishes clatter to the floor and a bowl rolls away with a *whing*. I wonder if she kicked the table. There's a heavy silence. I wish I could see what's happening. And then she's sobbing, practically wailing. I imagine her plopped on the floor, clutching at the guy's pants, screaming at him. But I can't picture Sŏn—where is she, is she pressing herself against the door to the loft? Those eyes of hers looking up at me were so chilling.

"I guess that's all for today, but if he should contact you please be sure he turns himself in. He's only hurting himself if he tries to hold out. The times have changed and everything could get dumped on him. Finally, bear in mind that harboring a fugitive—"

"I know that—will you please get out!"

When will she ever stop sobbing? One of the men clears his throat. Footsteps recede. I wait for the *ding-a-ling*. There it is. The cramp in my leg releases and a tingle goes down my back. I waddle on my knees to the top of the steps, reach way down, and lock the door. Holding the doorknob I heave a sigh, the lower half of my body on the floor of the loft, my upper half hanging over the steps. My thigh is cramping up again. I pull myself back up. Suddenly I'm getting hard, my blood gathering. What the fuck?

The tension is stiffening my member, standing it up. It didn't respond to tender loving care and sweet-talking, but now it's alive and moving on its own. I lower my briefs and the big guy pokes its head out as if it's been waiting.

It's a living thing, no one's going to boss it around, the rest of me doesn't matter. It twitches and grows, puffing itself up. There you go, blow your top—and out dribbles the spit. It's a beacon of power, inspiring fear with threats of violence, commanding the organs linking the blood vessels and the nerves, directing the blood to pool, the muscles to contract, my lungs to inhale. All my bodily organs cower in the presence of the savage ruler, swearing loyalty to him.

I hear howling dogs. I'm a fugitive running through a field, on a mad charge toward a single objective. But what for? More howling. You sly, slippery snake, sticking your head into a dark, moist hole. All right, snake, take my mind too. You snarling dogs, bite down on the head of that snake. Sink your teeth into that filthy, frantic member with its flicking tongue. Draw out the venom that's clouding my soul. Bite, tear, rip until all the blood spews out.

"Dear—are you all right, dear?"

She's knocking at the door, her voice nasal and clotted after she's cried her heart out. What am I doing? I feel like I've been sleepwalking, like I was caught up short in my fugitive escape.

Blood surges to my head, my legs feel unsteady. The door rattles, the window shakes, and my body shudders.

I'm back in the real world, in my cramped loft where I can't stretch out. At my feet are the overturned soup bowl and gnawed chicken bones, on my crumpled-up quilt are fat rice grains that resemble wriggling maggots. Over there the half-empty urine container and stale chunks of pastry. I'm in my lousy hideout with the wall of boxes and the ceiling so low it almost touches my head. I'm a cowardly fugitive hiding out in a loft and trembling with fear.

My erection was not of my own will, and the baying of those savage dogs controlled me. My body wagged in response to the howling of the dogs that were chasing me. My body is no longer mine—has it been waiting for those dogs?

I shudder one last time. Tears are forming, my nose is running. I wipe my nose with the back of my hand and look at the slimy spit that remains there—clear evidence.

"Dear! Will you open the door? Did you get hurt? Are you all right?"

On the other side of that door are my wife and my girl. The look in my girl's eyes flits across my mind. It was only momentary, and I know now it wasn't directed toward her father. She was looking instead at an insect, or maybe a dog in heat, determined to deal contempt, hatred, despair, detestation, revenge, punishment.

Sŏn is no longer in my bosom. Just like my member is no longer mine, she's removed herself from my control. I hear her voice.

If he committed a crime, he has to accept punishment for it—isn't that right? He himself taught me that, remember?

I'm afraid of her, she scares me to the bone.

I curl up on my side and feel a cold draft. I'm desperate for that little bitch and her warm, whispering breath that tickles my neck, I crave the snap of the belt on my back, the slap as it coils around my bottom. I smell rot and decay.

CHAPTER 8

"Aren't you going?"

The duty apprentice has finished cleaning up and stands at the entrance to the hair salon, trash bag in hand. I can't believe we're done already. I close my hairstyle scrapbook and throw my stuff into my backpack. As soon as I'm through the door she locks it and without so much as a *see-you* she's running down the steps. "Take care," I say to her back.

It's the largest hair salon in the city center. There are seven stylists, seven apprentices, and seven interns, along with five adjustable chairs for shampooing, a room for manicures, and a room for makeup sessions. A day at the Greenfields Beauty Salon starts with soft music from the radio. Here it starts with twenty-odd women chanting a slogan. From morning till the neon sign goes off at the end of the day there's a steady stream of customers and a constant flow of pop music top hits from the speakers. If business is slack I work on my scrapbook, cutting out material from magazines, and write reminder postcards for appointments.

Who's the duty apprentice for today? Stylist Song's apprentice? Or maybe Stylist Kwŏn's? I've been here a month but still I ask myself these questions—it's impossible to tell who's under whom. Everyone seems friendly enough, but they never remove their watchful eyes from me. I somehow missed out having to go through an internship and started out instead as an apprentice—which makes me wonder if I was handpicked by the lead stylist.

Not until later did I learn that getting special treatment also meant being subjected to spiteful looks. A long internship would have been nice.

Intern is such a nice word—how come I missed out on it? For the most part we helpers don't like the term, but it sounds cool to me, part naïve and part mature, part lively and part clumsy. It's like the tart and tangy taste of Aori apples. What was the name of that song about the intern that I heard at the university—was it at the retreat, or in that smoke-filled Student Association office? Whichever, I was quick to erase it from my memory, even though the words and the music kept running through my mind.

I tiptoe down the steps. The bulging trash bag the duty apprentice took out sits at the bottom, where she dropped it. She didn't tie it either. A manikin head is sticking out from it—just the thing to scare a passerby silly. For fun I rehearse an explanation.

Why is a woman's head sticking out of a trash bag? Well, don't be surprised. It's a manikin head, and we have more of them inside— one for red hair, one for blue, one for curly hair, one for long. The heads were in the show window until yesterday, but they've become an eyesore—they're no longer in fashion and they're collecting dust. So we replaced them with a cactus. Cactuses don't have seasons, they don't go in and out of fashion, and they don't need much water. On the other hand, manikins don't have needles. There are lots of things you can do with manikins, you know. You can do their hair, you can talk to them, you can apply makeup. Would you like to have one?

I look around. No one in sight except for some drunken men, arms around one another's shoulders. The shops are either closed or are in the process of closing. No one's going to be interested in a bag of trash. I open the bag and take out the manikin head with the long hair. Sticking it under my arm, I walk off.

Mom will give me the evil eye again when she sees this. I think about her expression the last time I showed up with a manikin head. Her jaw dropped—maybe she thought it was a chopped-off head. And she didn't attend the graduation ceremony after my six months of beautician school, where we each had to make a presentation about a hairstyle we created. Nor did I inherit her favorite pair of scissors—not that I was expecting much in the way of a present in the first place. What I did get was a quote from my dear, departed grandmother—there's no rest for the weary if you're a woman who's good with her hands. I remember Mother sending me a look of suspicion and jealousy whenever I played with the hair rods at her beauty parlor.

The cold wind reminds me that the season is changing. All my winter clothes are in the loft, a sour thought. I raise my jacket collar, then reach into my pocket and loop my fingers through the handles of my scissors.

Tsubasa scissors. My guardian angel.

It's because of a pair of scissors that I decided to be a beautician. I was sitting in the dark beauty parlor one evening when it occurred to me that I'd like a nice pair of scissors. It wasn't a case of like Mom, like daughter; I simply made the decision on the spur of the moment. The day I registered for beautician school I spent all my money on a pair of those scissors. The same brand as the ones the school director proudly displayed. They were too much for someone like me who was just starting out and for the time being was using them for newspaper clippings for my scrapbook. But I wanted to splurge on a fancy item just for me, a lovely pair of scissors I could cherish.

Tsubasa scissors are beautiful. Except for the blades, there's nothing threatening about them. Even the tips are gently tapered. The transition from the straight blades to the curved handles is alluring. Just below the pivot is etched a Japanese castle, simple yet formidable.

Scissors embody danger, and therein lies their beauty. They're dangerous but not threatening. And the element of danger calls for prudence and composure—in other words, tranquility. You mustn't be disturbed with scissors in your hand—you have to be at peace with yourself.

Thinking about the scissors in my pocket relieves me of fear, even on dark streets at night. If I'm feeling victimized or I'm in a nasty frame of mind, I loop two fingers through the handles. Those metal handles rein in my arms and legs, which tend to run riot when I'm bitchy, and they settle me down.

I pass the area with all the clothing shops and head down to the underground shopping arcade. The warm, moist air smells like food gone bad. I stumble over boxes and trash tossed from shops that are shuttered for the night. I need to walk slow and easy. And that I do, striking up a conversation with the boxes and the trash.

I've always ended up back at the Greenfields Beauty Parlor. I have a standing invitation with which I proudly march into this single solitary place. No matter how late I hang around the hair salon, no matter how far I roam through the streets and alleys, no matter how slowly I walk—and sometimes I count the steps—it's the Greenfields to which I return. The seasons change, a new year is here, but it's always the same at the Greenfields—frigid.

I put my key in the lock and steady my breathing, hoping something terrible has happened. I hope the place has been ransacked, that there's a long dark shadow hanging from the ceiling, or the door to the loft is wide open with blood streaming out, or I'll encounter a man lying still in a dark red puddle or a dismembered corpse with the members still present, or witness a fatal knife thrust to the neck.

I open the door. *Ding-a-ling.* The tinkle echoing in the darkness tells me I'm back. Bewitched by the bell, I close the door, make sure it's locked, and heave a sigh.

All I ever feel returning to the Greenfields when the lights are off is an awful stillness. Everything is neatly arranged, no magazines strewn about, no hair left unswept, every object right where it should be. Absence of change. Pretense of neatness. I give the storage cart a kick. It rolls a short distance and fetches up against the coffee table. Again the beauty parlor falls silent.

I go into my room and flick the switch. The fluorescent light comes on but it always feels dark. My room is spotless—of course. I take off my coat with its hint of perm chemicals and hang it. Everything's the same as when I left this morning except for a note lying in the middle of the floor.

I open the half-folded note. He reminds me about the electric floor pad and barbells he's been demanding for days. He wants dry cereal and it has to be sugar-coated—and he's kindly indicated the brand name. Is it my dear father I'm serving, or a little boy? Next, scissors and glue—for what? An arts-and-crafts session for Dear Father. *Women's Home Journal* for July and August—for God's sake. I already delivered him September and October. You like the novel they're serializing, Father dear? I crumple the note and toss it off I don't care where.

I set the new manikin head on my desk and comb its tangled hair—much better. Shall I give you the unbalanced look? Or just a light layering effect? A certain customer comes to mind. And then it hits me—something is missing. The manikin head that was on my desk this morning. The bald head—I took off the wig, which I'd clipped so short while practicing. I'm sure it was here this morning. Hmm—and then my head whips around and I glare toward the loft. What's he up to?

I get up. A single stride and I'm at the door to the loft. I try to pry it open with my fingernails. It's locked. I knock on the door. *Kul-lunk*—the door unlocks, then opens. I steel myself and catch my breath.

"Give me my manikin." No response.

"And my boxes."

Silence. I hear only a pattern of regular, utterly peaceful breathing. I bite down on my lip and glare into the darkness.

Finally, his voice: "When you bring me those things."

"Then give me my box of clothes. All my winter clothes are in there—and it's winter, in case you didn't know!"

"First bring me those things. Then I'll give it to you."

Coward—it's not enough that you take over my loft, but you think you can use my belongings for bargaining chips! What a dirty trick.

"Is this what you're looking for?"

Out of the darkness something clatters down the steps and lands at my feet. It looks like a bird with outstretched wings. *Captured Angel.* The first book I ever bought with my own money—it was back in middle school. One of the young-adult romances that kept me company, stories about the obstacles that loom when you're learning about love and the inevitable, glorious instant when boy and girl find peace together. The painful, thrilling adventure of achieving the perfect love. My beautiful romances. He's opened all my boxes. He's got the nerve to put his hands on my belongings, to contaminate my prize possessions.

"You think I sent you to school to read crap like that?"

Another book shoots down the steps. It's thick and hard, and the corner practically impales my instep. *Hangŭl: Spelling and Usage*. A gift from Dad along with my penmanship workbook. *It's important to write neatly and use correct grammar.*

That's what he said when he gave them to me. He bought the same text and workbook for himself. I put my heart into filling that workbook—I felt I was competing with him.

My poor angel and my grammar book, tossed from the loft by Father. My angel, torn and broken, falling to earth, and your esteemed spelling book, armored with regularity and neatness.

"Get me the heating pad first—it's freezing up here." There's no room for compromise in his voice.

You can freeze to death for all I care. I barely manage to choke back the words.

Silently I close the door. I feel capable only of closing that door and cutting off his voice. I feel so powerless beneath him.

Father in the loft operates according to his one rule: tit for tat, and it's based on his wants, not mine. Benevolence is earned not through prayer but by completing my assignment.

He wants to be a savage god, and like all gods he uses the pretext of salvation to demand sacrifice, self-denial, and devotion. Lower your head and accept the commandments, bite down on your lip and receive your charge, be loyal to your father and benevolence will be granted you.

I fulfill Father's written demands. Up goes the electric heating mat, down comes my winter coat. Up go scissors and glue, down comes a sweater. Gloves and scarf are my reward for the sugar-coated cereal and home-delivered milk. The box of cereal specified by Father bears our Olympic tiger mascot flexing his muscles and grinning. The remainder of *Captured Angel*—the cover and a few pages that were torn off—takes longer for him to produce. I reattach them with glue and tape, but still the book is tattered. My angel captured by Father has finally returned, wounds and all.

When Father needs nothing, I get nothing. Before long I find myself aching for another demand. What if I offer up a sacrificial item before the command comes down? Could I escape from here? When will I recover my belongings held hostage up there?

How long must I live a predetermined existence for Him? I'm his only child, his gateway to the world, a loyal minion for my niggardly coward of a father.

Snow flies through the air. I'm crouched outside the beauty parlor looking down at the milk and newspaper. They're delivered every morning without fail, my father's daily bread. Snowflakes accumulate on the milk carton.

I'd like to bury myself in my toasty quilt on this winter morning, but instead I'm on the corner of an alley of untrammeled snow, little questions accumulating in my mind like the snow on the milk carton. Questions about my automaton of a body, moving by reflex in response to his knock. About my duty to deposit his daily bread at the door. About the taste of the milk and the contents of the newspapers that pass thorough my hands to his. A motorcycle roars past.

I pick up the milk, open the carton, and drink. The cold milk chills me all the way down. I finish it and close the carton, set it on the pavement, and raise my foot high. I've always wanted to do this, like little snots trying to scare girls. I expect a pop and get a hiss of air instead.

***

There he is again. Just when I thought there was a respite, he's back. The man with the bloodshot eyes who's looking for Father. He didn't show up for a while and I assumed he'd given up. He'd become part of the scenery outside the Greenfields Beauty Parlor. Standing like a still life in front of the record shop across the way. Arriving without a word, standing there without a word, then leaving.

I'm not afraid of you now, I don't get anxious any more. I've turned you into a speaker outside the record shop or a rack of shoes outside the shoe store. And here you are again. I guess it's time. People need to revisit memories they've temporarily forgotten. Oh yes, how can we forget that damnable man? That human butcher? That devil incarnate? Where could the bastard be hiding? How can his family survive? They don't deserve peace and quiet. The reporters will be swarming around again. The reward will go up. That's right, everyone should remember Father, Father who's now in the loft. We should commemorate the day when this estimable personage vanished. Every day will be a battle again.

But I have no time for the man—I'm off to the hair salon. I have a place where I can get away from the Greenfields Beauty Parlor. I'm the hot apprentice of the number one stylist at the biggest hair salon in the city. I love the title *apprentice*. And my stylist is awesome when it comes to competition. The word has gotten out, and unless you've booked her in advance, you'll be waiting hours.

I arrive to find everyone gathered around the new electric curling iron. From now on we'll heat the irons with electricity rather than coal briquettes or a gas stove. The retro look is in, and since you get that look with the irons, they decided to purchase the machine. But now that it's here they don't know what to do with it—they're just staring at it. It's impossibly bulky compared with the irons my mother mastered after two decades of curling and styling.

"What do we do with these?" asks Stylist Song's apprentice, indicating the pincers. I remember asking Mom the same question way back when. Stylist Song doesn't try to hide her embarrassment at not being able to answer. The lead stylist keeps quiet too, arms folded across her chest.

"They're used for *sodemaki*." Damn—I should have kept my mouth shut. "I mean, for curling the tips in or flipping them out." That must have come out sounding strange too. So I add, "You know, my mom runs an old-fashioned beauty parlor."

You make a mistake, you try to recover, recovery involves an excuse, and the excuse leads to a lie. I'm sure I'll be on the receiving end of unfriendly stares. Silence follows, and following the silence there's a vigorous rendition of today's slogan. We split up, go to our assigned stations, and get to work. The new curling iron takes its place next to the hair steamer.

So much for good intentions and trying to be helpful. I don't dress right for this place, I talk out of turn, I sound like I'm joking when I shouldn't be joking, I'm going to catch the heat, and it's a burden on everybody. This is what I get for my poor judgment. How much longer before I don't have to feel this way?

It's a war zone on Saturdays. We have to coordinate the walk-ins with the appointments, the perms with the styles, and the throng of customers doesn't leave us time to blink. We grab a bite to eat in the utility room and reek all day of perm solution and coloring agents.

The man from a week ago is back. Was he unhappy with his straight perm? No, he just wants some coloring. He doesn't need a cut, he had *that* done the week before his perm. There in the mirror the stiff face of the man and the playful countenance of the stylist. And stock still behind them, my usual expressionless self. I've actually practiced smiling, but it doesn't come easy.

The stylist's comb gently lifts his hair like a rock skipping across water. She lays it on the aluminum foil, adds the coloring, folds the foil with the hair inside. She does the same with a second swath of hair, then turns him over to me with a few instructions, before moving to a customer who wants a cut. The passing of the baton is too quick for my liking.

I silently get to work with comb and coloring brush. The man's eyes are closed—I think he's nodding off. Good—he's sparing me a stream of conversation I'd have to keep up with. An intern arrives offering to massage his hands but he waves her off. I keep up a conversation but it's silent and directed to the back of the man's head. *How do you like your perm, sir? Your hair is quite thick, it could probably stand some thinning. You've got a little tail, but it shouldn't stand out if we leave the back a bit long. Ooh, look at that pimple on your neck. It's red and swollen—I bet it hurts. If it was yellow I could probably pop it for you. But it's not quite ready.*

I finish the coloring, then move to the woman my stylist has just cut, and give her the finishing touches. Then, while the man is getting his hair washed, I seat my next customer—a style. The man's coloring isn't quite what I expected, but it's not bad. The stylist dries his hair and styles it, then applies gel and he's done. Seeing off the customer is my responsibility—while he's paying I stand off to the side, hands gathered before me, watching his expression. He includes a tip. Middle-aged women will tip the apprentice for a hand massage, but it's rare for a young man to leave a tip.

It's late to be having lunch, but I grab myself a bite. There on the table in the utility room are *kimpap* and assorted side dishes. Judging from the amount of *kimpap* that's left, I'm not the only one taking a late lunch. I put some of the rice rolls on a small plate and take it to the storage room. In the utility room I have to put up with the watchful gazes of others while I eat. Here it's peaceful and I can take my time. I'm among boxes—my new loft. I perch myself on one of them and plop a piece of *kimpap* into my mouth.

Voices outside. Stylist Min's girls? I chew slowly before swallowing.

"Did you see that man—he came again." A voice from the utility room. I crunch down on the radish pickle in the *kimpap*—it makes too much of a noise. I stop chewing, pause, then swallow. Should I let them know I'm in here? "Must be hot on her—can't wait a week and he's in and out again." Another voice: "Who knows? Maybe he thinks she's a princess the way she keeps her eyes down and her mouth shut. Or maybe it's her curves." The first voice: "That look of hers is bad news. '*Sodemaki*'—did you hear that? And 'flipping out'—who asked her anyway? She thinks we didn't say anything because we're idiots? She won't associate with us and she's a brown-noser. Don't let that innocent face fool you—I bet she's full of surprises. You know, I wish they'd give us something besides *kimpap*. Madam goes out for lunch, and we get stuck with *kimpap* or else sandwiches? Hey, let's go out for clams after work—I know a new place and already it's absolutely packed."

I need to pee.

Our next booking is a woman who wants a style. I start with a dryer to fluff her hair. *You're not going to a wedding on this cold winter day, are you, ma'am—I'll bet you have a hot date. Wow, who did your makeup, ma'am, was it you? It looks really natural. Hmm, your hair could use some attention—perhaps you'd like to try our treatment. . . .* No matter how I rehearse these lines, they just don't want to come out.

As I curl the sides, I sneak glances at the big mirror to see what's going on around me. If I'm lucky, I can even check out the faces of the stylists and their customers I'm back to back with. Wait, who's that in the mirror behind me? Mirror to mirror, eye to eye. My back stiffens. It's Chini. She looks down, then back up and into the mirror. The set of her mouth seems to be saying, *Oh, it's you.*

You're here for a straight perm. You must be one of Stylist Song's regulars. Chini, are you doing anything that's getting your heart pounding? You don't hear my heart pounding, do you. That's because you stepped all over it and it hardened—it remembers. And you've brought that beast back to life and he's raging. I never expected Father in the loft to show up like he did. He can make his divine entrance anywhere. Hiding inside me, watching over me, popping out when I least expect it and punishing me. I didn't perform my duty as I should have, I took from Father his daily bread, and now he's punishing me. And all my fears, dormant inside me, have come back to life. Thanks to Father in the loft—

"Hey! Didn't you hear me? It's too hot!"

"Wake up!" says someone else.

I hear music. I smell of singed hair

"Are you trying to burn my hair, you crazy bitch!"

Someone snatches the hair dryer from me. I'm just standing there, my roll brush in my other, upraised hand. Go on, apologize—tell her you're sorry. It's easy to say, but then why don't the words come out? I'm frozen, even my mouth.

"Idiot—what are you trying to do!" She yanks my hair, hits my head. She's pounding on my head, no one's stopping her. I can hear her panicked breathing.

Ow, that hurts. No one's ever hit me before. I must have really burned her.

Chini has drifted out. She quietly lowered her gaze, quietly had her straight perm, quietly drifted away.

***

I'm being beaten. Beaten like a drum by a gang of faceless people. What did I do? I must have done something wrong and so, eyes closed, I take all the punches and kicks and slaps without resisting. I feel a chill, it brings my eyes open. People's heads are hanging from the ceiling. Flaming heads, heads dripping blood, howling heads. I close my eyes and the heads start screaming at me. *Where are you hiding your father!*

And then I'm awake. My nose tingles. A fierce wind rattles the window. The heated floor has gone ice cold and is drawing the remaining warmth from my quilt. I burrow into my quilt, every bone and joint aching. My head feels like a giant squeezebox, expanding and contracting with a monotone whine.

Thump thump—heels beating on the floor of the loft. I fling the quilt aside. Cold spreads through my bones. *Thump thump.* I sit myself up. My squeezebox head expands, drawing in cold air. *Thump thump.* I go out to the washroom. The *thump thump* rings in my head, as if Father's heels are hitting me instead of the loft floor. *Thump thump thump thump.* The signal from on high is more demanding.

Fuss and squall and tantrum all you want, you're not getting anything until I get warm. I go out and check the hot-water heater—the red warning light is on. I try the hot-water tap and hear the on-demand system click, but then nothing. Now it's the heating system that's ganging up on me. *Thump thump thump thump.* Keep that up and you'll kick holes in the ceiling.

Back in my room I put on my coat, stick my hands in the pockets, and loop my fingers through the handles of the scissors. I look up toward the loft. *Thump thump thump.* More loudly now. *Thump thump thump thump*—the sound is drawing out the beast in me. *Snip snip.* Quietly I work the scissors.

What's up there isn't my dad, it's a beast, a growling, agitated beast, bare fangs dripping. No, actually it's the rotten meat of an animal slaughtered by a beast—what's left of the carcass after the eyeballs and innards have been devoured. No, actually it's the clouds of shitflies buzzing and swarming around that rotten meat. What's up there in the loft is the maggots hatched by those shitflies. Wiggling, crawling, sickening maggots burrowing into flesh. They reek of decay.

That afternoon my energy level plummets. Every movement reverberates in my squeezebox head. My eyes are hot and swollen and feel like they're going to pop out of their sockets; my tongue is parched and burning. There are many more customers for styling than usual—it must be the year-end rush—and they continue to stream in after closing time. I sneak a hot drink whenever I can, and barely keep up with my work. Not until ten at night am I able to clean up and leave the hair salon.

Back to the Greenfields Beauty Parlor. Isn't there anywhere else I can go? The frosty Greenfields. My icebox room. That disgusting beast oppressing me.

I feel like there's a thick elastic cord around my ankles. So that the farther I fly off, the faster I'm jerked back. I can't snap it and I can't wrap it around my hand and control it. Or is it actually me who holds that cord and yet I don't realize it? Maybe I'm holding myself like a yo-yo, letting myself out, bringing me back in, out and in. I can't throw that yo-yo away, and I can't hold it and make it do what I want.

Into my room I go, and bury myself in my quilt, coat and all. The room is still frigid. The hem of the quilt touches my cheek and I startle, the chilly sensation spreading throughout me. I feel like I'm sinking into the floor. I'm drifting off to sleep. And then the door to the loft is flung open—he's been waiting.

"Have you been drinking the milk?"

I don't move, don't acknowledge that I've heard.

"It's been days since I got the milk and the newspaper—I want to know why," he barks. "Aren't you going to answer me?"

He's not going to give up.

"They weren't there."

"I saw the milkman come and go."

"Maybe he forgot?"

"What about the newspaper?"

"I don't know."

"What do you mean, you don't know. The milk and the newspaper come every day—what happened!"

"For god's sake . . . would you . . . ?"

Please stop. Your voice is like a screw in my eardrums. Like thunder and lightning in my head. I hurt all over. I feel like bugs are crawling over me—digging into me, sucking out my blood. I'm on fire: my throat is burning, my tongue is like a parched leaf, fire is shooting out of my mouth. But I can't get rid of this damn chill. I'm numb from head to toe. I just want to rest. My eyelids are heavy. I need to sleep. I've had a long day. Hair dryers are still whirring in my head. Will someone please get the chemical reek out of my nose?

"I'm hungry—make me a pot of ramen."

I don't respond.

"Did you eat?"

Never mind. Don't pretend you're my dad.

"We can eat together, hmm?"

I turn so my back faces him. As I do so a grunt escapes me.

"Are you sick?"

That does it—I'm not going to give in. I sit up, my back to the loft, and recite into the darkness, "There's no ramen. The gas is off. Do you really have to have ramen, right now, at this very instant?"

"Go buy some—is a two-minute walk to the store going to kill you?"

"Why me? Why don't you ask Mom? Are you doing this on purpose? What did I do to deserve this?"

From the darkness a sigh.

"Your mom is not here. And she didn't make dinner for me. She had some hens over and they were clucking and fussing all evening . . . they must have gone out somewhere. So let's have some ramen, okay?"

Is that thunder I hear? A clap of thunder from far off? The thunder brings an image of menacing clouds; I imagine myself soaked already. I rise to my feet like a ghost.

"Maybe there's still a noodle place open?"

Meaning noodles with black-bean sauce. I walk out the door. "Here, take some money."

I don't look back as I close the door, slotting the eye and sticking the spoon handle through it. I walk the length of the beauty parlor and I'm outside. The *ding-a-ling* has a sharpness to it. The icy wind layers my bare face before moving on.

There he is again. It's close to midnight but there he squats, like another speaker propped in front of the record shop, elbows resting on his knees, head wrapped in his hands, gazing at the pavement. I stop and watch. Cigarette butts are scattered about his feet. *You're pathetic, all of you. I'm sick of you there, sick of the gentleman in the loft.* The man registers my presence and looks in my direction. I approach, each step heavier than the one before. I stop in front of him. He looks up at me.

"It's almost midnight—what are you doing here? Don't you have anywhere to go? Are you waiting for a handout?"

No answer.

"You're trying to catch my dad?"

Silence.

"And if you don't catch him, does that mean your life is not worth living anymore? You're one of his victims too? And you want to find the son of a bitch? Yes? All right, I'll show you where he is. And then you can take him away!"

He turns his head away.

"What's wrong, you don't believe me?"

Still no answer.

"I said let's go! I'll take you to him!"

I grab his wrist but he doesn't budge. We're having a tug of war. I grit my teeth and pull harder. That gets him a few inches off the pavement. I lift and he resists. The seesaw tilts his way—he's stronger. He struggles to free himself, twisting his wrist like a fish I've grabbed hold of. I've got him with both hands—I'm not going to let this fish get away.

In my palm I feel the pulsing in his wrist. Faint but definite, his heart is pumping. It's an ardent movement—a fearful, sob-like trembling.

"Are you afraid?"

Silence.

"You are, aren't you? Here I am, giving you your opportunity, but you're scared."

Still no response.

"Why is it me you're harassing? Am I an easy target? Do I look weak? But you can't act on your own, you don't have the confidence. You're not brave enough to catch him. So instead you're acting the big bully with me."

You're a coward. People like you are the bad ones. You hide from the strong and you bully the weak. A pseudo-cop. A self-appointed director wearing an armband. Proudly putting on the noble face of the oppressed and the wounded, screeching for truth, duty, and justice. Sacrifice? That's something you get others to do. Out of the goodness of your heart you want to chase down the bad guys, bring them to justice, see them punished. But you're worse. Dad didn't do anything wrong—he was just doing his job.

So now it's the man who's bad and Dad is blameless. I should be more understanding. Dad was only following orders. He had to punish people—it was part of his job. And just like I'm programmed to react to his heel thumping in the loft, he's programmed to respond to the heel thumping of his bosses—at least I want to understand it that way. Because that gives me the crazy notion that maybe Father didn't do those things they said he did.

The strength drains from my hands. But not because of my ridiculous hope. Instead, some strange force has sucked all the venom out of me. Why am I pulling this man? I let go of his wrist. The instant he's free he lunges and grabs *my* wrist. Wow, that was quick. I struggle to free myself but it's no use. And here we are back on the seesaw, but the roles are reversed.

"The radio is killing me. My body's like a radio, ever since I don't know."

He's still clutching my wrist as he says this. His face is purple with fright, the color of someone reliving an oppressive, uncontrollable experience.

"My skin remembers that place before my mind does. It lives inside every cell of me."

He's glaring into space, his bug eyes a spider web of blood vessels. I feel what he says—that every cell of him is alive and moving in that place. He's desperate to keep the liquid from gathering in his bloodshot eyes. He has a blood-raging desire to hide something, like people who bite their lip, using pain to block the flow of tears.

"Every time I moved I could hear the national anthem and even when I was still I heard the announcer's sweet voice wrap itself around me. 'You're listening to Radio Korea, broadcasting from Seoul, capital of the Republic of Korea....'"

He lets go of me and his hands come back to rest on his knees. Silently he lowers his head, and silently I look down on him. The back of his head looks so heavy.

"Your name is Sŏn," he drawls. "Your birthday is April 21. I always wondered what presents you got."

Now he's looking up at me. I can't read his expression. Maybe it's involuntary, he feels like bursting into tears but he can't, or maybe it's a smile, he's suddenly remembered a happy moment. Whatever it is, it's amorphous like a dream.

Finally tears pool in his eyes. I've never seen such a sad expression. It's like a brand on my chest. Some day that brand will destroy me. I don't know where that sad look comes from, or why it's so ominous. All I know is that it came the instant his bloodshot eyes began to flow. I know that something has been put in place and will always be there, and that maybe I will seek out that something.

I reach out, gently take hold of the back of his hand, and slowly draw him close. He looks up at me and takes my forearm with his other hand. My hand on his arm, his on mind are like a pair of snakes intertwining. His gaze and mine meet and exchange positions. Looking straight at the man, I draw him toward me again. He rises to his feet, not removing his gaze from me.

I move back a step, the man moves forward a step. Are you

scared? Yes, I'm scared. Like the first time I encountered the man, one of us retreating step by step, the other advancing step by step. Are you frightened? Yes, I'm frightened. Silent footsteps, no shouting, no terror. And the clear *ding-a-ling* of the door to the beauty parlor.

Tell me. Tell me what Dad did. I want to know. I have to know. Tell me. Don't leave anything out. That place that lives inside every cell of you, bring it alive in my body too. Make your tongue remember what every cell of you remembers and inscribe those memories on my tongue. It doesn't matter if you slash at my throat, crush my heart, rip out my innards. If that place is hell, then I'll go to hell. If it's heaven, then give me the taste of heaven. And seal it inside me with those blue lips of yours. So that once your story is inside me, inside my every capillary, my every cell, it will never escape. Only then can I betray Father in the loft.

A fateful kiss. All sensation gathers in my tongue. Flames engulf me, like a witch in the fires of hell. The fathomless sensation of sucking and releasing. Tongues in each other's mouth, whistling and singing, sealed by lips so the song can never escape. The song focuses all sensation so that it circulates forever inside your partner. One fateful kiss.

Look, Dear Father in the loft. Look upon your sweet daughter, look upon what she does beneath you here. Or else listen. Listen to the panting. Listen to the man you broke break me down. Listen to him inscribing in me the pain you inscribed in him.

His body tells my body a story. Of the radio playing inside him. The fire stinging and burning his shoulders. The blood streaming down the insides of his thighs. The chill spewing from his heart. It's the story of what you, Dear Father, inscribed in his body, the story of your flicking tongue.

. . . You're listening to Radio Korea, broadcasting from Seoul, capital of the Republic of Korea. Our mission is to provide you our listeners with the most enjoyable and entertaining programs in accordance with Broadcasting Committee standards . . . .

A small room with a radio, and a tub, a bed, and a desk. The door opens and in you come, holding a large leather briefcase. You place the briefcase on the desk, remove your jacket, loosen your tie, and take off your shoes. You open the briefcase and consider the contents, like a technician selecting the proper tool to repair a broken item. You take out a sheaf of papers and tap the bottoms against the desk to get them perfectly aligned. You place that file on the desk, and next to it two dictionaries, a Monami pen, and a ruler, everything in order. Sporadic screams come from outside, dying out then erupting again, poignant as the howling of a beast.

Good morning, everyone, and welcome to kog'u, *rain for grain, the last of our six spring periods, and wouldn't you know it, we wake up today to a nice soaking rain. The baby green of the new rice shoots looks all the greener, doesn't it? How about a song for our morning musical stroll into the spring rain.*

Let's have a look at your face. *Aigu*, what a handsome young fellow. Do you know who I am? Have you heard of Number Two at the Funeral Home, the man who gets rid of the dead bodies? If you're a good boy and listen to me, that won't happen—we wouldn't want any dead bodies, would we. So let's not make things difficult, that's what I say. Lies don't work with me. Understand? I see the boys worked you over pretty good. They should have been more gentle. How do they expect you to talk if they beat you to a pulp? Let's have a look at your balls. Can't very well work on them if they're playing hide and seek. Does that hurt? No worries, if one of them ruptures, you've still got the other one. So, you didn't know there was a radio receiver in the hardware shop safe? What—you son of a bitch, you didn't know what the receiver was for? A radio *receiver* is for *receiving* contacts from people. If you don't know something, asshole, then find out and drill it into your head. The beating you just got should help. You're starting to come around? Let's get you something to eat first. Anyway, you don't know what the money was for, you were just the delivery boy? And you didn't know about the code in the account book? You thought it was strange, right? So, you didn't do anything wrong, you just did what you were told, correct? You know, I've got a soft spot for you because you're so handsome. The place we're ordering from stinks, but the bone-marrow soup is just the thing—don't bother with the beef-and-rice soup. And after you get out, stop by and I'll take you out for lunch—on me. Nothing beats bone-marrow soup for your aching joints.

You're finished. You look so peaceful sitting there at your desk, looking through the Chinese-character dictionary open in front of you along with the Korean dictionary as you write your report. So involved with your writing, like a boy who's just learned that skill. Fixated on writing in straight lines, which is what the ruler is for. You're absorbed in thought, then you look up and check a spelling with him. You're nonchalant and cruel. Gentle and vicious. Absent-minded and lucid.

"The pain I could bear. But not the radio. There I was crying and screaming while that sweet, gentle voice talked about leaves soaked with spring rain—I couldn't stand that voice. She and the other announcer, they were laughing and having a great time. What was I to them? They had all the time in the world, and that world was peaceful—that's what really scared me. It was hell until the national anthem and the beep when they went off the air for the night. But that was just a few hours."

The man bites his lip and tries to rub warmth back into him. I'm cold just looking at the blueness of his lips. My body feels like a windpipe.

He retrieves a newspaper clipping from his jacket. It's creased and tattered—how long has he had it? He fumbles with it, distracted, before offering it to me. The paper is soft against my skin but feels like a razor blade. I almost drop it because of the chilling sensation, then manage to clutch it.

"That's my crime. Not his but mine. I wish I knew why I keep coming here. I never think about it, I just walk and this is where I end up. When I'm next to that speaker it's like the radio inside me turns off."

And then he's gone. The wind has died down. The radio is off, the man's voice extinguished. I'm left by myself. Everything that's been tying me down is snapping loose, the rope around my wrist, the elastic band around my ankle, they're all undone. I'm floating in zero gravity. No place to set foot, nowhere to hold on. With nothing to touch, there's no pull and no push. Time flows by, weightless, and when I come back to earth I'm colder and lighter.

CHAPTER 9

It's the size of a fingernail but I'll be damned if I can open it. I can see through a rock and yet I can't open the lock on this kids' toy. Sure I could rip it open, but then the girl would give me hell for the rest of my life. So I find a hairpin and try to stick it into the hole in the lock, but it's too big around and it won't fit. I bite down on it, make it thinner, and try again, tapping it into the hole, working it around, trying to pull it out. For God's sake. The lock's so damn tiny it keeps slipping out of my fingers—it's a real bitch.

Finally the treasure chest pops open and I see a small notebook with a pink plastic cover—the secret door to my girl's life. I rub my hands in anticipation. Carefully I open the notebook to the first page, a picture she drew of five girls lined up left to right holding hands—Four-Eyes, Piglet, Prissy, Sunshine, and Scaredy-Cat. There's a different personality to each face, so even if my girl hadn't added the nicknames, I could tell who's who. I never knew she had such talent. The girls must be her friends. Prissy—that has to be Sŏn. Each of the girls must have had one of these notebooks and they swapped them—how cute.

The next page has nothing, and the next page and the one after that, blank to the very end. I've been wasting my time. She must have cherished it so much that she wanted to keep it in its original condition. Or maybe she lost interest. But it obviously meant something or she wouldn't have tucked it away in the chest. All those blank pages have gotten me thinking. I'm sharp enough to review a statement and catch details that slip by the analysts, and yet I'm stymied by a child's notebook. When it comes to little girls I'm clueless about their feelings.

I set the notebook on my quilt. What's next in the chest? Glitter stickers, a notepad with a floral theme, postcards of cartoon characters, a scented dayglow pen. She liked red in a big way. That pearl earring with the broken pin—she must have gotten that from her mom. And here's a necklace with a photo locket, a hairpin studded with tiny colored stones, a white lump of God knows what, and a smooth, shiny pebble. Worthless girly treasures. So much for the first box.

I'm going to snack on all these yummy boxes hidden in the loft. I can spend an afternoon on a single one, taking out the items one by one then putting them all back.

So, back in the box we go. Wait—what's that hiding at the very bottom, the small velvet container? I open it. A commemorative coin? No, it's a medal, the Justice Award. Aha. There was a modest ceremony in the Town Hall conference room. Afterward I gave her a ride on my shoulders and we proudly marched home. She put the medal around her neck, pumped her arms in the air, and shouted, "Gold medal, gold medal!" She wouldn't let it out of her sight, she even slept with it. She wore it like a garland, or sometimes like a bracelet, and she put it around the neck of her teddy bear and babbled to it. And here's where she kept it, in a treasure chest.

I loop the medal around my neck and the warm applause from that day comes alive in my ears.

It happened on a sultry summer night. The curfew was drawing near and the streetlights were dimming. I was on my way home from a night of drinking when I heard a woman scream for help. The scream came from around the next corner, and the thought of a woman in peril set my righteous heart to throbbing. My alcohol haze cleared and my body tensed, ready for action. Balling my hands into fists I charged. A taxi came into view, a woman half-hanging from the passenger-side window. She had one hand propped against the pavement and with the other was trying desperately to pull herself back in. I realized someone inside was trying to push her out. And then it hit me—the driver was trying to rob her.

I sprinted to the taxi, my thick hands yanked open the driver-side door, and I grabbed the guy by the neck. He had a knife and was about to slice free the woman's handbag from the straps. The blade flailed at me, the tip grazing my forearm. But the robber's hand was no match for my stout heart, and the knife fell from his grasp. I took the guy by the scruff and yanked him onto the pavement, where I put his hands behind his back and kneeled on him. So there. God in heaven created judo to subdue assholes like this one.

I hoisted the guy up and marched him off to the police box nearby. He made no effort to resist—I had dislocated both his shoulders. I opened the door to the police box and pushed the guy to the floor. "I caught a robber!" I shouted. The scene is still vivid: the slack-jawed, bug-eyed policemen trying to make sense of the situation, the taxi-driver robber squirming on the floor and whimpering, the woman who had pranced there behind me hovering like a shadow.

With my righteous heart, my fast legs, and my stout forearms I had saved the woman. I was a righteous man and physically I was up for the job, a notion that did not register completely until a few days later when, with the Justice Award hanging around my neck, I was invited to apply for the position of policeman. A light went on in my mind—with a righteous heart and a strong body I should be doing police work, not selling books on monthly installments. And that's how I joined the force.

I was thirty-one, an age when neither robbers nor tigers can faze you. And now I grip these forearms of mine. No way could they be the firm forearms of my thirty-one-year-old self. And what has happened to the muscles of my steely legs? All I do is crouch in this loft—no wonder my body is breaking down and the gold of my medal, stuck here in this loft, is tarnished and flaking.

I remove the medal from around my neck and close my hand around it. Put the notebook back first? No, the treasure chest has to go in first, down at the bottom. Then her stationery. And then the sticker set to the right, the postcards on the left. I put everything back in the reverse order in which it came out. Except for the medal, which I leave on top, above the notebook. Finally I place the lid on the box.

"Daddy, gold medal, gold medal!" How old was she when she started calling me Daddy? Roughhousing may work with boys, but girls are different. When she was young, even though I took the gentle approach and tried to reason with her, she was a handful, a prissy little pouter. But I have to admit there's some fun involved in raising a cute little girl. *Daddy*—those two syllables draw me into a recess of my memory, back when I sold books door to door. When I came home late at night, exhausted from lugging my briefcase all over town, her greeting was like a breath of fresh air. "Daddy, get me some cookies," she'd say, rubbing her sleep-filled eyes. The next night on my way home I'd make a detour to the place that made *sembei* cookies, more specifically the kind that look like a spinning top, and buy her a bag of them. Even if it was late and I'd been drinking I was drawn to the cookie shop like a sparrow to a mill. One time they gave me a bag with a hole and I didn't realize it—I must have left a trail of cookies all the way home. If she was asleep I'd place the cookies under her nose and the next thing I knew she'd be munching on them without even opening her eyes. And then she'd talk in her sleep:

"Daddy, they're so yummy." Sometimes, just to see her wake up, I'd put a ginger-flavored cookie in her mouth. She'd wake up scowling a hundred different ways, and did she ever bawl—that voice alone could have made her a general.

Yes, I remember the smell of those cookies, hot from the mold. Sweet fragments of distant recollections. I keep being drawn back to the past—it's like taking out the contents of the boxes. I like the way time goes backward here in the loft, the footsteps of my memory returning me to scintillating moments from before. I want to linger in those moments. Only then can I endure the long hours. I *have* to endure.

One year, stick it out for one more year. Come next spring my time in the loft is over. Just be patient one more year.

***

For the third day in a row the old woman hasn't shown up. The first day I wasn't concerned, I don't think her absence registered. But yesterday I got to wondering if something happened to her. Just three days ago she had a slight limp, but as usual she moseyed through the alley with the Bible tucked under her arm. She stopped to stretch her back beneath the streetlight and took a deep breath before continuing—nothing different from her usual routine. With old folks, though, one moment they may look to be in perfect working order and the next moment they croak. And when it's biting cold like now, they get so fragile they can collapse while they're on the pot. My last glimpse of her is sharp in my mind. The alley was icy and she kept bracing herself against the wall. If spring is fixing to arrive in this alley where the shade breeds ice, it won't be anytime soon.

Pak's been found guilty at the re-trial, a year and a half after he was found innocent on appeal. Granted he's on parole now, but his luck is running out for sure. As for Paek, Ŭn, and Nam, their trials are pending. Because without me there's no basis for a trial. The boys could have dumped everything on me but sure enough, they didn't betray my trust in them. I would expect no less from the boys I raised—they didn't tarnish their father's name. My first order of business is to survive. That way I benefit all the others.

Dinner arrives late. My wife has brought the stovetop grill with the butane cartridges and is cooking meat. I dip a spoonful of rice into the bean-paste stew and pop it into my mouth.

"The wild *naengi* smell nice, don't they? The old woman across the way said she was on Kanghwa Island and dug those greens herself. You name it, she's got everything for sale in that big basin of hers. She'll have squash leaves and that new curlicue eggplant this summer."

She places a chunk of meat in my rice bowl. I ignore it as I work on my stew.

"It's going to be noisy tomorrow. I'm adding an adjustable shampooing chair to the washroom. We're the only beauty parlor for miles around that doesn't have an adjustable chair. And I figured I might as well put in a new floor there too. So if you can be patient for a couple of days. And . . . "

I silently spoon my stew. The *naengi* do smell pretty good.

" . . . next week I need to make a trip to Kaya."

"What for?"

"Father's memorial—you know. The last two years I didn't go. And . . . I hired a new girl."

"You'll have to pay her. What do you need a helper for anyway?"

"I need someone young to help me get by. Even the old ones prefer young hands—they have a different fashion sense, or something like that. I'm stuck here, I don't have time for anything else—"

"What about Sŏn? Why not ask her—"

"No way, she's stubborn as a mule. Besides, she's cooking up something with the manager at the hair salon. And she's been pestering me to teach her how to use the hot irons. But I don't feel like going out of my way to hire her. And am I supposed teach her for free? Plus there's the cost of the construction work, so—"

"You mean you'd charge the girl for lessons so you can pay for the construction? Why?"

"No, she offered—she stuck her pay envelope right in front of my nose. I didn't ask her, *she* asked *me*."

"What about the money Pak gave you? And didn't you say Paek and the others promised you money every month?"

"You know as well as I do that Pak's money is long gone. And Paek's is a drop in the bucket."

A neglected piece of pork fat sizzles on the grill. Whatever else my wife was going to say she's not saying it. Instead she keeps wiping the rims of the side-dish containers.

"Why don't you go see Pak? Apart from the money issue you can ask him what's going on."

"I don't want to."

What am I supposed to say to that?

"I don't want to see his good wife and I don't want to meet with him. It's disgusting the way they look at me, it's like everything's your fault. No, I'm not going to do it."

"How could that be. You must have misunderstood—"

"You know what the good wife said last time? 'There are people watching, so kindly refrain from visiting us so often.' Or else I should go there around the time their housekeeper arrives. As if

134

I'm one of their maids—so I don't create suspicion."

"Well, their circumstances are difficult and so—"

"And so I need to be one of their maids now? That's ridiculous! Back when she used to come all this way for a curl and carry on about how her hair held up for three days, four days—all that sweet-talking makes me want to throw up."

"Just put up with it another year."

"And then what?"

I don't have a good answer.

"And then they'll take you back?"

Good question.

"You're part of our family now." So said Pak as he gave me a pat on the shoulder after the first time I grilled a guy. Being part of a family meant one mouth, which meant in turn eating the same food and saying the same things. I wondered if that was possible. Not only would I belong in his world, I would be part of his family—I was mightily obliged.

When I first met Pak I was a bodyguard—the lowest rung on the police ladder—and my first assignment was to protect him. I had always imagined being on the move in that job—breathless chases and quick arrests—but the reality was that I had to dress up and dog the footsteps of the man I was guarding. Not a job that had me jumping for joy. But Pak's world seemed so cool, so tough and righteous, I was able to put up with it for half a year. It couldn't have been more different from the world of my father, whose artificial leg and sparrows symbolized a loser.

My father had tried to make a living catching sparrows and selling them in town. On the ground he would spread a trail of grain leading to the trap he'd made from a bamboo basket, and then he waited. Holding the cord to the basket and nodding off, he looked like a fisherman sitting beside a lonesome lake. But when opportunity struck he pulled the cord—end of story. One time he caught five sparrows all at once. In town there was a row of *makkŏlli* houses known for their roasted sparrow, and men came from far and wide to sample it. When grain got to ripening on the stalk, catching sparrows was the village pastime. The other men used BB guns or nets, but all Father could do, having lost a leg in the war, was set out a few more traps.

Whenever Father caught a sparrow he built a fire on the spot and roasted it. He was a real pro at burning off the feathers, cutting open the belly and removing the innards, and skewering the bird. And the entire process—setting the trap, catching the sparrows, and roasting them—he did sitting.

You have to learn to wait patiently. Never, ever be hasty and always be alert. Let them enjoy the grain. Let them enjoy it till all their suspicion has evaporated. That's when you pull the cord. And you pull quickly. It's all about speed—don't hesitate, don't shilly-shally. Once you make up your mind, yank. Move faster than the bird. He emphasized these last words as he placed the cord in my hand. Yank—move faster than the bird.

That was all my father taught me.

I wanted to belong to Pak's world. I wanted to dump my pathetic father and serve a new father. "Please let me catch Reds!" I declared to Pak as I handed him a resignation note. Without a word Pak smiled and returned the note to me. I had to submit that note twice more before my chance arrived.

"Want to give it a try?" Pak said casually. It was a golden opportunity for me to replace my father. We were with an investigator who was taking a snack break. "That guy is one tough bastard," he said, waving in exasperation. "He won't blink. He'll play with you, absolutely drive you up a wall." His words whet my appetite to go one on one with the guy and come out on top. I rushed off to the interrogation room. The guy was just about to dig into his lunch. When I saw the generous meal on his tray my blood boiled. I flipped over the tray, sending the metal dishes clattering to the floor, and a cloud of steam rose. I let a few seconds go by before resuming the attack.

"The police get stuck with rice and soup while a son of a bitch like you porks out on stew and grilled fish. *And*—an apple for dessert? Hey, I've got some news for you—you're going to go fetch yourself a bowl of soup and rice!"

The guy raised an arm to protect himself. He still had his spoon in his hand. He remained frozen like that until the apple from his tray came to rest near my feet. Then he lowered his arm and that's when I caught an indication of his cowardice and his willingness to betray. The corners of his mouth had that little twitch that told me he loved to meddle in other people's business, and he had the lines beneath the eyes and the thin lips of a sex fiend. I knew at that moment I needed to draw out all of his cowardice. I picked up the apple, crushed it in my hand, and threw it in his face. It bounced off, leaving pulp streaming down his cheeks. Then I grabbed his balls. Didn't squeeze, just held them as I looked him in the eye. And that did the trick. When I gave him paper and pen he spilled out more than I expected, then filled his empty stomach with a cold bowl of soup and rice.

That guy's lost meal turned into the sumptuous feast I earned from my new father. He and I ate from the same dish, we spoke the same language, and we became a true family. But there was more—I was pointed out by others as the son who was certain to succeed my father. "You're the spitting image of me when I was younger." When Pak put his arm around my shoulder over drinks and said this, I vowed I would safeguard my father's new world forever.

The world I live in now is not my father's but that of my wife and daughter, a life of exile or homecoming I'm not sure which. The world sheltering me now is a world that smells of *naengi* and soybean-paste stew. Will I ever return to my father's world and inherit his seat of power, and if so, will I remain forever in that position?

I mustn't doubt my father. The moment suspicion encroaches, my world will collapse. The world of my father that I've watched over is formidable and also beautiful. I can't get wrapped up in the trivial concerns of little women. All I have to do is wait one year, just one year.

The loft is rattling. I lie here, eyes closed, feeling the hammering in my head and hearing the drill whining for dear life. I can understand replacing the old hot-water heater and adding the shampoo chair, but new tile on the floor? That's not going to be cheap. Why is she so bull-headed about this earth-shaking renovation, to the extent that she's using Sŏn's money to help fund it? And the damned racket—I can't sleep, and the words in the book that lies open in front of me aren't registering. The workers are in and out the whole day through, which means I can't budge or let out a peep. I'm in a vicious frame of mind.

Suddenly everything's quiet. The stillness is more ominous than the noise. Since I can't see what's going on down in the beauty parlor, I might as well be blind. Noises are my only source of information about possible danger. Well, sometimes smells too, like the ones coming from down below right now: the aroma of noodles in black-bean sauce—equal parts sweet, greasy, and smoky—and the smell of sweet-and-sour pork. A bowl of noodles in black-bean sauce from the Hyangwŏn was heavenly when I took a break from giving a guy the third degree.

I take the lunchbox from beneath the quilt. What with the construction I've had to pull up the electric cord from the washroom, so the electric floor pad is cold as ice and even inside my quilt my meal has turned cold. Taking in the smell of noodles in black-bean sauce, I eat my cold rice. Thanks to that aroma, I have a hearty appetite even though I'm in no mood to eat. And so I finish my meal down to the last grain of rice. If only I were slurping those noodles instead.

I look down at my empty lunchbox. All those times I waited in ambush I never felt as lonely as I do now. I've slept out in the open, surviving on rock-hard pastries—rice was out of the question—but have never felt as cold as I do now. Back then I was full of energy, always passionate and excited about my work.

It's not easy waiting days on end, armed with conviction, for an enemy that may never show up. You're working against the clock but you have to be prudent, you have to catch the enemy before they know you've found their base. All we could do was wait, with no end in sight. And it's all the more difficult if your hideout is some damp, abandoned place up in the hills. We'd found the evidence in the firebox—a wad of money, a radio, instructions left by their advance team. Sooner or later someone would show up to retrieve those items. The monsoons had arrived and it rained the whole time we were there. We never set foot outside the gate. For nature's call we used the firebox. For food we made do with hard pastries and soft drinks. No smoking at night—the glow from the cigarette would show. We took turns sleeping, couldn't be bothered with washing up. It was damp inside and I hated the chill. The stink was nauseating. You have to lock yourself up to catch the dogs you want to lock up. To corner those dogs we had to become dogs ourselves.

Around the time I was beginning to doubt my convictions, on a morning when the loathsome rain had stopped, just as I'd unzipped my pants to relieve myself in the firebox, we heard the squishing of feet in a puddle and someone clearing his throat. I signaled my two boys and positioned them, then went into the kitchen and waited by the door. We were all set. There—a man and a woman dressed for a hike. Now who the hell goes for a hike on a small hill with no path and no road leading to it—and during the rainy season? They weren't your typical hikers.

Without a word they sat down on the veranda and drank from canteens, taking their sweet time, as if enjoying nature in all its glory. I was itching to move, but haste makes waste. Holding our breath we watched their movements. The rat got up and inched his way toward the kitchen. I hugged the wall, waiting for him to come around the corner. The door opened and the guy stepped down to the firebox. And when he bent over to look inside I jumped him, lightning quick, just as my two boys went for the woman. The guy tried to wrestle free but I subdued him. The woman didn't put up a fight. And that was the end of a long and tedious stakeout.

We had hit the jackpot. The couple we caught that day were the main contacts for a ring of twelve, and it didn't take much to persuade them to give up the names and whereabouts of the others, who soon fell under our net. My accomplishment brought me a special promotion as well as a medal.

Those were the days when I got thumbs-up all around and everyone said I was the best. What a charge it gave me to shove the guy's head into the firebox we used as our crapper. The click of my handcuffs was music to my ears and I felt a surge of triumph and relief. I can see it now, the quivering of the guy's blue lips, the fear-ridden face of the bitch. The sun felt so warm and dry as we marched the two of them down the hill. Even my unwashed body smelled sweet. I wonder if crows still perch on that wall. Now that their hideout had been exposed, the dogs would steer clear of it.

Can't she stop tittering, for Christ's sake. She's flirting with punks who are young enough to be her sons. She used to be cautious to a fault, but now she's being careless.

She's even got herself dolled up and showing her neck line. Her makeup, the clothes, nothing escapes me. What with the remodeling and the new shampoo chair, there will be a constant stream of women. What is she thinking! My intolerant suspicion and my fussy complaints are snowballing.

I look down through the hole made for the electric cord. The washroom looks so lonely now that it's been emptied. But it's all I can see. I wish the interior of the beauty parlor was within range. I stick my fingers into the hole and try to enlarge it. I wish I had a file but the toolbox is down below. Instead I find my girl's scissors and work away at the opening. The scissors are for cutting paper, not much use here. With my fingernails I work at the edges of the wooden veneer, scraping away one thin ply at a time, careful not to make a sound. Ouch, damn it! A sliver beneath my fingernail.

I hear the hissing of cement being applied by a trowel. I look down through the hole. Back in the old days you could make a living as a plasterer. Men needed a skill if they wanted to feed their family. I watch the guy mix and apply the cement, producing a smooth, even finish, no irregularities. Not bad. I can see the gentle dance of the tendons on the back of his hand as he applies the cement. With every movement of those tendons, those on the back of my own hand twitch.

What if I take your fingers holding that trowel and wrench your wrist—that would be one way to stop the plastering, wouldn't it. Then press with my fingernail on your cuticle and you'll feel electricity shoot to the top of your head. No, the tip of a pen casing would work better for that. No, the blunt end of a needle. No, the point of a fountain pen—more to hold on to, and the business end is finer. No, inside the fingernail is better than pressing down on the cuticle, isn't it. No, the inside of your wrist would work better. No, the inside of your elbow or the inside of your knee. Like the fellow says, *Knees, don't fail me now*. My implement of implements, my Monami pen, I wonder if it's still in my office drawer. The fountain pen tip I stuck into the bottom of it for scratching out spelling mistakes proved useful in other ways. I got so much information from my invention. The little jolt the kids got from that tip had them pissing their pants.

The punk down below is sitting on the threshold of the washroom having a smoke. Nothing like a cigarette once you've cleared a hurdle in your workday. You take that last puff, flick the butt to the ground, inhale, and the bitter taste makes you tingle all over. Crushing out the sparks from the butt, you go back to war feeling the goose bumps of anticipation that you wouldn't know if you'd never been on the battlefield.

He takes a couple of drags, purses his lips, and just when he's started blowing smoke rings he looks behind him. Then reaches for the doorknob to my girl's room, taps on it, and cracks open the door. He peeks inside then sticks his head in. That son of a bitch, peeping into my girl's room—I've got half a mind to beat him to death.

What the hell do you think you're doing? Sniffing for lingerie? Where does a shithead like you get off scoping out my girl's room. Shut the door, you're letting cigarette smoke inside. I wouldn't think of going in there—so how come a piece of shit like you does? I ought to gouge your eyes out, I ought to wring your neck, and then if you're lucky I'd put you out of your misery.

Before I know it I've kicked over the half-full urine container by mistake. Down the steps it tumbles, banging into the door to the loft. The guy looks up, then nonchalantly closes the door to my girl's room. But he continues to look up, and then crushes out his cigarette and gets to his feet. He taps on the ceiling—the floor of the loft—a *tap tap* here, a *tap tap* there. I move away from the hole and put my ear to the floor like a mangy mutt. Or maybe I'm a frightened mouse, because that fucking punk gets into the game and yowls at me like a cat.

***

Two days later I'm stiff as a bone. I couldn't move around during the renovation, had to lie still the whole time, practically holding my breath. Now it's nighttime—no radio from down below, no women gabbing, none of the cackling from my wife that led to my idiotic suspicion. The loneliness of being left alone is more difficult than the fear of being discovered. When I'm alone even the distant honking of a car is a welcome sound. Any human activity gets the chill of my body dissipating.

I take two boxes down to my girl's room—the box with the medal and a box of books—and leave them on her desk. I'm bartering to ease the tension between us, starting with the two boxes and a tiny glass doll I discovered among the other boxes. I wonder if it's enough for me to begin retrieving her.

What to make of her books? They're not quite love stories but they give you an itch. Like *The Naked Thief*, the novel I'm reading in *Women's Home Journal*, they're fun, but in a different way. Maybe her books have more integrity than this novel, which glorifies thievery. But there's no fundamental difference between the two types—whether it's love or thievery, you're chasing and being chased, or else you're wandering. Going through her books, I get an idea of the subject matter from the blurbs on the back cover. "A stifling love arising from ridiculous suggestions and cowardly demands." "A painful love born of an attractive but self-destructive other." "Punished by an unforgettable love." "A stunted love between two who hide their feelings for each other." Romances are supposed to get you squirming and tingling with anticipation. What more do you need? Why dwell on the stifling, painful stuff?

I move the boxes from the desk to the floor near the door. That way she'll see them as soon as she walks in. Next I stick my hand inside her quilt, then feel the floor. Ice cold. The hot-water heater must be out. I had no clue. Now we're warming up the floor rather than the other way around. I bring down the electric floor pad, spread it over her sleeping pad, then cover it with her thin quilt. All set. When she comes back we need to do some bonding over a pot of ramen. Just like in the old days, we'll use the pot lid for the noodles we slurp. Just thinking about it gets my gastric juices flowing.

Ding-a-ling. She's here. I lean back against the door to the loft and count the steps. One. Two. Then it's quiet—how come? Where's the scuffing of her shoes? She should have walked the ten steps by now, the door to her room should have opened, but I don't hear anything. Are my wide-open ears manufacturing sounds?

I hear something get knocked to the floor—did somebody bump into it? What the hell? I open the door to the loft, bound up the steps, banging my chin on the steep risers, climb up onto the floor, and put my eye to the hole. Nothing. Was that a scream? I open the window just enough to peep out. My reward is a blast of cold air in the face—not so much as a rat to be seen in the alley. Is that someone sobbing? Something's happening to my girl.

Back down to her room I go, and push at the door—locked from the outside. Back up to the loft, back down, back and forth, to heaven and hell. If only I knew what was going on. A million thoughts swirl through my mind—horrible crimes, terrible accidents. What in God's name is happening? More crying? I never should have sent a full-grown girl out in the middle of the night. Rousting her out of bed just so I can indulge myself in a luxury—what good does that do anybody? Your dad's here. But not really. Obviously he's here but he's not supposed to exist. Where did his righteous heart and his strong legs go? A righteous sack of shit who can't even take care of his daughter. A wretched sack of shit bound and tied and locked up. Scream, my baby, shout so someone can hear you. Or break a window. Don't worry about me up here, just shout, get someone to help you.

Suddenly it's quiet. I hear murmurs, the voice of a man and the voice of a woman, two people for sure. The woman—is it Sŏn or is it my wife? Maybe it's not what I thought. Somebody turned the radio on. I hear the screeching of violins. More murmurs. In the pitch darkness I can't even guess what's going on. Damned radio, damned music—turn it down! What the hell is happening?

All night long I see a procession of faces I don't recognize, severed heads all of them, floating in air and dripping blood. Faces full of righteous belief and faces of servility, faces pale and fear-ridden and faces sun-darkened, faces clean and dirty, faces without eyes or lacking a mouth, faces of ice and faces in flames, faces silent and faces screaming, faces of children and faces of old men. One face disappears and the next one takes its place, each new face bringing new blood to wet me. Are those faces, that blood, all from the same

143

person, a joker who keeps changing masks? In between masks I get a glimpse of the real face, and from whichever angle, it looks like mine.

All night long sounds travel through me—shouting that immobilizes my limbs, outcries that peck at my head, panting that penetrates my blood vessels, drilling, hammering, the honking of cars, the click-clack of train wheels, screaming. Listening to these noises, I scrape with my fingernails at the hole in the floor as if I'm digging my grave, and manage to pull up a floorboard. My bloody hand covers my mouth so I won't scream, then pushes me toward the hole. A hand with a hole buries a stake in my chest. Hand with a hole, chest with a hole.

In an interrogation the questions and answers become a head game. It's my convictions against the other guy's, mask to mask, me wearing the mask of dispassionate interrogator and him wearing the mask of righteous belief. I have to bulldoze him with my convictions and make them into the truth. I never lost at that game. Except once.

Labor unions were springing up like mushrooms after rain, and when they joined forces it was a headache, especially with all the college kids itching to work in the factories and stir up trouble. I didn't need the analysts to tell me that this particular kid didn't go to the factory for work. His hands weren't meant for oil and grease, they were meant to play with a pen or flip through a book, soft hands with not a scar to be seen. The only place that wasn't soft was where the pen rested against the first knuckle of his middle finger. And then there was his handwriting. I had gone to penmanship school and yet my writing couldn't compare with his. I never expected to have to rough up a kid with handwriting so refined.

This kid, the first time I saw him, looked meek, the kind of kid you could scare shitless with a single glare. His milky skin, the gentle curve of his chin, the red tinge of his cheeks—his face radiated boyishness. I figured he would submit in no time, wetting his pants as soon as I shouted, clinging to me and saying he'd do anything I told him. He wasn't the main target, so all we needed from him was a few names. I'd tell him a name and all he'd have to do was nod. The picture was drawn, needing only a few last brush strokes from him.

But it worked out differently. The kid played dumb from start to finish. When I asked why a guy with an economics degree was dirtying his hands in an auto-parts factory, he said his family was needy. When I took a different tack and tried to touch a nerve asking about his widowed mother down in the countryside, he said, *Well, isn't that why I have to earn money?* And when I told him all his buddies had come clean, he said how could that be, there was nothing to come clean about. The kid's answers were consistent, they were all planned out. When he wrote his Life Account—in other words his confession—it stretched to ten pages, twenty pages, forty pages, and there wasn't a hole in it.

The kid wouldn't take off his mask, and eventually I couldn't tell if I was seeing his real face or his mask of righteous belief. At one point it occurred to me that maybe the innocent face I saw was genuine. Maybe he really didn't have any names to give up, maybe he really didn't know anything. If his convictions were true, then I was willing to retract my convictions, even if our contest ended with my defeat. After all, my territory had never included these kids fresh off mommy's tit, so why not protect this kid with the elegant handwriting? I was a spy-catcher and my convictions were enough for me to bring in spies. So with this kid I thought I would make things just hot enough to teach him a lesson and then I'd let him go.

But just for the hell of it I thought I would mention a few more names, names that weren't on the list the analysts had come up with. That's when the kid let his guard down and made the fatal mistake—he smirked when he said he didn't recognize them. There's a difference between a guy who says he couldn't possibly know and a guy who says he really doesn't know, a difference between a kid wanting to protect someone and not needing to protect someone, a difference between his attitude when he knows something and his attitude when he doesn't know. The trace of scorn on his lips gave it all away, and at that instant I realized the kid was playing me, he'd been laughing at me all along. The convictions I was about to retract were the truth after all.

I lost my head and jumped him. I was braying like a donkey

running wild, howling like a mutt that's eaten rat poison. I smashed his face, I stomped on his head, I slammed my chair against him, threw a file cabinet drawer at him. *You little son of a bitch, your poor mom sent you to Seoul to study, not demonstrate! Your widowed mother worked hard to keep your hands pretty, and now you want them mucked up in a factory!* I had to torment this kid, I needed to rain down punishment on those hands that were toying with me. I grabbed the first thing I saw and stabbed at the backs of his hands. The kid's screams echoed through the room—my weapon was the awl I use for making binder holes in my documents, and with it I impaled his hand on my desk. *I don't know anything, really I don't. Please, let me go to my mom, I'll be good to her, I'll stay with her.* A whimpering little kid, running at the nose.

That was my one and only loss, the only time I lost my head. If Paek hadn't stopped me I might have strangled the kid. Another team ended up with him. I heard no more about him, only that the team made a big score.

I think of that item at the Rehab Center. Maybe the filthy hand that was scratching his body was soft and lovely once. Did the back of that man's hand have a scar? Maybe I saw it but looked away? Is that the only thing I looked away from? Well, who cares—the guy's dead and buried.

Ding-a-ling! Is it for real? The damned radio finally goes off. I sit up. The door to the room down below rattles. I spring up, rush down, and push it open. It's my wife.

Clutching the edge of the door, I stick out my head. There's not much light from the beauty parlor, the blinds must still be drawn, but things look to be in order. So what was all the commotion last night?

"Where's Sŏn! Can't you keep an eye on her! She's all by herself here at night—shouldn't you be checking on her! You're her mother, aren't you! Answer me!"

"Dear, what's this—"

"Listen, woman, your mind is somewhere else—focus! Why do you leave the door to her room unlocked during the day—so any punk who wants to can peek inside? And yet you never fail to lock it at night!"

"Now listen, dear!"

"What were you so busy with that you couldn't check in yesterday? If you've got time to flirt with those idiots then have them check on the hot-water heater. The floor's ice cold, there's nothing to eat, the girl's supposed to be here and she's not—"

"Hey!" she screams, fists clenched and eyes closed.

"Hey what? Are you—"

"Aren't you the one who's here with Sŏn? Aren't you? Why are you asking me? My girls are bugging me to use this room for our card games—should I bring them here, is that what you want? So you can join us, and show us how to win? Why are you jumping on me first thing in the morning? How about me—don't *I* have anything to say? What, you think I don't know how to shout back at you? Tell me, dear—have you ever yelled at me before? Really, dear, how could you? What did I do? What! Why me! Why!"

She's panting, lips trembling, chin twitching. She turns away, steadying her breathing. I watch her anger cool.

"It's been extended."

Leaving me with this cryptic pronouncement she goes back out to the beauty parlor. Where she was standing lie my newspaper, milk, and meal. I feel my mouth watering. Gathering these items I return to the loft. What the hell, what the—hell? Every goddamn thing that could go wrong . . . .

I spread open the newspaper. What is it, exactly, that's been extended? North–South relations? Are we getting a green light, are we supposed to hold hands with those Red sons of bitches? I flip through the national news, the economy section, the city pages—nothing. Back to the city pages. *Environmental Laws Broken, 50 Arrested.* Oh shit, there it is. *Statute of Limitations for An: Extended to September 1995.* 1995?

It was announced that the statute of limitations for the fugitive An has been extended by three years. The four police officers who were brought to trial as suspects in connection with this case are awaiting final disposition. According to Article 253 of the Criminal Code, the statute of limitations for an accomplice is not in effect between the time an accomplice is arraigned and the final disposition of his case.

That means three more years plus the time it takes for Paek and Ŭn's trials to finish. Which means at least four more years in the loft—not one year but four! And possibly longer depending on their trials. What the hell? What in God's name!

CHAPTER 10

I open the door to the sound of feet scurrying up wooden steps. I imagine the scuttling of cockroaches and the scampering of mice and I feel like retching. Two boxes lie inside the door—fortifications. I push them aside and go in. My bedding is as I left it. The newspaper is scattered on the floor, the door to the loft open half a hand span. I kick the quilt to the side of the room and sit. Back straight, I scowl at the door to the loft.

If you're going to hide, then hide for God's sake. If you're going to escape, then why leave traces? Don't leave a trail of slime. If you want to put up a wall, then it needs to be higher and stronger. What are these two little boxes supposed to accomplish? You make walls with bricks and you reinforce them with steel. If you want to interfere with my life, then don't hide like an insect or a mouse. Don't let me hear your scaredy-cat steps.

All right, you can ask. Why didn't the daughter you sent out on an errand in the middle of the night come back here till now? You can ask about all that moving around you heard. You can ask me what the hell I was up to. Go ahead, I know you're dying to. That's your specialty after all, isn't it, Father dear, making people tell you what you want to hear? Well, I have some good news—you won't have to break a sweat with me. You won't have to put your feelers up, I'll spill everything for you like the obedient little girl I am. Go on, ask. Why hide? What are you afraid of? What are you waiting for? You need to press me, don't you—*Whathaveyoubeendoing? Wherethehellhaveyoubeen? Whywereyououtsolate?* What happened to your voice? Where's your fatherly nerve? No more heel-kicking tantrums?

Silence. No rustling, no thumping on the floor. The stillness is driving me crazy. But then he touches the door. It opens halfway. A pause. I hear a sigh, followed by his voice.

"I want you to do something for me."

What? A favor? You don't you need to interrogate me first?

"Go see Pak. Your mom knows where to find him."

Of course. You're not human. All you care about, Father dear, is your own safety.

For everything else, it's see no evil and hear no evil. And those boxes—what you're asking is worth more than a sweater or a pair of gloves, it's worth two whole boxes. That's my dad. That's your survival scheme, Father dear.

I press the intercom button and identify myself, then wait outside the white-painted steel gate. Inside I see a tidy landscaped garden. The house is surrounded by a lush growth of trees and rock steps curving up to it, so the roof is about all you can see. It's a desolate neighborhood. I feel cold sweat on my forehead. The silence is broken by the call of magpies flying over the crests of the trees. The flapping of wings ceases and again the huge home is locked in stillness.

Why am I here? Is there something for me to learn? What is it Father wants to know? Maybe I should just go home—what good is this visit supposed to do anyone? Should I press the buzzer again? Just then a man in a dark suit appears from the house. The steel gate opens. The man sticks his head out and inspects the surroundings, then steps aside so I can enter. For a moment my feet fail me. The man clears his throat, urging me through the gate. As soon as I'm inside, he closes it then bounds up the stone steps ahead of me. There's no wasted motion, he's done this before. A neat array of Chinese junipers follow the steps up; they look like they've just been pruned. The man enters a number on a keypad, opens the door, and admits me.

Inside there's a sharp smell that prickles my nose. A smell

of cleanliness but annoyingly strong. For furnishings, only ponderous furniture in a beige color, practically nothing on the walls. The living room feels creepy, neurotic, fastidious. A man sits on a leather couch reading a book, spectacles perched at the tip of his nose. Before I know it the man in the suit has locked the door and parked himself by my side, hands gathered in front of him. I remove my shoes and venture into the living room. The coolness of the marble floor penetrates the soles of my feet.

I sit down on the couch as far from the man as I can. He closes the book, removes the spectacles and places them on the coffee table, and looks at me. He has the face of a broken-down old man whose energies are flagging but who remains obstinately, pathologically self-centered.

"Ever read the Bible?" he asks, pushing the book in my direction. The Bible. The gilding of its pages is worn and faded.

"I've read it four times, you know, beginning to end. Four times. One of these days you should give it a read, young lady. When life seems too much, you know, I find myself reading it."

His mouth makes a squishy, lip-smacking sound when he speaks. And it's repulsive the way the corners of his mouth sag and bounce. I look away and fix my gaze on the Bible.

"You go to church, anything like that?"

I don't respond. The Bible's leather cover has begun to warp.

"I've read the Bible four times, you know, but I've never once been to church— you want to know why?"

I look up at the man. He regards me intently, smacking his lips. "Well, do you or don't you?"

The corners of his mouth twitch. His brow furrows and his expression hardens. I don't care why he doesn't go to church but I don't want to be pressed for an answer so I mouth the words *I don't know*.

"No, of course you don't, young lady. Why would you? The hardships involved in the line of work we devote ourselves to— why would anyone know about that?"

The man slaps his knee and straightens, as if he's been waiting for this moment.

He points toward the ceiling. "Up there, you know?"

Up there?

"From up there they send down specialists. Assassins. I've put away so many kids from their side—every time they send one down I get him, you know? So imagine—if I'm out of the way, then hallelujah for them. You think I should go out whenever I want, with those assassins waiting for me? Who do you think benefits if I leave for church and catch a bullet along the way? Isn't that right, young lady."

I smell something rotten. Something familiar. A musty, unpleasant stink. The smell of Father rotting away in the loft.

"So . . . is An getting along all right?"

I don't respond.

"So . . . you need money, do you? Already?"

I remain silent.

"I don't have anything for you today, but I'll arrange a delivery first thing. But this is it. Puts me in fix, you folks coming over all the time. Everyone thinks I've got him tucked away here, and you and your mom taking turns visiting doesn't help matters. God, what a family. . . . " And he makes his squishy sound.

"You put him up to everything, didn't you? Said you were one big happy family—you were all on the same side!"

"Well, well, young lady, you sit there so nice and quiet but you've got a temper, don't you? Well, why not, considering whose daughter you are. I put him up to it? How could you say such a thing? He knew what he was doing. He could have stayed on as my bodyguard, given me a massage now and then, that would have been fine with me. I didn't volunteer him to catch Reds—*he* did, your father. Make no mistake about it, he was amazing with his hands—I knew it the first time he gave me a massage. Amazing how well he knew the human body. Joints, muscles, nothing he didn't know."

This was your life, dear Father? Kneading the carcass of this dirty rag of a man? Is this how you survived? Is this what you did for the organization you believed in? And for what, Father dear? What exactly did you do for them anyway? What did you want me to find out by coming here?

"What did he do there anyway!"

"You really want to know? You mean electricity, water, and whatnot? That's what you want to know? Beats me. Not my line of work. What I *can* tell you is that a lot more went on there than you could possibly imagine."

"Not my father."

"Oh, let me tell you, An was born with a gift. You have any idea how strong he was? And you've seen his hands—my oh my were they huge. He'd slap a guy upside the head and rupture his eardrum, or else an eye would pop out. One hard look from him and they'd wet their pants, the kids who didn't know any better. I was a pretty strong fellow myself back when the Japs ruled, but I couldn't have held a candle to your father. Me, I don't have much strength left, just a shell of my former self. I'm an old man and I'm not getting any younger—isn't that the truth, young lady."

He gives me a disgusting grin. Everything about him smells rotten, even his gaze.

If I stay here much longer, I'll start rotting myself. I get up and head for the door. "Speaking of the organization. . . ." It feels like his voice is yanking me by the hair. "It's like a starfish. You know what a starfish is?"

A starfish.

"It loses one of its legs and a new one grows back—that's a starfish. Well, if a leg gets rotten you can cut it off, same with a hand. And occasionally, you know, you cut it off on purpose—when you need a new one. It happened to me. It happened to people above me. And people above them. Well, it's all over. Go back and tell him it's every man for himself now. We've lost—we've all lost. Other starfish are in place now. They're everywhere. So tell him good luck."

The rotten leg of a starfish. Cut off on purpose so a new leg can grow. Father is the cut-off rotten leg of a starfish.

"Tell your father he ought to read the Bible. Lots of wisdom there."

I open the door and go out. The man in the suit pops out robot-like and leads me away. Like before, he opens the gate, inspects the surroundings, and moves aside. I hear the gate close behind me. I take a few steps, then look back. The house is like a prison floating on air, only its roof visible above the high wall and the dense growth of trees. Inside that prison is a large starfish rotting in its death struggle. The rainwater splotches on the wall are like the slime oozing from that starfish.

I raise the seat to its maximum height and look in the mirror. There's a creepy silence in the beauty parlor that makes the reflection in the mirror seem distorted. I step down on the adjuster and hear a pneumatic hiss, and down goes the seat. Feels good, that momentary descent. Push down again with my toes and back up goes the seat. As the unfamiliar face in the mirror rises and lowers, lowers and rises, her expression vanishes.

I turn on the radio and return to the chair. I move my feet in time with the music, kicking in the air like a little kid. Every kick brings a metallic groan, the chair getting into the rhythm too. Now it's me who's hearing the radio, and riding the chair along with it.

I take from my pocket the newspaper clipping he left and open it fold by fold.

Handling it like ancient parchment, I pretend to shake off the dust and wipe the mildew and then I spread it out, as if I'm performing a ritual that will open a secret door. Before me is a diagram of events layered in the form of a pyramid. The top is labeled North and branches fan out beneath it. At the end of each branch, suspended like fruit, is a face.

Paired with each fruit and hanging next to it is a kind of caption, the letters sticking out like twigs, some in larger type than others. The passage of his hands has left the photos and the lettering hazy, but I can read the larger type and distinguish the faces. The page number and date are missing. All I can tell from the faces and captions are names and ages. There are twelve faces, ranging from a 22-year-old man to an elderly woman aged 89. Judging from the single family name and the kinship identification—cousin, cousin's son, and so forth—I'm looking at a family tree. The older woman and the middle-aged woman have faces you could encounter anywhere in the countryside. There's a stony-faced farmer and a girlish woman in a polka-dot blouse. But where's the face of that man? When he gave me the clipping he said it was something he did. Not something Father did, but something he did. I wonder what that something was.

I consider the handwriting on the clipping. A fine, clean hand. Father's handwriting, symmetrical and precise. The vertical lines are powerful but not overbearing. Each letter is a story in itself, the broad lower strokes firmly supporting the other strokes to produce a finished, majestic syllable. The man composed the diagram and Father wrote what appears below it. Where in this pyramid is the man hiding? And where is Father? From the base of the pyramid the 89-year old grandmother smiles at me.

The phone rings. I listen to the cadence—ring, silence, ring—then pick up and carefully place the receiver to my ear. "I'm sorry, Sŏna, but I won't be coming—I'm staying here for the time being." And then she's sobbing. Mom is crying. Her whimpering pierces my ears. As I listen to her cry I look into the mirror. In it is the smiling face of the 89-year-old grandmother. And above it the girlish woman. And above that face, me. I touch the mirror and raise the corners of my mouth reflected there. The faces in the mirror are more lively now. The grandmother, the woman, me—we're all beaming.

The chirping of birds signals the hour, followed by the strains of the national anthem—the radio is announcing the start of a new day. *You're listening to Radio Korea, broadcasting from Seoul, capital of the Republic of Korea, providing our listeners with the most enjoyable and entertaining programs.* . . . I bid farewell to the women in the mirror and climb down from the chair.

I raise the blinds. The radio announces a new day and I fling open the door to the street and step outside. Fresh, cold air surges in. I take a deep breath, go back in, and close the door. When the sun comes up I'll open it again, just a crack, to help warm the interior. I stop in front of the cabinet and remove the neatly folded towels. With the towels out of the way the circuit breaker panel appears. I open the panel and throw all the switches. The radio falls silent. The refrigerator motor wheezes and comes to a stop.

At the door to my room I unfold the clipping and stick it

in the gap between the door and the frame. The 89-year-old grandmother and her family are going inside. I see them off, then look up toward the ceiling.

No more deals, Father dear. You can keep all my items—I don't need them anymore. Our transactions are over. No more dark dealings. You come down only with my permission and you take what I give you. I'm declaring war.

I open the beauty parlor, then sit while I wait for the man, the prop in front of the record shop. But it looks like the prop's been removed. Let's walk over and see. Hands gathered behind my back, I take ten slow, short steps. Then ten steps back to the beauty parlor.

This time I try swinging my arms like a soldier marching to an officer's cadence. It takes me eight steps. Same distance, fewer steps. The third time over is seven steps. I crouch where the man was squatting. Resting the back of my head against the wall, I look over at the beauty parlor.

Greenfields Beauty Parlor. A corner has broken off from the sign, and half the silhouette of the woman whose wave is flying in the wind has faded. I wonder what he's been looking at all this time. Neglected green fields? The flaming structure rising out of them? A woman sifting through the ruins? The smoke rising behind her?

There he comes, hands in his pockets, head tilted against his shoulder, eyes to the ground. He's very dependable. A truck passes, horn blaring, but he doesn't react. I go out into the alley to meet him. He looks up, sees me. I look him in the eye.

"I have no place to go—take me somewhere."

***

"We're the only team that knows how to use the curling irons. We get so many appointments at the hair salon we have to work way beyond closing time. You ought to see the stylist—she's brilliant with her hands, it's like her scissors are dancing. But I have to wonder how much of it is just for show."

"Big Hwang had the largest boat on Kwi Island. His wife made good fish relish and his mother could really belt out a tune. His younger brother ran a hardware shop on the mainland. But you know, there's always the monkey that falls from the tree."

"Yesterday one of the customers gave me a ticket to see a totally famous singer— it's his first appearance in Korea. To hear the customer talk, he had to go through fire to get the tickets. He wants to meet me this Sunday at Seoul Olympic Stadium, that's where the concert is. This guy comes in for a weekly cut. I have a lousy voice, you know."

"Little Hwang who ran the hardware shop got to go to Japan, thanks to his youngest son, who was studying there. Big Hwang and Little Hwang were close as two coats of paint—so close Little Hwang took his brother's family along for the ride. Grandma with the nice voice passed away during the Olympics. So did Big Hwang. Followed by Big Hwang's good wife the year after."

"They jacked up my pay thanks to my aptitude with the curling irons. So I don't have to do scalp treatments or sell hair products. But I'm not a schmoozer, and that's my biggest weakness. Everyone thinks I'm stuck up. I wish I could just work with the hair rods and cut hair. But what if the youngest son had studied somewhere besides Japan?"

"I'll tell you what a good man Little Hwang was—he fronted me two months' pay at the hardware shop so I could find a place to live. And I could kill for his good wife's hotpot. You know, it's better to keep your trap shut than say something stupid."

"I don't eat dumplings. You know how people hate biting into ginger when they're eating kimchi? Why is that? Some people treat me like ginger—they want to pick me out from their kimchi. But if you didn't say anything you could have died, right? Being forced to talk, that's worse."

"That reminds me of the ginger tea that Grandmother Hwang made for me. It had ginger, bellflower root, and pear nectar. Each one's tasty by itself but when you simmer them all together . . . anyway, you're safe from colds all winter long. It's all about jealousy—because you're pretty. Kimchi without ginger? No way. I love ginger—ginger preserves, ginger tea, ginger cookies."

"No one's ever told me that. I'd hate to imagine what would happen if I acted stuck up. I absolutely hate ginger cookies. They're so sugar-coated, but when you eat them they're bitter. What's that scar? It looks like a crescent moon."

"I fell off a swing when I was seven. Banged my chin—there was actually a crack in the bone, but I didn't feel it. My friend who was giving me a push started bawling. I guess he cried enough for both of us. Ginger cookies are like that. Bittersweet. Sweet and bitter."

"I have a scar too. It was winter solstice and my mom sent me next door with some red-bean porridge. They had a great big dog. It had a collar so I thought they kept it tied up. I didn't want to spill the porridge, so I was practically tiptoeing, and that's the last thing I remember. That dog took a bite out of my leg, up here on the inside—dogs do that when they know you're scared. No, don't look. I wish it had a nice smooth shape like a crescent moon, but it's all messed up—because of the dog bite on top of the burn mark from the porridge."

"It looks like a map of the Moon. That white area lower down is the Tycho crater, and that there is the Sea of Clouds, and then the Sea of Tranquility. I wanted to be an astronomer, you know—that was my dream when I was a boy. I wasn't sure what astronomers do, I just liked stars. I used to lie on Turtle Rock at night and look up at them."

"So, my scar's all mapped out? And it's bright as a full moon, that's a first. The next day he slaughtered the dog. He said that's what it gets for not respecting people. *My* dream was to be a mom. But when I told my mom, she said anyone could be a mom and I should come up with something else. And how did you get that scar on your arm—is it a puncture wound?"

"Too bad that full moon put a spell on Big Hwang. Otherwise he wouldn't have chased that school of milkfish so far north, and then he wouldn't have gotten lost. He taught me how to predict the weather by looking at the moon and the stars. Maybe that dog was afraid of you. Or maybe he liked you too much."

"I wish people had tails. So when they wag their tail they like you, when they tuck it between their legs they're scared, and when it sticks up in the air they're mad. Then you'd know right away, you wouldn't have to read the other person's eyes. You know, I must have stumbled and that's how I got the porridge on me. And *then* the dog bit me. I wonder if I had a hole in my arm too—maybe that's why I dropped the porridge."

"I'd choose a feeler, not a tail. A feeler could guide you in the dark and tell you when danger is coming."

"Did you know that some insects have two thousand hairs on their feelers? But snail feelers barely sense light and dark. I learned that in biology."

"Then I should have snail feelers."

"Why something that barely works?"

"If you can sense light and dark, what else do you need."

"Can I feel those things?"

"Sure."

"They look weird—are they like that on other guys?"

"Nope."

"What's so funny?"

"I was thinking about the hands that made them look weird."

"How did you know my birthday, anyway?"

"Your hands are so much smaller."

"Want to hear a story about a birthday party?"

"Where there's a birthday there has to be a party. So are you going to that Olympic Stadium concert?"

"It was the class monitor's birthday and she was having a party."

"Sounds like fun."

"I had some new pencils in my drawer and I used them for my gift. I didn't feel bad about giving them away, I just wished I had more of them. I picked out my prettiest clothes and left for her place. There were yummy smells and girls cackling and music— wow, this is a real birthday party, I thought as I went in. But when her mother took me by the hand and led me into the living room all the voices stopped. I waved and said hello and all I got in return was a bunch of puzzled faces. Well, stupid me, I didn't know it was invitation-only. The class monitor drew the invitations herself.

Needless to say, I hadn't gotten one."

"I just thought of Big Hwang's sixtieth birthday. The party was on the mainland and all three of his children were there with their families—his number-one was a fisherman, number two was a fishmonger, and his youngest, the daughter, had just gotten married. And Little Hwang was there with his family too. They got the buffet from the biggest restaurant in the area and they even had a band playing. He must have gotten bored just sitting there in his nice *hanbok* because he grabbed his good wife and they started kicking their heels up. Big Hwang knew how to catch fish, but he sure was out of his element on the dance floor. But you have to shake a leg when you're celebrating your sixtieth. The only one who's still alive is the daughter."

"I offered her my gift. I thought she'd like it. She took it like she didn't know what else to do and opened it right there. It bothered me that I'd just slapped some scotch tape on it and didn't use a ribbon. As soon as the pencils came into sight I heard, very clearly, all this sneering. She didn't look thrilled over a handful of pencils—maybe if they were a set and hadn't been kicking around in my drawer? Anyway, she tossed them on the table and turned her back on me. And of course without a thank-you. One of the pencils dropped to the floor. No one cared except me. The rest of them went back to their dancing and singing while I picked up the pencil and put it back on the table. I felt I was more pathetic than my present. She didn't give me a second look. I tried to say something but no one bothered to listen. If I giggled along with them they stopped. If I tried to sing along with them they changed to a different song. I shut my mouth and inched away from them. There was no place for the uninvited guest except off to the side of the television. I stood next to the wall, hands gathered behind my back, and watched the joyful occasion. I was a ghost—existing but not felt, and therefore not acknowledged. But I wanted to be with them even if I had to be a ghost. And so I stood my ground till the party was over."

"Sometimes it's the people on the guest list who ruin the party. They're ingrates—they look down their noses at the food, they're hurtful, and they sneak off with the gifts. You were quite the brave ghost, looking after all of them."

"Maybe I should have walked away to salvage my self-respect. That experience taught me a lesson. I don't go where I'm not invited. The problem is, I'm still not sure when I'm invited and when I'm not."

"I think you can go to that concert. You got an invitation."

"And now I have a ghost living with me. He's self-invited, just marched in, a rotten low-class ghost."

"Everyone has a ghost inside him."

"Was he a devil?"

"A devil?"

"Didn't he show you what hell was like?"

"He promised me heaven if I sold my soul."

"Did you ever have the urge to kill someone?"

***

I cut out the face of a woman, focusing all my energy, like I did my first day at beautician school. It hurts, I feel I'm cutting out part of myself, and so my scissors keep stopping and my eyes keep closing. But even with my eyes closed I can see the typed names— they're in motion, like the blood circulating inside me.

The woman is sobbing, a woman who lost her husband. A long time ago, in a room somewhere, she was sobbing as I see her sob now. She sobbed wanting to know where her husband was. She was scared, frightened, terrified. She sobbed because there was nothing else she could do. Because if she stopped sobbing she would hear you shouting. Because through her sobbing her husband might soon return. She wailed not knowing her husband was close by and listening.

The woman is sobbing not because her husband was released after her and then died. And she isn't sobbing in vexation at her husband's unjust detention. She's sobbing because she blames herself for sobbing that day. If only she hadn't been there, if only she hadn't been sobbing, if only she had betrayed him and fled. . . . Ever since then she has wept without a sound, hurt with never a moan. Tears are sure to flow when that day comes to mind, but the tears are always silent.

You would probably say you didn't know her, Father dear. Because you never laid hands on her. Because she never saw you in person. Because you were with her husband in the next room and all you did to her was leave the doors to both rooms open a crack. Would you really not remember that woman?

I paste the face onto a page in my sketchbook and pat it down. I jot down a date. The faces pasted in my sketchbook are a chorus. They say you are not human. They say you're a torture machine, that no blood runs in your veins, that you're incapable of tears. A butcher. A devil. Is it true, Father dear—are you?

I didn't know what you were doing. I didn't want to, I never wanted to. I had to not know. I wanted to live my life not knowing. I believed I could live a life separate from yours. But what I didn't know was that not knowing can be a sin.

You were a god to me, Father dear. A benevolent god who looked after me, caressed me. A god who brought electricity to the loft and removed my tooth without hurting me. But the father who took over the loft rages at me, he's the master of my fate. A merciless yet servile god who shakes me by the collar he's put around my neck. I wanted to resist my fate but I couldn't get away from you.

You were contraband, and like the stickers I sealed in the wall you were the physical evidence of a nagging sin from which I can never be free. I want that contraband discovered, but I lack the confidence to extract it myself. I connect you, Father, with my masochistic desire to be part of a group, and with my obstinacy in keeping secrets. I've sealed those stickers and erased my memories of them.

I wanted to forget you, Father. I wanted to disdain you, avoid you, believe you were never there. But every time I was about to forget you, your name would appear in the newspaper or else the reporters made their annual visit to the beauty parlor to memorialize one of your victims—a reminder to me that the person they sought was you. You were that person, the ghost in the loft, a presence unseen but stern, using a signal or leaving a trace, your floor creaking in the dead of night, to imprint on me your existence.

You were a god, Father, you were contraband, a wandering spirit, the embodiment of fear. That fear in all its variety you implanted in me, and there it incubated. You were a ruthless beast that broke me open, collared me, suffocated me. A beast that taught me excuses and lies. That taught me to shift blame and cover up mistakes. You made a prison and induced me to confine myself there, and in that prison I developed a murderous intent.

I couldn't see you as you really were, a Father dear full of fear. Because that fear froze my blood and hardened my body. Because the instant our eyes met, I became a rock and shattered. I could never confront you in the totality of your being. But I wanted to, heedless of all you represented. I wanted to engrave in myself the evil you worked, the fruit of that evil, and the hell you inhabited, even at the risk of shattering and scattering like dust on the wind. And that's how I opened my eyes and unblocked my ears. The moment I finally confronted you I was no longer afraid of you.

I tear the page from the sketchbook and stick it inside the door to the loft. In goes the sobbing woman. Listen again to her weeping. Look again at the hell you inscribed in her. Listen carefully, look squarely. This is your hell.

"What the hell is going on? There's no power and no food. And what is *this*."

We stand there, the door between us. He bangs savagely, rattling the door. You're panting, Father—would you like to stomp on my heart, make it colder and harder?

"Open the door. Where's your mom?"

"She's not coming. She's staying at Kaya."

"Did you see Pak? Open the door, will you."

"He said not to come any more."

"Stop lying. How can you behave like this to your father? Open the door, now! What did I do to deserve this? How dare you!"

"He said you were rotten—the rotten foot of a starfish."

"You don't think I can open this door? Where do you get off lying to me like that—you're testing me!"

"He's cutting you off. The starfish is rotten to the core. You didn't know? And that magnificent organization of yours? It's long gone."

"You little twit, how dare you—what do you know—how can you—"

"You're on your own now—good luck. That's what your father asked me to pass on to you."

Sparks fly and lightning strikes. The next instant a hot liquid is streaming down my forehead and onto my cheeks. Blood. Your blood, flowing within me. Pump and pour, no stopping until it's drained. Down my chest, over my navel, between my thighs, down to my feet. I drop my gaze and watch the blood flow down me, dripping like tears onto the face of the woman, who has reappeared as the door opens.

And here you are. Panting, leg outstretched but frozen in place. The beast is collapsing. You're crying. You're sniffling, your voice is catching in your throat. Your face is buried between your upraised knees. You're hunched over, shoulders heaving. You look up, reach out toward me. "Sŏna."

In Father's face I see the dark eyes of an old fish, and beneath them tears filming on sagging flesh. They're the tears of a boy who's perversely resentful, whose muttering is foolish, the false tears of a spoiled brat pleading to his mommy, whining that he doesn't want to give up his toy. The tears aren't directed at anyone, they're the residue of a man who feels sorry for himself. I should have known. They're tears of obsession and narcissism. Slime from a rotten starfish.

I turn my back to him. Live on forever and ever, Father, leaving a trail of slime, rotting in your starfish prison.

CHAPTER 11

That hardcore craphound was the last hurdle I had to jump to inherit my father's seat of authority. To secure my position I had to make sure my father's position was rock-solid. And to do that we had to protect the king's position. And to do *that* we had to eliminate more enemies, which meant we needed more sons. The new sons brought in by Father that year numbered in the hundreds. Success is everything; the organization will take care of the cleanup. That's what Father emphasized to all his sons, just as he had to me, his oldest. We were all one family. To earn their father's love, all these rookies, recruited from far and wide, were bent on boosting their accomplishments. Concrete results were needed, which meant big fish and not just small fry. The hardcore guy was a big fish and if I could get him to submit, then none of the other sons would dare take over my position. And that's why I volunteered to work on him, even though he hadn't been assigned to me.

It wasn't easy. The craphound was determined to be top dog, and his mask of conviction was thick and hard. How much pressure, threat, and terror would I need to strip him of that mask? I was on the hot seat, and that became the decisive factor. The guy held on for dear life, but I met him head on. While he clung to the façade of his grand convictions, I relied on my bread-and-butter, marshaling all the skill at my command, and ultimately his convictions couldn't stand up to my mastery. At the end of our long, tedious faceoff he knelt down to me. No one else could have made him submit.

And so it was, on the most glorious spring day of my life, with blossoms flying in the air, that I served him up on a platter to Father. With the capitulation of that big fish the organization expanded—three new departments, nine new sections—and Father was promoted to head of national security, with special authority for capturing Communists. This omnipotent position was created just for him. I was Father's number-one son, the one and only apple of his eye, and every step he took brought me one step closer to the inheritance.

Round them up, the more the merrier. Don't worry about the cleanup. I take care of my own. Hearing these words, Father's sons developed grand notions. Believing in these foolish sons was Father's big mistake. Yu and Wŏn joined Father late in the game, bastard sons brought in before the Asian Games because of a manpower shortage. I never did care for them, I thought ill of their youthful bravado, their sloppiness, and their tendency to run amok. I smelled trouble when they were added to Team 3 and Paek and Ŭn were left out.

They ran rampant, there was fallout, and then, idiots that they were, they got caught. Father did his best to preserve their anonymity. In the media photos their faces were blurred. And when they were taken into custody he had body doubles made of Paek and Ŭn and added them to the entourage. Father looked after those two fools until the end. Then why me? My face alone was exposed to the world. I never killed anyone. If I did anything wrong, it was that time I left marks on a man to whom I'd given the shock treatment. I never expected those little marks would turn around and bite me in the ass.

Why only me?

I should have been more careful when those rookies started running wild—they didn't know shit. Father's mistakes were to love the netting of the fish caught by those novices instead of appreciating my hard-earned catch. And to entice his other sons with the seat of authority he had promised me. He should have believed in me alone.

The organization was more fearsome than the king himself; the king was someone we made. That's what Father said. *Results are everything; don't worry about the cleanup.* Well, who's cleaning up after me? Who can protect me? Am I getting *any* protection?

Who are my enemies? The dogs? The father of the dogs? Do I have a different father now? Who is taking care of my father anyway? Is he safe? If the organization is protecting him, then why all the media coverage? When the king's head was cut off did my father lose his head too? Who is the father of my father anyway? Is it possible the organization ditched my father?

The light has disappeared, taking with it my warmth. What's unbearable now is not the darkness, the cold, or my hunger, but the loneliness that sinks into my bones. I put my ear to the floor. How I wish the doorbell would sound. There's no sign of my girl. And I miss my wife's laughter. I need someone's watchful gaze, but I'd settle for the girl's cold, contemptuous look and whatever harping she might wish to add.

Sŏna, don't leave me alone. I'm afraid of the howling animals. Hurry back to me, tell me what my father really said, bring some good news, tell me it's all a lie.

Finally you're back. For god's sake kill the radio, turn off the music, and let me see you. Open the door and let in the light and tell me it's all a lie. Please, don't keep your poor dad waiting.

I hear a soft pop and the light in her room goes out. I flip the light switch and look up—nothing happens. The radio's dead too. Everything is silent—it's eerie. Her footsteps arrive at the door to the loft. I hear a sigh. What's that in the crack of the door. A tattered clipping—the diagram of the Kwi Island spy group I attached to the report, complete with ID photos, titles, and job assignments. We used that diagram until we made the media announcement. How did she get hold of it? I rip up the clipping.

First the power and now this goddamn article. What the hell does she want from me?

***

Sŏna, don't force me to make a bogus confession. I didn't do anything wrong. Don't try to hurt my pride or rob me of my dignity. Just because I'm in hiding you can't deny my contribution to the world. The world my father looked after and that I look after, the myth my father's fathers forged so long ago—we can't rewrite history. What's this stupid piece of paper supposed to prove?

It's only paper. And those lumps of leather and lard you see on it aren't even human, they're rats infested with germs that incubate in damp, dark places, seditious little creatures that live in darkness and dream of the day they can create havoc and overturn the system. The word *humanity* doesn't apply to them. They're inanimate objects, they feel nothing, they're no different from rocks. And I took on the responsibility of wringing tears from those rocks and eradicating those germs. It was my job to forbid them humanity.

I had to warn those who dreamed of the impossible. Does a single chittering swallow mean spring is on the way? Spring doesn't come because of swallows. It's the other way around— spring brings out the swallows and their chittering. I had to crush the false faith of those who believed that spring would come if they themselves were chittering. The spring they crowed about was not spring, it was a wasteland barren of ideals. The spring they dreamed of was a world of evil. I couldn't let them have their way. That was my job.

Do the forces of evil acknowledge they're evil? Do they fly the white flag of surrender and confess? No, they wear a mask of goodness, armor themselves in faith, and cry out, *Resist and Fight, Death or Glory*. I had to unmask them, and be quick about it.

Because evil can instantly summon more evil, expanding its might and protecting itself. To obtain a confession from the forces of evil it's sometimes necessary to turn their evil against them. It can't be helped. I was operating under time constraints and it was either strike or be struck. They were agile, cunning, vicious rats and they were well trained. If I was too rash in my attack and they slipped through my fingers, they would dig a deeper hole and God knows when I'd get a second chance. If I didn't do it, someone else would have to. They are evil, I am good. I employ only the power of good. Isn't it natural to punish evil for the sake of goodness? How in hell could there be a problem with that? I punish evil—it's the job my father entrusted to me.

I didn't do anything wrong. I was only doing my job. I don't reflect on crimes I didn't commit, and I don't break my faith. Any ordeals that come my way I'll endure. Sŏna, don't pay attention to the whisperings of evil. One shouldn't be suspicious of one's father. A father's world can't be allowed to collapse. To deny my father's world would be to deny my world, to deny my very existence.

It's a nasty night. I'm confused by what I used to do with my hands, I miss human contact, even if it's with the ravaged flesh of a lifeless body. I didn't do anything wrong.

Morning arrives, the day passes, and by nightfall not a soul has visited, not even a mouse escaping the cold. Two nights I lie forgotten, like a corpse in a coffin. Am I dying in vain, a war-games soldier hit with a stray bullet, a make-believe Dracula buried forever before he can wait up? As I lay dying I wait for she who would open the lid to my coffin and breathe life back into me.

I'm a boy crouching in a dark, damp cave, listening to the distant approach of thunder. Worms crawl toward me. I smash them with a rock but still they wiggle. I squish them until they stop. I gnaw on my fingernails to forget I'm scared, I bite until I draw blood, I suck as if they're nipples, and then I fall asleep.

The *ding-a-ling* filters through my sleep. I think of bells tolling a funeral procession as I clamber to my feet. I'm ready to go, even if it's the messenger from Hades. But it's my girl, I know her footsteps. She stops outside the door to the loft. Silently I place my ear to the door panel; I sense a heavy weight. There, my little girl breathing on the other side. She heaves a sigh, then breathes normally. I time my breathing with hers. It's a cozy feeling.

I didn't do anything wrong. But I have to prove myself capable. Who cares if those germs have to be sacrificed? It's only right that they disappear. What's wrong with stripping the forces of evil of their humanity? They're germs that spread disease and infect the world with evil, and it's my job to prevent them working their mischief.

It was the springtime of my life and we were given the freedom to identify and punish evil. Why shouldn't I enjoy the springtime of my life? All I wanted was to be the sole possessor of my father's love. To love someone is to love and maintain his world. I loved my father like others love themselves. I sustained the world I loved and I have no regrets. My love is sincere and everlasting, even if its object has a change of heart or dies.

Success is everything. As my father's number-one son I had to read the hidden meaning in this mantra of his. Catching Reds was not enough, and even assuming we captured the top dog we'd only be met with more howling from those base beings, which after all pose no threat to our king. The enemy we see in the open is not the real enemy. The real enemy hides inside the most innocent-looking people, Reds that don't look Red. So *that's* what he meant—he's talking about the enemy inside us. Inside the best people lie the makings of the worst fear. Most fearful of all is evil that doesn't look evil.

The more the merrier. One or two was not enough, I needed a good dozen. Well, why not those fisherman who were taken north? They came back after ten days and we put them through the ideological litmus test. I spent two months trying to figure out if they were taken north or went there voluntarily, and released them. But then it struck me that the skipper's elderly mother was from the North, somewhere in Hwanghae. I needed those five after all, and more besides. So I looked into their background and investigated their close relatives, and here's what I came up with: *Taken North, Travel to Japan, Hwanghae Province.* Throw in the pro-DPRK Koreans in Japan, connect the dots, and bingo. If I hadn't released those five only to have to reel them in again, I'd probably have a perfect record. In any case, purity of heart has a way of purifying one's past.

"We went through hell up north—why would I want to spy for them after that? I *hate* Commies, even the word 'Red' makes me shudder. And didn't you agree, sir? That we had a devil of a time and we just need to be more careful from now on? And you sent us on our way. So why are we back here? 'Cause we been spying in the meantime? Did you let us go 'cause you wanted us to spy? I'm an old man at the end of my rope, what do I know about spying, am I out for glory? Instead of making Commies out of my kids I'd rather bite through my tongue and bleed to death, right here and now. Better yet, you could kill me, eh?"

"No, I'm afraid we can't let you off that easy. But if you're determined to do yourself in, don't do it here. You can do whatever you want with yourself but I'm going to live. And if I live, you do too. I'm not trying to kill you, I'm trying to save you. So don't blame me, blame your own greed. You steered your boat north just to catch a few more damn milkfish. You were the sparrow that went into the trap just for a little ear of grain. You went the wrong way and crossed over—that's your fault. Everyone should know what you did so they won't make the same mistake. They won't make a wrong turn and go through hell up north. Your death would teach your pack the true meaning of danger and fear. You'd be a savior. Aren't you going to thank me? What, you don't understand? You're not going to give up? How about we bring your pregnant daughter here—that would make her a spy, it would make her daughter the daughter of a spy. Wouldn't you rather give up instead?"

You need to show some respect. How dare the likes of you doubt the world I rule? Where do you think your rambling is going to get you? If I say you're a spy, then you're a spy. I am a god. Kneel before me.

"He said not to come any more. You're on your own now—good luck. All right?"

I'm collapsing. My love is collapsing, and my world along with it. I'm dying and so is my world. Tears stream from my closed eyes. My girl is crying—I can't hear it but I can feel it. She's struggling to hold back her tears. Hold my hand, hold me and never let me go, comfort me.

Sweetie, all I ever wanted was to keep my love—and I was willing to die trying. We're both crying, we both lost a father. I stroke my hair, thinking it's yours. Here we are, each of us in mourning, neither of us able to comfort the other.

CHAPTER 12

You're no longer the fear that hides inside me, Father. No longer a god, contraband no more, no longer a ghost. You're a dead beast, crushed by a collapsing wall. You're a swarm of maggots crawling from a decaying body. You're the stinking excrement from that body. The day you left the imprint of your foot near my eye, that stench followed you back up to the loft and you haven't appeared since. You haven't made your demands, you haven't kicked the floor to show you're still alive. You want to hang on to your rotten life, but who cares?

You're a handful of ash. Ash in a funeral urn, inert and trivial. The loft is a mausoleum of such urns, a place of desolate repose. I sometimes wonder, are you dead?

As an experiment I left you a meal. When I came back I found the dishes empty, which told me you're still alive—damned if you're going to die. And so I live on, tending to your mausoleum. Again today I mourn your death, placing flowers at your door, pasting a photo, writing your obituary. Tedious hours pass, my cold hands working the scissors. Sometimes I clip photos, sometimes newspaper articles, sometimes from a flyer or maybe a memoir. I'm working on sketchbook number twenty but there's still way too much to paste—who knows how much longer I'll be clipping.

I rip yesterday's sketchbook from its pad, place it on my desk, and leave. Today's newspaper, today's milk, and the sketchbook— your daily bread.

A month after she left for Kaya Mom returned with her arm
in a cast. And I left the hair salon and made my debut at the
Greenfields Beauty Parlor, the new beautician. How did this come
about? First, Mom couldn't handle scissors, and second, I had a
little accident at the hair salon. I was looking over my customer's
shoulder at the ladies magazine she was absorbed in, and there
you were. And next to your photo, one of Mom from the rear as
she was going into our building. And what do you know, I nicked
my customer's ear. Your stench was doing its best to follow me.

It wasn't much of a nick, and we pacified her with a coupon for
a free massage. But I'd always been a thorn in the side of the other
apprentices, and now they had their big chance. Out poured their
reproaches and their grievances, and what could the owner do? I
didn't think twice about leaving. I'd felt all along like the rotting
leg of a starfish and I wanted to amputate that leg and let another
one grow. And I knew that if I stayed there I'd become a monster.

I lasted two days more after I decided to leave. The least I could
do was stay on until my replacement arrived. But the others
found my considerate gesture fishy, even the owner, the same
person who at one time had given me special treatment. The
appointment book, which anyone was allowed to see, got locked
in the safe, and if one of my regulars arrived she was assigned to
another team. Did I care?

A few people still hung around outside the beauty parlor,
eager like that man to learn Father's whereabouts. Sometimes
the reporters showed up, and sometimes the groups that posted
a reward for Father's capture. Like the dignitaries who plant a
commemorative tree on Arbor Day, they would make their little
fuss, leave a placard behind, and I'd never see them again. I was
left with a profusion of placards in my heart—placards of anger, of
resolution, of scolding directed at Father.

The man still planted himself at the record shop. Sometimes
he'd shove a bag of fruit at me and disappear without a word. Or
he'd hand me scrapbook materials to clip and paste. We exchanged
stories—him about a new job, me about my time at the hair salon.
Or we sat side by side in front of the record shop after it closed,
watching the Greenfields Beauty Salon and listening to the sounds

of silence.

His visits began to dwindle—from once every three or four days, to once every week or week and a half, to once a month, and then one winter they stopped. Inside the beauty parlor I'd be combing someone's hair but taking every opportunity to look across the street, waiting for this man who never came. He was the only one who should have returned to look after the tree he'd planted, the only one not to have left a placard.

A newspaper article stated that the statute of limitations for Father was being extended another five years. People were quoted who, citing a special law, were calling for an indefinite extension. And sure enough, next to the article was a photo of Father and a tidy list of the deeds he had committed.

As always, the photo was of a man in his mid-thirties, his eyes full of mischief but the line of his mouth and jaw decisive—the face of my father starting out as a policeman. A face both familiar and unfamiliar.

Spring came and it came again and it came several more times, with Father seemingly enjoying an eternal rest in his mausoleum. Again today I do some clipping, me and my guardian angel. Time drags and my sketchbook pasting never ends. Will my cutting and pasting ever be over?

All is quiet. I take his breakfast tray to my room, set it down, return to the beauty parlor, and sit in one of the adjustable chairs and listen to the radio. A man opens the door and walks in. His salt-and-pepper hair is neatly cut, his skin clear. His glasses have rounded rims and his deep-set eyes have double folds and a sparkle. He scans the interior; I can tell from his silence that he's not here for a haircut. He stands with his hands gathered before him and utters my father's name.

"I don't know where he is."

"I just want to help."

He wants to help? Hmm. Cursing, sobbing, shouting I can understand, but helping? He's volunteering? Being helped isn't something I associate with Father.

"It's not going to work. He'll have to be a fugitive for ten more years—actually forever."

"What are you saying?"

"There's no statute of limitations. Better for him to pay his dues and be done with it. How many years has it been anyway?. . . I'm not talking about revenge or punishment. If we try to bury the mistakes of the past, they eventually jump out like ghosts and repeat themselves. I can't be free from the past either. The names I spilled, the names of innocent people I had to sacrifice to protect someone—that's the reality, as much as we try to deny it. History, you know, is made by the ghosts of the past. . . . Anyway I just want to help—like An helped me."

"You want to help. I can't imagine why. He was a devil."

"Yes, he was a devil all right. But he wanted to be respected too. Respected for his skill and for everything else about him."

"Maybe he wanted to be a god."

"The An I remember—of course I was afraid of him, he scared me—wasn't a monster, at least back then. So when I read the articles about him I couldn't believe it. I hope he's the same man I was reliant on at one point in my life. Hard to believe he could turn into a monster."

"I'm not sure what you want from us, sir."

"I'd just like you to tell him this—like he once told me: 'Say, "I did it," and say it proudly—that's what you do if you're a real man.' If you should see your father, would you tell him that for me?"

"Tell me about him. Tell me about the man who wasn't a devil, who wasn't a monster. That's a story I've never heard."

You may not remember this man, Father dear. Without a photo of the college kid he was twenty years ago you probably won't connect him with the middle-aged man in this magazine clipping.

Twenty years ago copies of a leaflet were scattered from the rooftop of a university building. It was a political statement, and the young man thought long and hard for three days before writing it. He and the other students who launched the leaflets were taken away in handcuffs, jackets covering their heads. He remembered hearing a steel door creak open, being walked down a long hallway, and deposited in a room. It was a small room with no windows, and he was greeted with a round of kicking and beating. It was like a formality, no explanation given and no demands made. And when the beating stopped, you came in. He had to prove to you that he wasn't a spy. For three days the young man wrote a statement. When he finished, you pointed out shortcomings and had him rewrite it from the beginning. The statement got longer and longer—three pages at first, then ten, then twenty. It was a mind game as well as a statement. You asked questions and the young man answered, and you decided if what he said was true or false.

And then the young man flashed on the realization that you had come to a conclusion. Maybe your glaring eyes breathed a sigh of relief and turned gentle. It was the moment you were convinced he was not a spy. The moment you started believing in him. The young man saw the look in your eyes and thought to himself, *I'm safe*. It was the moment you decided the young man was connected not with a spy ring but with the underground student movement. He was cleared of the spying accusation but that wasn't the end of it. You needed a diagram of the underground network. *I'm not here to hurt you*, you told him—*all I need is some names*. And you read him some names. The young man was in a fix—some of the names he recognized, others he didn't. And so the names he ended up mentioning were of people he didn't think had a relationship to the network. He thought that was his best option. He had no idea what might happen as a result. He was sentenced to two years. The underground network consisted of dozens of people, including him.

That weekend you happened to be home with us, and another team worked over the young man in hopes of getting better results. All during that torture session he awaited your return. It wasn't a family member he awaited, or a buddy, or a lover, but you, the only one who believed in him. That knowledge helped him survive the torture.

Do you remember the face of the young man as he clung to you, sniffling like a boy, when you returned? Do you remember wiping that bloody face? And do you remember what you said then?

Do you know who I hate the most—the sons of bitches who do something wrong and then weasel out of it by lying. If you're a man you say, "Yes, I did it—so what!" You stand tall and proudly admit it, and don't you ever think about lying to me, understand?

***

This is the last sketchbook I will offer up to you, Father dear. I would like to have added a few more items but I'm calling it quits. All the people you'll see here, without exception, pointed you out as a devil. They blame themselves for selling their soul in order to survive the hell they experienced. They were desperate. Can you tell me why it's the ones who were beaten, not the ones doing the beating, who pound their chest and despise themselves and have to live with a guilty conscience? I hope you remember this young man. I hope his face revives your memories and brings back the words you said to him. If not, then I'll remind you, I'll make one last effort in remembrance of the dad you swallowed.

Who are you, Father? What's that rice bowl doing in your crotch? Look at you scarfing your food, your slack cheeks bobbing up and down with the effort. Your eyes flit around—are you afraid someone's going to snatch your meal? You're so intent on eating, bits of rice clinging to the little white patches near your mouth that show you're malnourished. What are you?

What happened to your body, your breath, your voice, your lively eyes and the firm, tight line of your mouth, the hard shoulders and the straight back? You look like a worried hunchback the way you slouch. You used to have a sparkle in your eyes—now it's a murky beggar look. I used to feel your warm breath, but all that comes out of your mouth now is a woeful tale told by a lip-smacking, nose-to-the-ground monster that makes me retch.

My father who wired the loft and took out my tooth with his Monami pen—where did he go? And what happened to the cold-hearted devil who infused me with terror and pain? If you're not the father I remember, then it's better you're a cruel, vicious devil or a hideous, terrifying monster, and not a pathetic old disgrace of a man.

Look at those liver spots festering with sorrow and loneliness on a body bloated by obstinacy and excuses. Look at the grimy hair so quickly turning gray, the stubborn furrows in your oily forehead. Look at your filthy hands and your feet swollen with grudge and resentment, your mangled fingernails and gnarly toenails. You're a greedy old man.

Behold the devil I've loathed and detested. Behold the essence of my father, who can't kill himself yet can't survive, whom we can't get rid of and who won't run away, whom we can't hate and yet can't forgive. Look as he drags out his life in hiding. Watch him transform to break my will whenever I make a decision. If only I could hate you as much as I wish. For heaven's sake, will you please come out?

What's that, a death robe—for me? No, it's an opportunity. What opportunity? An opportunity not to turn your daughter into an informant. No way would I do that. Yes you would. If you wanted to report me you could've done so a long time ago. Why do you suppose I didn't? Because I'm your father. My father died—and so did your father. If you report me you'll feel guilty the rest of your life. I don't feel guilty about you. Then it's because you didn't want people pointing fingers at you. No, it's because I was afraid you'd be tortured, like you tortured them. You think I'd submit to torture? You know as well as I do that torture can result in the fabrication of crimes that never existed. I don't remember anything like that. Then I'll help you. What's that in your hand? Scissors. Are you threatening me? Just lie back and I'll wash your hair. That ceiling is filthy. That filthy ceiling is your floor.

The water's too cold. I'll make it warmer. Now it's too hot. Yes, it feels hot. I didn't do anything wrong. Beating up people is bad. They weren't people. Yes they were. All right, they were twisted people. Not twisted—different. They deserved a beating—if the shoe fits, you wear it. You forced them to believe that, and that's worse than beating them. It was for the sake of justice. It was for the sake of you. It was for the sake of my father. Your father deserted you. Because he had to look after his family. That's why other families disappeared, isn't it. It's going to end soon. There's no end to it. Why are you doing this to me? Why did you do it to them? It was my job. A job you should never have done. You want me dead? No, I want you alive. Can I have a towel? I'll give you the mirror too. I don't want to look. You have to. That's not me. Yes it is. I didn't do it. Yes you did. It wasn't me. It was you, all right.

I hear the snip-snip of her scissors. There's a hair on the tip of my nose, making it itch. I feel the cut of the scissors and the feather fall of my hair. Soft hands pass through my hair, remove the gown, and rest against my shoulder.

I remember the touch of a hand on a lazy spring afternoon. Sunshine came through the window and wrapped itself around my cheek. A woman's tiny hands came to rest on my shoulders. And I remember a day when my thick hands came to rest on those hands resting on my shoulders. All sound vanished except her faint breathing and mine.

I feel gentle puffs of air on my neck. Falling hair brushes my earlobe. Warm breath touches my ear. I remember that warm breath, and the faint whispers that soothed the tremors in my back, and a moist kiss that warmed me to my toes.

"All done."

I open my eyes and see my daughter's face in the mirror. And the face of an old, weary beast, bloodshot eyes shooting me a look. That's not me. I punch the mirror. Blood spatters the shattered face. The back of the hand is sliced open, the bone is showing. My hand. A human hand of blood, bone, and flesh. It hurts.

I remember the first time I saw someone's blood on my hand. And the feel of mushy flesh and the chilling sensation of blood spraying like shards of glass as the skin burst open. And a hot, anguished cry. I felt a strange buzz, a sensation like a full bladder suddenly released, unpleasant yet refreshing, bringing relief alongside embarrassment. My hand dropped to my side and I felt liberated.

I sat by myself in the dark room gazing at my bloody hand. I could still hear the guy whimpering like a little boy. Every breath I took brought the smell of blood, and I had to pinch my nose shut. One day I realized I was getting anxious if I wasn't kicking, punching, or shouting at someone. Blood, tears, submission—the necessary conditions for my peace of mind. But since when? At some point the odors of blood, urine, and burning flesh began to smell sweet. The interrogation stimulated my appetite and loosened my bowels. Oh, how I could focus when I was writing the report, how the energy surged inside me when my results went up. That's when I began to turn into a beast.

But the feelings didn't last long. No matter how many punches I threw, how many times I drew blood, how many bones I broke and joints I dislocated, it couldn't quench my thirst. As I got faster at making a guy submit, my relief from anxiety grew shorter. It got to the point where my head spun and I broke into a cold sweat when I left the interrogation room. Times of quiet made my ears ring. I needed a place where I could breathe freely and stop second-guessing myself and go home spent. And I needed submission of a different sort. So I always ended up in the room with the red windows.

There I could empty my mind by grabbing a girl's mane and dominating her, kneading her flesh, stuffing myself into her, beating her. But that wasn't a solution either.

Which brought me to that wasted little bitch who was always scratching her scab-ridden body, fearful and shuddering like a mangy dog. Who drifted off to sleep to her own lullaby as she rested on my back, her rib cage making itself felt with every breath she took. My body remembers her delicate quivering and her whimpered breathing after the lullaby faded to silence. I need that little bitch.

"Get me a pair of shoes."

This is a first. It's one of his items, not mine, that's come down from the loft, a pair of old shoes, stiff and deformed from disuse. How could they have known they'd be stuck in the loft so long, harboring the memory of a fugitive's breathless escape, warping like you with each passing day?

The shoes I buy are two sizes larger. Plain, soft, dark leather shoes. I hope they give you confidence. Even if you can't be stately and graceful when you walk, don't slink like a cowardly fugitive.

Instead, endure the rocks and the kicking and stomping that come your way. I hope, Father dear, this concludes my dealings with you.

I set down your new shoes toe outward, then sit in the adjustable chair observing them, visible beneath the washroom curtain. The sun sets and darkness descends.

Meaningless time passes. Finally the door to my room opens and your feet appear on the threshold. Pause. Here they come to the washroom floor. Pause. What are you waiting for? Go on, put on those beautiful shoes and leave. Pause. Finally your feet slip into the shoes. Try them out. Take a baby step, that's it. The curtain opens and the hesitant shoes venture into the beauty parlor.

I was hoping those shoes would deliver you from your monstrosities to a court of justice, that in your lifetime you would pay for at least a fraction of your crimes. But you lack the appearance of one who wishes to turn himself in. You look like you're still in hiding. The felt hat, the surgical mask, and the muffler make a shabby disguise. Why bother? The way you look now, how could anyone connect you with the infamous photo? Or attach grace and forgiveness to your name? It's spring now. Spring. But it's not for you that the buds are opening. When you go out that door, take with you the burning hell you will forever inhabit, and even if you turn yourself in I hope you never return.

Where to? I stop and place my hand on the wall. Still trying to get my land legs under me. There's a huge department store where the train station and its small plaza used to be. Where's the entrance to the subway? I walk past brightly lit display windows, past a manikin with its arms posed outward and so much light on the face it scares me. I slide down the wall until I'm squatting, and gape at the people.

Young lovers pass by hand in hand, giggling. A woman in a short skirt makes a detour around me, heels clattering as she hops along. Someone drops a couple of coins in front of me and walks on by. I look at the coins and am reminded of something I need to do. I gather the coins, get to my feet, and look around. There used to be phone booths outside the station. There they are, at the far end of the department store.

I pick up the receiver. Where's the coin slot? Oh, it only takes a phone card. It's the same with the next booth and the one after that. I park myself in a booth that has a seat, uncoil my muffler and stuff it in my pocket, then remove my mask. Not a soul is about, no one to gape at. But sitting suits me better than walking—it's quieter that way, and I've gotten used to silence.

A couple of high school kids stop at the next booth and have a smoke. Here we go. One of them sticks a hand in his pocket and poses with his cigarette while he shoots me a look.

"What, you want my ID? Would you kindly get a move on, sir, and find someplace else for your lecture?"

"Could I borrow your phone card?"

The boy tosses his cigarette to the ground and searches his pocket.

"Phone card? Are you serious? No one uses phone cards anymore. I tell you what, here—but make it quick, all right?"

"Don't you know who I am?"

"Should I? Maybe you were a famous singer back in the day? Would you hurry up. Hey, give me another smoke while uncle here makes his phone call."

"Sir, I just want to get it over with. The attorney thinks I'll get two or three years—but there's a chance I'll go on probation instead. Worst-case scenario is five years. I can handle that. I should have made up my mind a lot earlier—then at least I'd have some peace. I'm sick of it, can't remember the last time I had a decent night's sleep. Actually I'm afraid to go to sleep, those guys I worked over keep coming back in my dreams. And the next day I end up slapping the wife around. Well, she's gone now—had a couple of miscarriages and took off. She's had it here, said she'd go the U.S. and wash dishes for a living. So I let her go. I'm done, finished.

"You've been deceived. It was all planned out. It's not that they couldn't catch you—they decided not to. You were just doing your job, and they knew it. Why upset the apple cart? You remember how Chŏng, the district prosecutor we used to work with, took over Pak's position, right? The last thing he would have wanted was for you to get picked up. And now he's a national assemblyman with the gold pin. So now you know. Why stir up a bee's nest. I'm very sorry, sir. It's not going to end until everything changes. And even then, who knows? One thing I *can* tell you, I don't think anyone's going to forgive us. Sir, I think it's time.... Sir—I have a favor to ask. Could you please keep out of sight until our trial is over? We're taking the just-following-orders tack— which won't work if we're together in court with you. All I have left is my mother and I'm afraid she'll have a heart attack. Please, sir."

***

The area around the station where I caught that train all those years ago has changed so much I can't figure out the streets. But the alley with the red windows is still there, frozen in time, including the building at the end with the mirror-walled room. The little bitch is gone and no one's heard from her. Lying on the bare floor and looking at the mirrors, I try to recall her face, but all I remember is her sleepy voice.

Can I tell you about Whitey? The first time I saw him was next to an old storage shed where the reed fields start. He must have been a newborn, I could tell from his puppy fur. And he had red marks— maybe he was abandoned or got hurt. My mom said he was going to die. I tried to put rice I had chewed into his mouth, but he only looked at me and tried to hide in the corner. So I crawled up close and blew warm air on him and petted him nice and gentle on the back. I guess I dozed off, and the next thing I knew, I felt something warm on my tummy. I woke up and there he was inside my shirt with his head in my armpit, whimpering. Finally he quieted down and went hoo, *very softly. And then he shuddered. I thought he was dead. But when I listened closely I could hear him breathing like a baby. After that I let him come under my shirt every day, so I could feel him shudder just before he fell asleep. I always waited for him to go to sleep first.* Hoo.

I always waited for the end of the story when she did that little sigh. And I put the little bitch on my back just like she held Whitey inside her shirt. Her faint whimpering would go away and I could feel *her* breathing like a baby, in and out. My own breathing settled down too. I wanted to remain forever on the verge of sleep, a boat rocking gently on the water.

So what happened to Whitey?

He got bigger and bigger and bigger. He was quick and brave. And then rat poison got him. There was so much rat poison back then. Rats ate rat poison and dogs ate rats that were killed by rat poison and the dogs . . . .

And then?

Whitey ran through the village. And along the river, this side and then the other side. And through the drainage ditches next to the paddies. And through the reed fields. His tongue was hanging out, and he ran and ran and ran. I never knew he could run so fast. He was like a warrior of the wind. I tried to pant like my warrior. And then he came home and broke a sauce crock and knocked over the washbasin and fell over in the yard with his legs stretched out, foaming at the mouth. He died in my arms. And when he took his last breath I heard that hoo *sound. And I felt him tremble. I just thought he was sound asleep. I didn't know that soft sigh comes when you die, too.*

I blew my warm breath on my cold Whitey but he never warmed up. I wish I could have tucked him inside my shirt but he was too big by then. So I heated some water and poured it over him. You should have seen the steam come up. I thought I saw his eyes peek open. All night long I was in and out of the kitchen fetching warm water to pour on him. Thinking that tomorrow he and I would run out to the paddies so fast we'd pant like the whistling of the wind. Tell me, when people die do they go hoo *too? How can you tell when a person's dying and not just going to sleep? Is dying kind of like sleeping?*

And then she did her little sigh. I found it so relaxing the way she breathed, and I sighed myself. I tried to remember if that sparrow that died by my hand so long ago went *hoo*. Did I give myself up to her and fall asleep the way that puppy did with its nose in her armpit? Did I pour warm water over the dead sparrow?

I think of the autumn sun in our yard where I used to look after

Father's basket trap, dozing off as I waited for the sparrows. In my sleep I heard them chirping clear as day. I yanked the twine cord and realized I was drooling. I felt the tension as I reached carefully into the basket and took the sparrow. I felt the warmth of that living sparrow, the palpitations of its tiny heart, the faint tremors from its breathing. Those tiny movements startled me and I flung the bird away. But instead of flying off it fell to the ground. And I had been so careful.

I buried that small bird that had died in my hand. I built a little mound over the grave, gathered leaves, and covered it. And I watered it as I would have a seed. Yes, I remember.

Hoo. I remember when my father was on his last legs. He struggled for life up to the very end. He was whining about how itchy the sole of his missing foot was, so I did the next best thing and scratched his arm. *It itches*—those were his last words. And in fact his eyes held a mixture of agitation and pain.

There were no indications that the end was near. For a brief instant his pupils grew big and then they contracted. There was a tiny disturbance in the whites, like a fluorescent light that brightens in the instant before it turns dark. And his eyes shining lucid one moment turned smoky. And finally his itchiness. I kept scratching his scrawny arm, hoping relief would come like a blessing to his expression.

I wish I could go to sleep just like I am. Not a shallow, hungry sleep, but a deep, warm slumber. Not a weary, helpless, fear-ridden sleep but a peaceful sleep nestled in warm sun, gentle breezes, and tranquility.

"Hey!" Followed by knocking on the door. "Hey mister! Time's up! I know you're all alone in there, but if you're planning on killing yourself do it somewhere else. I knew it the moment you came in—you're not here to get laid. Sick, perverted son of a bitch."

***

I wipe my face with a towel. The towel stinks. It's been laundered so much it's getting threadbare and developing little loop-like snags. I pull at one of the snags. It straightens into a thread and snaps, leaving a tiny gap. It's fun how the loop disappears so fast when you straighten it. I take another loop. Pull it slow and careful so I don't break the thread. But it doesn't come all the way out and eventually it too snaps. Not much strength in the worn-out threads after all those washings. Let's try another one. Control the hand, do it slowly, gingerly. It works! There's a one-thread gap in the weave. I feel like I'm out in a paddy making space for the next row of seedlings. I guess I should say I'm harvesting the thread. It's like when you unravel a sweater you've knitted—regret for all the time and effort you put into the knitting but at the same time relief that you can do it over.

Anyway, I've discovered another mindless way to kill time. I find another loop, then pinch it and pull. Slowly, carefully, gingerly so my thick fingers don't end up pulling two loops.

I pluck out the loops and in no time the towel is half scraggly. Long, empty tracks run from left to right. Without those horizontal threads you can see the vertical weave.

That's the towel's structure, the way it's made. Even when you pluck out the vertical threads the horizontal ones are so strongly attached to the borders that they don't break. If you pull out a loop from a knitted sweater you'll end up unraveling it, but with this towel the weave merely loosens. The fluffy pile of thread in my lap is more than I expected. And it's feather-light. Pulling idly on thread like this I could go through ten towels a day, easy. I take a loop from the pile and wrap it around my finger. I do the same with a few more threads, but then the other ends of these threads, still part of the pile in my lap, get tangled. To kill time you can't beat unraveling tangled thread. How about I make a spool of that unraveled thread and weave a towel out of it. Just think—a spool of unraveled thread.

***

He's back. I'm drying a customer's hair and applying hairspray, and when I look out the window there he is. He's just lit a cigarette and is blowing out the first deep drag.

In the mirror I show the woman how her hair looks in back, and then I'm done.

The woman puts her face close to the mirror and checks her

makeup, then leaves, beaming in satisfaction. I stand in the open doorway and look across at the man. Our eyes meet and he looks off down the alley. He's gotten thinner.

Another of my customers, an elderly woman with her head wrapped in a towel, is ready to finish up. I loosen the rubber band around one of the curling rods to see how her permanent is shaping up, then add neutralizer to her hair. He's still there in front of the record shop. I wash her hair, then usher her back to her seat. As I dry her hair I hear waves washing up onto a small island. Now he's in front of the shoe shop. I puff up her hair to cover where it's thinning out on top, and she starts to rattle on about how she ought to learn this part of the process herself. The perm solution smells like the ocean.

After the woman has paid me I slip two thousand *wŏn* back into her hand.

"You look so lovely, grandma, I want to give you a ten percent discount."

It never fails—even elderly women blush when you tell them they're lovely. What's even more lovely is the way they straighten up and march out afterwards. It's early but I turn off the sign and close up.

"Let's get something to eat."

He nods, and I set out ahead. We keep our distance, like lovers anticipating a parting of the ways. I hear a great big tree sinking its roots deep inside me. We come to an intersection and go into a restaurant, a place I've always wanted to try.

I didn't expect the low lights and the vines snaking along the walls. The servings are huge and I finish my meal in silence. He tries a couple spoonfuls of soup and merely pokes with his fork at the meat and vegetables.

"You're not eating?"

"I've got a bad tooth and it hurts when I eat meat."

He passes me some chunks of meat and I finish every last one. The table is cleared and coffee arrives. A ponderous composition for piano is coming over the sound system, adding to the dark oppressiveness of the interior. He takes a small box from his pocket and places it on the table.

"I wanted to give you this for your birthday."

"My birthday—I'd forgotten."

"Did you ever wonder what happened to me on your birthday?"

"You mean there's still something you haven't told me?"

"Actually, nothing happened—not a thing."

"Then how do you know it's my birthday?"

"I overheard it. It was something he didn't want anyone to know, especially me."

"So tell me what happened that day that nothing happened."

"I was really scared of him—I kept wondering why he never laid a hand on me, just sat there working on his model car. It felt like the calm before a storm."

"Really?"

"I was sitting there buck naked, nodding off, and he went out in the hall with the phone. The door didn't close all the way because of the cord, and I could hear his voice. 'Yes, I'm going home—it's Sŏn's birthday. Can't *you* do it?' Then someone comes down the hall and says, 'How come your shop is so quiet, did one of your machines break down?' And he says, 'Listen, dickhead, it's my girl's birthday tomorrow, I'm not going home with the smell of some Commie's balls on my hands. How about we knock off early?'"

"Just that one day? He always took at least two days off for my birthday. He never missed it."

"What happened was, I let him know I knew his secret. I got overconfident. I asked him what he was getting his good daughter, and earned myself a beating for my trouble. 'How dare you—your mouth isn't fit to speak her name. You think you're a smart guy?' It was just before he left for home—he went absolutely nuts. I was shitting blood for days."

"Is that when you got the burn mark?"

"That was compliments of the little welder he kept on his desk."

"What about your arm?"

"All I could think of during that beating was tracking down that prize possession of his and destroying it. But I have to admit, that was a red-letter day for me. I got the next day off and that gave me the strength to stick it out. I hated you insanely, but I'm thankful for it. As far as I'm concerned you were a godsend."

A music box, and inside it a ballerina making a pirouette— that was Father's present for me, a small, lovely dancer made of porcelain. I was afraid his thick fingers would crush the ballerina as he lifted the box, so I snatched the box from him. He laughed and then wound the box so I could hear the music. That was also the day he put new flooring in the loft and ran the electric cord up from the washroom. The same day I was given that ballerina doll I watched my very own palace come into being. I never knew my palace would hide a devil for so long. I'm sorry for what happened to you, but I'm not going to repeat the *I didn't know* line. I only wish I hadn't been born that day. I'm ashamed I was born at all. I'm sorry I haven't told you I'm sorry. Instead I want to say thank you for that brief moment when you were thankful I was born, and I thank you for sticking it out. Honestly. I only wish I could say this out loud to you.

So many seasons have passed, and he's never returned. The record store and the shoe shop were torn down and replaced by a supermarket. The speakers with the soft music have been replaced by speakers making nonstop announcements about today's sale items and those to follow. That restaurant where he and I first ate is now a spaghetti house whose pastel interior is plainly visible through its one grand window. Once and only once I went there and had a meal at a table beside that window. The sun was so bright I thought I would cry. It was the day Father's life in the loft came to an end, a year after he returned from his brief outing and went back into hiding. It had been 10 years and 11 months since his face had exploded in the media—meaning I who was then 19 am now 30.

I've replaced the broken acrylic sign with a new one made of clear-grain wood. The top is inscribed with my name, *Sŏn*, and the bottom, in smaller print, *Hair Salon*. And the interior decoration is new. It's roomier now, with the back room and the loft being converted into a lounge. Before the back room was taken down I made a visit to the washroom and gazed at the ceiling. The middle was sagging under the weight of the loft, and the mold and the stains were spreading toward the corners like they were trying to escape. My ceiling, your floor, was so low I could stand on my toes and my head would touch it.

The workers gather their tools and leave. I lower the bright yellow shades and set flowerpots beneath the windows. From a distance a person might mistake this place for a little café. Why don't I put a café table outside. I'd want to add speakers too, like the ones in front of the record shop. Then, if I can't handle the noise from the supermarket speakers I can always play some soft music.

I take my hands from my apron pocket, stretch, and yawn. Spring is here.

CHAPTER 13

"You're back—you look so happy, does that mean good news?"

"Happy? Well, your dad asked for solitary confinement—he doesn't want to associate with all those common criminals. And he said for us not to worry, we're being looked after—can you believe that?"

"How exactly are we being looked after?"

"I have no clue. But the bottom line is, we don't have to worry. He must have said it a hundred times."

"Then why aren't you staying? Aren't your legs tired? You said they were cramping."

"I'm off to change the world."

"What do you mean?"

"The world—it's all messed up, it needs changing, our tax money's going to the Commies. The world has to be put right for your dad to get out sooner. We need to make a better world for everybody."

"Is that what he said?"

"That's what he said."

"And how are you going to change the world, Mom?"

"I'll figure out something."

"Mom, for heaven's sake."